When LIFE gives you LEMONS instead of LATTES

RAYNA YORK

Toad Tree
PRESS

Published by Toad Tree Press.

167 Terrace View NE

Medicine Hat Alberta TIC-OA4

Publishers Note

This book is a work of fiction. Names, characters, places, and incidents are either the product of the author's imagination or used fictionally, and any resemblance to actual persons, living or dead, business establishments, events or locales is entirely coincidental.

ISBN 978-1-9990951-2-3 (paperback)

ISBN 978-1-9990951-3-0 (ebook)

Cover design by Rocio Martin Osuna

For my mother who always encouraged me, regardless of how unrealistic the endeavor. She is my hero.

1

"Mom, who are these people?" I demand, standing beside her in defense mode. A stocky looking man in a cheap suit and bad haircut looms in front of us while several beefy men climb out of vehicles behind him.

I was making a mixed-green, berry smoothie when the doorbell rang. It's not my usual practice to care who's at the door, but I'm expecting a delivery.

"Ma'am, I'm Special Agent John Stafford of the FBI." He flashes his badge before snapping it closed and attaching it to his belt. "When was the last time you saw your husband?"

"What? Um . . . this morning."

Several agents push past us into the house, one of them bumping into me. "Excuse you!" I give him my best you-are-lower-than-scum glare.

"He left for work at seven." A loud noise behind us makes her jump and has us both turning to see several agents ransacking our living room. "What's this all about?"

Harlow, my younger sister, suddenly appears and wraps her

arms tightly around my waist. "Mom, Kylie, what—what's going on?"

Seeing her distress has my claws coming out, which is never pretty. "Mom! They can't just barge in here. Get them to show you a warrant!" She can be so stupid sometimes.

Detective Stafford gives me a look like I'm irrelevant before returning his attention to my mother. "We might want to have this conversation in private," he says, indicating that "we" doesn't include me.

I cross my arms over my chest. "I'm *not* leaving!"

"Go ahead, detective. Whether they find out now or later isn't going to change things."

Good answer.

"If that is your preference," he says with cold authority. "Jared Mallory James is wanted for fraud and embezzlement. And as he has refused to abide by our summons, is now a fugitive of the law."

My mother gasps. "Are you sure?"

"That's total bullshit! Mom, they're lying."

Harlow moves to her side. "I don't understand."

"It's okay, honey." Mom pats her back in an attempt to soothe. "Why don't you go to your room and watch TV?"

"No. Just explain what he's talking about." She sounds panicky. She's nine. I can't blame her.

"Harlow, honey. Just give me a minute. I'll explain everything to you when I know more. Kylie, will you please go with her?"

"*No.* These people are destroying our house!" And I don't want her believing this guy's bullshit story. She's never had a backbone, and I don't trust her to ask the right questions.

Another agent walks up and hands Detective Stafford a

paper. "Thank you," he says, then holds the paper up in front of us. "As of this moment, all properties have been seized and accounts frozen. You have five days to vacate the premises. Nothing—"

"What?" I shriek.

He ignores me, continuing, "Nothing in this house can be removed except those items of a personal nature. You can keep your phones but all other electronics, including computers, must remain."

"Mom!"

"Kylie! *Please.* You're not helping. Where are we supposed to go, Agent?"

"That is not my concern, ma'am."

"You're just going to let him kick us out?" My mother holds up a hand, attempting to silence me. *As if* she has the power.

"I understand it's not your concern, Agent, but I have two children. What am I supposed to do without any money?"

He gives her a look of disdain before stepping past us into the house. The guy probably makes beans for a living, sees a multi-million-dollar house, and thinks we deserve what's coming to us.

"Thanks for your sensitivity and concern." I scowl after him, then turn back to my Mom, who's staring off into the front yard. "What's *wrong* with you? Do something!"

She turns to me. "What do you want me to do?"

Her expression has me pausing. I've never seen her look so beaten, dejected. "Well . . . for starters, you're not even questioning him. You know Dad couldn't have done this— whatever they're accusing him of."

She shrugs her shoulders and walks off, taking Harlow with her.

"Seriously?" I chase after her. "Come on! This is Dad we're talking about. He works his ass off. He would never steal money. Why would he? We've got money out the yin-yang!"

"So it would seem," is all she says before stepping out the back door with Harlow in tow.

I gawk at her as they pass our infinity pool and walk down the boardwalk to the beach. When they disappear behind the tall grass, I take my phone from my back pocket and call my dad. He's going to be so pissed when he hears what's going on. I squint against the brightness of the sun. And how can she just walk away from me like that?

The phone rings and rings with no answer, so I text him.

"Hey!" I holler as an agent fumbles a valuable glass sculpture. "You break it, you buy it!"

He tilts his head, giving me a bored expression before setting it back on the shelf.

Idiot.

I look at my phone again, willing it to ring or alert me that I have a text saying he's on his way and not to worry—that he will fillet these dickheads and serve them up a healthy portion of whoop-ass the moment he arrives. But there's nothing.

He's probably in a meeting. He always turns his phone off.

No. If he was in a meeting, they would have found him at work.

Maybe the meeting was somewhere else?

I don't know. *Whatever.* He just needs to freakin' respond.

Seeing agents start up the stairs to the second floor reminds me of what Stafford said about the computers. I rush up behind them, slither past, then bolt to my room.

"Hey!" one of them shouts, rushing up behind me.

"Gotta change." I slam the door in his face and quickly lock it.

"Open up!" He bangs on the door.

"Just a second! I told you, I need to change!" The doorknob jiggles and the banging continues. "You walk in on me naked, and I'll have my lawyers cramming a sexual harassment complaint so far up your ass . . ." The assault on my door ceases. I quickly grab a large Louis Vuitton shoulder bag from my closet and place my computer at the bottom—*they are* not *taking this from me*—then stuff a bunch of random clothes on top.

"Ma'am—"

I whip the door open and relish at his startled expression. "Fine!" I huff. "I'll just change at my friend's." I attempt to push past him, but he grips my arm, holding me in place. "Well, you won't let me change here!"

He yanks the bag off my shoulder and rummages through it. Not finding anything in the mess I've created, he shoves it into my arms. "You can go."

I bow to him in a dramatic flourish. "Oh, thank you, your mercifulness." I know I shouldn't antagonize him, but I can't help myself—I'm pissed.

I hurry down the stairs, anxious to get outside with my booty, when another agent stops me at the back door. "What do you have with you?"

"The man upstairs already checked my bag," I say, looking up at him, my blue eyes wide and feigning innocence. "He said I could go." This guy is cute and surprisingly young.

When he makes a move to look in my bag, I lean back against the doorframe, striking a provocative pose, then slowly glide one of the straps down my arm with a look that's put *many* boys to their knees. With the bag gaping open, I lift a brow, then motion with a quick glance at my bag to take a look, before returning my salacious gaze back to him.

At first, he looks a little stunned, then slightly amused before pulling at the edge of my bag, briefly looking inside.

"They're just clothes so I can change at Dalia's," I throw in at random. "We were supposed to go to the mall when this whole"—I motion with a wave of my hand—"shit-storm started."

He releases the bag. "Alright, miss, you're free to go."

"Thank you," I say, smiling, then give him my best we-should-hook-up-later expression.

"Have a good day, ma'am," he says over his shoulder as he walks away.

Well, *that* wasn't the reaction I was expecting.

"Thanks," I call out, before mumbling, "Your loss, loser."

I push away from the door, giving my long blond hair a flip and head outside, following after Mom and Harlow.

The weather is perfect as it always is in California—sun shining, calm temperatures, gentle breeze. Harlow jumps up as soon as she sees me and runs to my side, wrapping her arms around my waist.

"Hey, Bug. You okay?" I run my hand up and down her back, then give her a squeeze.

"Yeah. I guess."

"Don't worry," I say when we reach Mom's side. "Dad will call back soon. He'll be so pissed when I tell him what's going on. Heads will fly, I guarantee it."

Harlow looks mollified, Mom not so much. Figures. She's such a pessimist.

"What's in the bag?" Mom asks.

"Just some clothes. I was afraid they'd wreck my stuff, and I wouldn't have anything to change into if someone wanted to do something later."

"Right," Mom says with contempt, "because *that's* our biggest concern right now."

"You know what? I don't see *you* doing a whole hell of a lot at the moment. Shouldn't you be calling a lawyer or something?"

"I'm not the one who *needs* a lawyer."

"They're threatening to take all our stuff!"

"They have legal documentation saying they can seize all our assets. Besides, I don't have the money to retain one."

"You must have some." I wave my hand in the direction of the house. "I mean, come on."

"Not enough."

"But some, right?"

"Everything is in your father's name." She looks past me to the water. "He wanted me to have my own account, but never put over five-hundred in it at a time."

I'm horrified at the thought of being broke. "Why not!"

"That's irrelevant at the moment, don't you think?"

"So if you don't have any money . . . what are we going to do? Where will we go?"

"I'm not sure. This just happened, Kylie. I'm still processing."

"What about Dad's parents'? *They're* loaded."

"I don't know."

"*Mom*, you have to at least ask!" I yell, fear gripping my gut.

"Let's not talk about this now." She nods in Harlow's direction, who seems off in a daze. "Let's wait them out. When they leave, we'll go back in, I'll make some dinner, we'll get a good night's sleep, then talk more about it in the morning."

Only the concern for my sister has me backing off.

Harlow turns to us suddenly, eyes brimming with tears. "Mom, they're wrong. Dad would never do what they're accusing him of. Maybe he was set up or framed or something? You don't know. You can't give up on him."

Mom holds her arms open to her, and Harlow quickly walks into her embrace. "I know, baby. I'm sorry. This has rocked all of us."

"I'm with you, Bug." I smooth my hand over her sun-bleached hair.

"Please understand, girls. I don't think the FBI would go to this extreme if they weren't completely sure. And where is he?"

"Maybe something happened to him," I start, but it's returned with a glare from my mother. "What? Why not? Why are you always so down on him, anyway?"

"Kylie, stop!" Harlow shouts.

"That's why he's never home, Mom. You friggin' rag on him all the time!"

She releases Harlow and walks away.

Harlow wipes her eyes before piercing me with a cold, hard stare, surprising me. "Why are you so mean to her?" She swipes at the tears again.

"*What?* You know how she is."

"Maybe you don't know everything you think you do."

"And you do?"

"*Whatever.*" She turns and takes off after Mom.

Crap.

"Harlow!" I call after her as she takes off running. Either she doesn't hear me, or she's ignoring me, because she doesn't stop. I never snap at her. She's such an amazing kid.

I set my bag in the sand and sit next to it, then pull my phone out to text my dad again.

. . .

The sun is heating up, bordering on hot as I watch the waves tumble onto the beach, moving up toward me before being pulled back. Normally it would be calming, but the thought of potentially living on the streets . . . well, it'll take more than soothing waves to quell *this* level of panic.

My grandparents' never wanted anything to do with us, some sort of family rift or something, so the chances of them helping are slim. But if Mom doesn't have any money, it may be our only hope. *Hell*, I'd even go and beg. I'd rather lower myself to groveling than be broke. They'd have to take pity on me, right? I'm flesh and blood. Besides, I'm good at getting what I want. I'll concoct a tale that will have them drying their eyes and forking over a big, fat check.

Feeling a little calmer, I scroll through Instagram, liking several posts and commenting on others, then snap some selfies —my followers expect to see me.

Mom and Harlow eventually return, and we walk back to the house together. I drape an arm around my sister's shoulder, squeezing her to my side. "I'm sorry, Bug."

She looks up at me. "It's okay." The forced smile sends an ache right through me. She doesn't deserve this kind of stress and anxiety, and I've only added to it.

Walking up the boardwalk to our house, I strain my eyes for any movement. I hope they're gone. I don't want them to have another opportunity to look through my bag. I can't imagine they'd be happy that I filched my computer from under their noses.

I casually make my way to a seat at our patio table and place my bag under my legs while my mother checks the house. I figure if they're still inside, it wouldn't look suspicious waiting here under the umbrella.

Mom returns immediately and says the house is empty. I breathe a sigh of relief as I pick up my bag and walk toward the house. *I swear if they've tossed my room . . .* I stand frozen just inside the door. "Oh my god!" It looks like we've been robbed—stuff is everywhere. I run to my room. It's bad, but not as bad as the rest of the house. I go to Harlow's room next—pretty much the same as mine. I step into Mom and Dad's room—it's all but destroyed.

Mom comes out of her closet, tears streaming down her cheeks. She's startled when she sees me and quickly wipes her cheeks. "Kylie."

"You okay?" I don't think I've ever seen her cry.

She begins to pick up the clothes that are strewn everywhere. "All my valuables are gone."

Which translates to: We are now *officially* broke.

I stop a snarky comment before it leaves my lips. As much as I dislike my mother, seeing her in tears hurts. I wish I could go to her, but that's not our relationship, so I start picking up clothes and putting them back on hangers. Harlow comes in and does the same.

We work in silence for the rest of the day, doing our best to put the house back together. Since it's enormous, we only focus on the important areas—our bedrooms, the living room, and kitchen. The rest is irrelevant. They're kicking us out, anyway.

All the electronics are gone, so I give myself a mental pat on the back for having the foresight to smuggle my computer out. I guess they figured the tech would be the first thing we would hawk. Well, that and Mom's jewelry and Dad's Rolex watches. Even the art is gone.

Dinner was useless. We sat around the kitchen island, picking at our dinner. None of us had an appetite. Mom still hasn't told us what the hell we're doing—where we are going—nothing. When I finally go up to bed, I make several more attempts to contact my father, with no response.

Why is he ignoring me?

He must know what's going on. Maybe he was framed like Harlow suggested and needs time to figure out a plan before reaching out to us or the investigators? I mean, if someone framed me, I would want to gather enough evidence to help my case before I had to answer to anybody. If I didn't, everything would be in the FBI's hands, and I might not get a fair assessment or trial or whatever.

But what if he was coerced into a deal with some bad people—maybe the mob or something—and they made him run money through the firm or were blackmailing him and he had to steal money to pay them off? If it was something like that, we would all be in danger. Maybe he's hiding to keep us safe? Because there's no other reason he would ignore my calls.

We might be on our own for a while. Which gives Mom more of a reason to reach out to my loser grandparents'.

Why is it my responsibility to figure all this out?

2

"Kylie, Harlow. Let's go," Mom calls from downstairs.

She informed us yesterday that we could only take one suitcase each.

How am I supposed to do that? I have a massive walk-in closet —my shoes will take at least two.

I throw a large duffel bag over my shoulder and, pulling the biggest suitcase I could find, bang my way down the stairs, one mahogany step at a time. Harlow's already standing next to Mom, a small suitcase at her feet. She looks up at me with a crooked smile.

Yeah, she gets me.

My horrid grandparents' wouldn't return my mother's calls nor my own, but were kind enough to have their *lawyer* draft us a formal letter. It said that if they take us in, or help us in any way, the investigation would involve them, and they wouldn't *dare* do anything to tarnish their family name.

So basically, we're screwed.

Luckily, Mom is part of a support group—what for, I don't

know. They donated a car and gave us enough cash to get to where we need to go. The destination being my great-grandmother's old house in some podunk town in the Midwest. Apparently, she died about a year ago, and she left Mom the house. I never knew her—my dad said I wasn't missing much.

"Are you ready?" I ask Harlow when I reach the bottom step. She looks up at Mom, then down at her feet. "It's going to be fine, Bug. It's an adventure, you know?"

"I guess." She doesn't sound convinced.

"Okay." Mom picks up her suitcase. "I think we have everything, so let's get going."

I'm the last one out and debate whether to shut the door. Maybe a kick-ass storm will blow up, whip through it, and destroy everything inside. Or better yet, a drug dealer might come across it, turn it into a crack house, and accidentally blow it up. Either way works for me. I leave the door wide open.

I stop short when I see the car that is supposed to be transporting us all the way to Ohio. "Are you fricking kidding me? Where the hell did you find *this* pile of junk? It must be like five years old! And it's so tiny!"

"Don't be such a snob," Harlow says.

I raise an eyebrow at her like, *excuse me?*

"You're lucky we didn't have to take the bus," Mom bites back.

"And that's supposed to make me feel better? You sure it will get us there? It's not even an import." *And it's red! A color that should be reserved for sportscars.*

Mom stops what she's doing and glares at me. "Really?"

"What? What's wrong with me wanting to get there in one piece?" I swear the bumpers look like they could fall off at any moment, and there's a crack at the base of the windshield.

She shakes her head at me, unlocks the trunk, then moves to the driver's side. I lift Harlow's suitcase in, pushing it back as far as it will go. Mine weighs a ton, and Harlow has to help me load it in.

"*Mom*," I whine when my duffle bag won't fit, "there isn't enough room."

She comes around. "I told you to bring *one* suitcase."

"I did! One suitcase. This is a duffel bag."

"Your suitcase fills the entire trunk!"

"You didn't specify a size."

She growls. "Fine. I'll put mine in the backseat, which means less room for Harlow." My sister glares at me. "What's in the duffle bag?"

"Necessities."

She rolls her eyes. "I'll bet."

"Hey, don't get snarky. I already had to leave most of my closet behind."

"Well, you're going to have to store it under your feet because there's nowhere else to put it."

"Whatever," I grumble. Resting my feet on my bag of shoes doesn't seem like a big deal. Better than being shoeless in some shithole little town. It's not like I'll be able to buy anything decent there even if we *did* have the money.

We drive through the security gate of our Santa Barbara neighborhood and hit the highway. It's quiet in the car. I guess we're all in our own minds trying to cope as best we can. I worry about Harlow though. So much crap has gone down over the last week, and she's worried about Dad. I am too.

"We should be hiring an investigator to look for Dad," I say, breaking the silence.

"With what money?" my mother responds in a dry tone.

"Besides, I'm sure the FBI are better equipped to find him than any investigator."

"How do you know?"

"I'm not getting into it with you, Kylie."

It's her standard response to all our confrontations, and I'm sick of it. "You couldn't care less if they find him! Dad says you ignore him and treat him like crap. He says you don't love him anymore, that you just stay for the money!"

Mom's head snaps in my direction. "How dare you talk to me like that! You have no idea what you're talking about."

"I see it all the time. Do you think I'm blind? You're rude and cold to him. No wonder he's rarely ever home. It's because of *you*."

"Stop it!" Harlow yells from the backseat. "Stop fighting!" She's crying now.

Reaching behind me, I touch her leg. "Sorry, Bug." My heart breaks seeing the tears. "It's okay."

"Why do you always have to be so mean? I hate it!"

"It's okay, baby," Mom says. "Kylie is angry and scared. We *all* are. And she's lashing out because of it." She narrows her eyes at me before returning them to the road. "We need to band together and work this out."

Great motivational speech, Mother. I roll my eyes before staring out the side window.

"Want to play I-spy?" Mom asks, attempting to sound bubbly.

"What's that?" Harlow asks, sniffling.

"Only the best car game ever!"

I roll my eyes again.

She explains how to play, and they start the game. I'm a

reluctant addition, and after two trees and three signs later, I grab a pillow and fall asleep.

I wake up sometime later, sweating. Hoping I've killed a few of hours, I look at my phone and realize only an hour has passed. I look over at Mom who's focused on the road and then back at Harlow who's crashed out, head on a pillow with her feet up on Mom's suitcase. Being small has its advantages.

"It's hot," I complain.

"Yeah, the air conditioning is working hard. It's crazy hot out."

I want to growl at her, but what good would it do? Well, other than make me feel marginally better. Realizing I haven't posted anything on Instagram today, I flip down the visor in hopes of finding a mirror. Of course there isn't one, so I turn the rear-view mirror my way and almost cry out in horror. My hair is a complete disaster, I have mascara smudges down my face along with indents from the pillow.

"How much further?"

Mom takes hold of the mirror, adjusting it to its correct position. "Thirty hours, give or take."

"What?" I shriek. "You've got to be kidding me? Why didn't we fly? You could have bought a hunk of junk when we got there."

"What's going on?" Harlow leans forward between the seats, rubbing her eyes. "Is everything okay?"

"It's fine, honey. Kylie is just having another one of her temper tantrums."

"Bite me."

"That's uncalled for."

I lean down to the vent, getting some much-needed air on my face. "Yeah, well, so is baking in a car."

Mom looks back at Harlow. "Put your seatbelt on." She scoots back to comply.

"I still think flying would have been easier," I say.

"We didn't have enough money for flights *and* a car once we arrived. Remember this car was donated to us."

"Well, it's not like hotels or gas are cheap."

"Still cheaper than flying. Plus, I thought seeing the country would be interesting. Get you out of your little bubble."

Mom is always harping on me about being self-centered and caught up in my social life. It's not *my* fault she doesn't have one.

"I think the drive is fine," Harlow says. "It's been beautiful, so far."

Leave it to my sister to be diplomatically positive. I've always been impressed and a little envious of that little talent of hers.

"Yeah," Mom replies, "think of all the states we'll drive through. Nevada has been interesting so far. Don't you think? How about that one rest stop? I can't believe how deep the canyon was. And there were no guardrails, which I thought was *crazy*. Could you imagine if it was windy? You could blow right off the edge." She forces a laugh.

"Yeah, crazy," Harlow agrees.

I turn and stare out the window, not interested in Mom's attempt at making this any less miserable than it already is. I'm going to be stuck in this car for four days and my legs are already cramping up from no place to go.

I return to my phone and scroll through Instagram, looking at all the fun my friends are having—fun I should be a part of.

This sucks.

I start uploading selfies I've taken in locations that leave a vague impression of where we are and ramble off a bunch of crap about how fabulous our trip is.

When it starts to get dark, we stop at a questionable-looking motel for the night. I lift up the bedding.

"What are you looking for?" Harlow asks.

"Bedbugs."

She looks horrified.

"It's fine, Harlow," Mom says, throwing me an exasperated look. "There are no bedbugs. It's a perfectly respectable hotel. It's just not up to Kylie's five-star standards, so she's got her nose in a twist."

I'm caught between wanting to laugh at my mother's explanation and flipping her off. Not sure why I would find her insult funny. I'm obviously going a little stir crazy. Who wouldn't, being cramped up in a ball for ten hours of driving?

3

DAY two of our miserable trek and I'm awakened by a loud knocking sound. "I'm sleeping!" With eyes still closed, I turn sideways in the seat and pull my knees up, attempting a more comfortable position.

Mom swears as the sound gets louder. She never swears. I turn to her, eyes wide open. "What's going on?" Smoke is blowing up against the windshield, making it hard to see. "Oh my god! Pull over!"

"I am! I'm looking for a safe place."

I look around frantically. "We're in the middle of nowhere. Any place is a safe place!"

"What's happening?" Harlow cries out. She must have been sleeping as well.

Mom pulls to the side of the road and turns off the engine. "It's okay, baby. I think maybe the radiator needs water or something."

It's like a hundred degrees when we step out of the car and look around.

"Where are we, anyway?" I grumble.

"We're somewhere in Utah. Hold on." I wait with Harlow as Mom walks to the driver's side, then crouches down, disappearing out of sight. "I just have to . . ." The hood pops up slightly. "There," she says, standing up. Returning to the front of the car, she lifts the hood the rest of the way. We all take a step back as a plume of smoke rises with it. "Kylie, use your phone and see how far the nearest town is."

"Why don't you?" I snap.

"Mine's in my purse, dead, since yours has been charging the whole time."

"*Whatever.*"

"Just look it up, please."

Harlow rolls her eyes at me.

"*What?*" She walks away without saying a word and returns to the back seat of the car. I check my phone. "There's no service." Lifting it toward the sky, I move forward and back, then in a circle, trying desperately for a signal.

Nothing.

"Now what do we do?" I stare down the desolate road, watching it ripple through the waves of heat. "We could bake to death out here and no one would know."

"Relax," Mom says. "It'll be fine. We'll wait and hope a car stops to help us."

"*Seriously*, Mom? Wait and hope? That's your solution? We could be *dead* by then! You brought us to the middle of nowhere. There's nobody! Not one single car has passed."

"I'm doing the best I can!"

"Well your best sucks. We should have flown. Why would you buy such a crap car to begin with?"

"I didn't! *I told you*. It was donated to us by some very nice people."

"Not so nice when it breaks down in the middle of nowhere."

"Enough, Kylie!"

"*Whatever*. I'm going wait in the car with Harlow." I plop down in the passenger's seat. Leaving the door open, I push the button to make the window roll down, but nothing happens. Right. The car is off, no power. "*Uck!* It's so hot." I lean out of the car and holler. "Can we *please* turn the car on so I can roll down the windows?" She's way down the road and probably can't hear me.

"Kylie, I'm hot," Harlow complains.

I turn to see her bright pink cheeks. "Me too." I wedge myself between the seats and flip the cooler lid open. "Here, have some water." I hand her two bottles. Luckily, we filled it with ice and drinks at our last stop. "You can drink one and put the other on the back of your neck—it helps. And open your door."

"Okay."

I grab two more bottles. "Mom?" I hold them out to her as she approaches the car.

"That's okay. You go ahead."

I place one on the back of my neck and the other on my stomach. I groan in relief.

"Can you turn the car on so I can open the windows?" Even with the car doors open, it's stifling.

She slides behind the steering wheel. "No. I don't want to do anything until we get help. In case it's not the radiator. The last thing I want to do is cause more damage or set the thing on fire."

"*Great.*" I stare off into a large field of crops. The crickets are loud, but other than that we're in total silence. "Why aren't we on the highway? At least there would be witnesses when some psychopath tries to kill us."

"Mom?" Harlow's voice wavers, sounding terrified.

Crap.

Mom gives me a look. "Nice, Kylie."

"Sorry, Bug. I'm hot, sticky, and bitchy. Don't worry. We're totally fine out here." *Not. We're doomed crispy critters.* "Seriously. Why aren't we on the highway?"

"When the car started making noise, I looked for a service station and an exit sign said there *was* one, so I took it. But then the car started smoking. I could hardly see."

"Brilliant." I mutter.

We all turn our heads at the sound of a car. Mom hurries to get out, but gets caught up on something and tumbles out of the car. She recovers before hitting the ground and starts waving her arms.

"Real graceful," I call out.

An SUV pulls in front of us. The vehicle looks relatively new and I think I see two people inside. I smile at Harlow. "Fingers crossed."

There's a narrow opening between the dashboard and the hood. I watch as Mom runs to the driver's side window. She points to our car, then continues to explain. She steps back as an old man gets out and follows her toward us. I relax when I catch a glimpse of his face; he looks harmless enough.

Mom pops her head in. "They are going to help us out." She gives Harlow a wink before disappearing again.

I can hear noises and feel the car move as he pushes and

prods inside. "Stand back," I hear him say, and when they do, more steam rises.

"I need some of those water bottles," Mom says, leaning in. "We will fill the radiator and see how it goes. He's pretty sure it's just a leak. The radiator was close to empty. Harlow, can you hand me some?" She quickly loads Mom's arms. "I'll be right back."

"Can I get out?" Harlow asks.

"No, just wait here in the shade with your water."

"Okay." She scoots forward for a closer look. Both of us watching through the small opening.

There's more movement, but no steam. We sit and wait while Mom exchanges pleasantries with the man. I wish I had one of those tacky water bottles with a fan attached. That would be heaven about now.

"Okay," Mom says, getting behind the wheel. "Here goes."

We all breathe a collective sigh of relief as the engine comes to life without the horrible sound.

"Be right back." She jumps out and talks to the man again, then gets back in and shuts her door, immediately opening all the windows. "It was definitely the radiator. We need to take it into town to get fixed."

"*What* town?"

"It's another five miles. We are going to follow them."

"Can you turn the air-conditioning back on?"

"No. Frank thinks the car will overheat again if we do."

I stare out the window as she pulls back onto the road. At least we're moving again. The breeze gives a small amount of relief, but relief all the same.

Mom explains how Frank and June insisted we stay with them

since the mechanic probably won't be able to fix the car today. I think it's weird—they don't even *know* us—but Harlow seems fine with the change of plans. As long as she's okay, I can deal with it.

We are introduced to our saviors when we drop the car off. They seem nice, and after piling into their vehicle, Frank blasts the air-conditioning. Yep, I like him very much.

The town isn't more than a bump in the road and after about fifteen minutes of driving, Frank turns down a long dirt road with crops on one side and cattle on the other. We stop in front of a pretty two-story house with a wraparound porch, trimmed with multiple layers of vibrant flowers. I'm not impressed by much, but this is amazing.

We all pile out of the SUV. Frank is unloading our bags when I get to the rear of the vehicle. I drape my duffle-bag of shoes over my shoulder and attempt to lift my suitcase.

"I got that, young lady."

"No. That's okay. It's super heavy." I don't want to give the old man a hernia.

"I've got it. You can get your sister's." His smile is ear to ear. "I'm stronger than I look."

"Okay." I smile back, still unsure, but pick up Harlow's suitcase and follow him up onto the front porch, then into the house. Harlow and Mom are already inside. I guess Harlow really had to pee.

June greets me when I enter, and when Harlow returns from the bathroom, she asks us to follow her upstairs. The house is older, but still stylish and clean. I like it. She directs us to a bedroom with two twin beds separated by a large window and a flat-top steamer trunk that functions as a nightstand. The beds are covered with white, billowy duvets, embroidered in tiny blue flowers. The style is modern mixed with antiques, just like the rest of the house.

"This room is so pretty," Harlow says before I can get the words out.

"Thank you, Harlow. How sweet of you. My grandkids like it as well."

"The flowers around the porch are amazing," I say. "Do you have a gardener?"

She chokes out a laugh. "Yeah, me and the old man. Frank does all the heavy lifting, but still gets down in the dirt with me if I gripe at him loud enough."

"That must take a lot of work."

"It is. Weeding is a never-ending task. But it keeps us busy." She fluffs one of the pillows, then smooths out the duvet. "Now, after you girls get settled, why don't you come out and help me pick some vegetables for dinner? I don't know about you, but I'm getting hungry."

I'm about to say "no thanks" when Harlow looks at me, her eyes begging, *please.* "Okay, we'll be right down."

Pick vegetables? *Seriously?*

Walking in flip-flops on uneven dirt while trying not to get your feet dirty is a struggle. Trying to do it while swatting at things buzzing around your head is next to impossible.

Why did I let her talk me into this?

Harlow doesn't seem to mind the unsavory conditions, but I sure as hell do. Still, my little sister is excited and happy, asking *loads* of questions. So for that, it's totally worth it.

I follow behind and watch as they pull up carrots and gather green beans. I get a cute picture of Harlow with the shovel, trying to dig up some spuds. I had no idea potatoes are the bulging roots of a plant. It never occurred to me. Why would it? They turn into food and that's all I care about.

June gave each of us a basket to carry the vegetables, and since I'm not participating in the gathering, I've become the pack mule. *Perfect.*

I hold up the loaded basket and take a selfie, then set it on the ground arranging the stock and take a couple more photos. *Uck!* I'm taking pictures of friggin' vegetables. I leave the basket and take a couple more selfies with the house in the background. *Hmm, I could take one sitting in the flowers. I should—*

"You wanna join us?" June breaks me from my thoughts.

"Huh?"

June is holding an armful of something, maybe cucumbers, against her chest and has her free hand resting on her hip with Harlow snickering by her side.

"What?"

"I asked if you'd care to join us?

I notice that the basket they are sharing is overflowing. "Oh. Sorry." I pick up mine and stumble over. "My phone is almost dead anyway."

June rolls her eyes. It totally pisses me off when my mother does that. But when June does it, it feels different.

"What's wrong with taking pictures?"

"Wouldn't you rather live life than be a photo in one?"

Strange question. "I live my life pretty well, thank you." What's *her* problem? I slide my phone into my back pocket, anyway.

After the most amazing dinner ever, June gives us all homemade chocolate ice cream, which we eat out on the front porch. I wanted to refuse on account of the calories, but couldn't—it's too damn hot out. As I rock back and forth in a comfortable chair with my stomach *way* too full, I scroll through the photos I took today, seeing if any of them are worth posting. Mixed in with the selfies are pictures of flowers, vegetables, the barn, the cows, the house. My friends would laugh their heads off if I posted these.

I select all the irrelevant pictures, and for a moment, my finger hovers over the delete icon. I turn my phone off instead.

The conversation is easy as the crickets chirp, and a nice breeze blows—*finally*. A horse whinnies with another answering. Looking in the direction of the sound, I notice several horses eating grass in a field of bright green, lit up by the setting sun. I hadn't noticed them before. Harlow hadn't either, because she perks up instantly from the book June gave her to read.

"Um, Frank?" Harlow begins. "Can I go pet the horses?"

"Sure." He gets up slowly from his chair. "Let me get some carrots. They always have time to visit if you've got carrots."

He disappears into the house, coming back moments later with a small pail loaded with them. He steps off the porch and looks at Harlow. "Well? Are you coming?"

She jumps up and takes my hand, pulling at me. "Come on."

It's still so hot. The last thing I want to do is move, but how can I resist her excitement? Still, I slump my body and groan, putting on a show of indifference.

"Come on!" she says, pulling harder. "*Man*, you're heavy."

I jump up right away. "I am not! I was just making you work for it."

Everyone laughs.

"Uh-huh," she teases. I give her a gentle swat on the butt, making her giggle.

As we near the horses, Frank makes clicking sounds with his mouth and waves a carrot in the air. All six horses walk toward us at varying speeds. A white one is the first to arrive. He reaches his head over the fence, blowing his lips at us.

"Oh, quit being so impatient, Snowball. I don't move as fast as I used to." Frank winks at Harlow.

He shows us how to break up the carrots and hold them flat in our hands so the horses can eat them. Harlow laughs, then turns to me, "It feels funny. Come, try."

"No. I'm good. I'll just watch."

"*Come on,*" she persists. "Can you not be a moody teenager for one minute?"

I roll my eyes. "Fine."

Frank hands me a carrot which I break it up and place it on my hand. A light-brown horse with enormous dark eyes comes over, sniffs at the carrot, then starts nibbling. I can't help laughing. Harlow's right. The whiskers tickle. When it's all gone, I reach up and touch the white stripe on the bridge of its nose, then follow it down to the soft part of the muzzle. I quickly pull my hand back as its lips move.

"It's okay. He won't bite," Frank says. "He's just curious."

I reach up again and touch the side of his neck, which quivers under my hand. His tail swishes wildly behind him. "Is he mad?"

"No. He's just swatting flies."

"Smart horse." I've been swatting at a few myself.

As I stroke the horse's neck and rub around his ears, his eyelids droop, like he could fall asleep at any moment. I've never been around a horse before. They're beautiful. I don't even mind getting dirty.

Harlow turns to Frank abruptly, causing the horses heads to pull up sharply. "Oops. Sorry, Snowball." She giggles. "Can we ride them?"

"Not right now. It's quite a process, getting them saddled up and ready to go, and it's late."

"Yeah, Bug. And we leave tomorrow. Our car will be fixed by morning."

"Oh, right." Her face falls.

"I'll tell you what." Franks picks up the empty pail. "You get up early enough, and I'll take you out before you go."

"Really?"

"Absolutely."

She wraps her arms around him and hugs him hard. "Thank you!" I melt a little. Love is so simple as a child.

4

SINCE LEAVING the ranch in Utah, we crossed five more states before finally reaching Ohio. We stayed at another flea-bag motel in Missouri last night, then got up at the crack of dawn for another hellacious day of driving. It's been a rough haul, but by late afternoon, we finally reach our destination.

I'm sure Mom is happy to be done with all the driving, maybe even a bit thrilled to be back in her hometown, but it doesn't feel like it. The tension radiating from her as we enter the town limits is evident as she white-knuckles the steering wheel. I've never seen her this anxious—stressed, yeah, *many* times—but this is different.

"*Sooo*, this is where you grew up?" I say, looking at the low-end demographics with distaste.

"Yes," she says quietly.

"Poor you." And I sincerely mean it.

I wonder why they named it Foxall? More like Fox hovel. What a dump! The main street doesn't look like it's changed in the last hundred years. How could anyone survive here?

Oh my god. *Seriously?* This is where I have to live?

My mother points out familiar landmarks that I suppose meant something to her—the kissing tree, the railroad where she dreamed of jumping on the next train out of town, General Fitzwald's Grocery Store.

"I wonder if that grouchy old coot is still alive?" she says, looking first at the grocery store and then to Harlow in the rear-view mirror. "He used to terrorize us kids. The only person who could put him in his place was your Nana. She'd tear a strip off him if she ever caught him being rude to anyone, especially us kids. I think I saw him smile once, and I'm not even sure if it was real or just my imagination. It was just after Nana reamed him out for yelling at me, when all I was doing was standing there breathing."

After driving through what I assume is the downtown, we turn down a street lined with enormous trees that form a canopy of dense green over the road. All the houses are big and old but remarkably well maintained. The flower gardens are stunning, with each house rivaling the next.

After taking a couple more turns, the houses turn small again, but are still nice. That was until we pulled up into the driveway of a dilapidated old Victorian.

"This is it? Oh my god! It's such a dump."

"Shut your mouth, Kylie!" I stare at her slack-jawed as she turns off the car. She never talks to me like that. "This was home for me, my refuge. Nana was my saving grace. So get your stuck-up, little nose out of the air and be thankful you have a place to live that's not the street!" She gets out of the car and slams the door behind her.

"I think it's nice." Harlow climbs out and shuts her door.

She gives me a dirty look before following Mom up the steps to the house.

I open my door, but continue to sit, staring after them as they enter, the screen door slamming shut behind them. I'm so angry this is even a thing right now—eight days, and still no word from my father.

With an irritated huff, I climb out, reach over and pull on the bag of shoes that has been my footrest for the last bazillion miles. It's so jammed in there it takes several pulls—the final, an exasperated yank—before coming loose. I heft it over my shoulder and stare up at the house, shaking my head. Of course it had to be the dumpiest one on the block.

So Mom's saving grace couldn't take care of her house?

It's dark when I step inside and smells like old people. Dad said Nana was white trash, and he didn't want us associating with her. Looking around, I can see why.

The house had been closed up and, therefore, cool inside, which is a nice reprieve from the blistering heat. I'm not used to this much humidity. It's stifling.

I hear water running and Mom mumbling to herself. I drop my bag at the entrance of a small living room and walk through an open archway to my left. Mom pulls apart frilly, light-blue, checkered curtains over a kitchen sink, letting sunlight and a puff of dust into the tiny yellow kitchen. There is an ancient-looking stove and refrigerator against the far wall, and a small table that sits in the center of the room with a plastic tablecloth sporting tiny blue flowers. I cringe. It's hideous.

"Now what?" I ask Mom, getting more irritated by the minute.

"Well, there's no power, but luckily we have running water. The stove is gas, so I can cook tonight, and we can use the cooler to store anything cold. I will call the power company in the morning and get it turned back on."

I can't believe how far I've fallen.

"Let's open up all the windows. We need some fresh air in here."

"You think?"

She gives me a look.

"Wait. It's disgustingly hot out. Shouldn't we turn on the air conditioner?"

"There's no power, Kylie, and as far as I know there isn't one."

"Are you kidding me? It's like ninety-eight degrees out. There has to be! No one in the twenty-first century lives without air-conditioning."

Mom shakes her head at me. "I *swear* you live in a bubble. There are a lot of people out there who can't *afford* air-conditioning. It uses a lot of electricity, which costs money—something you've never had a lack of."

"Yeah. As you're always reminding me."

"I just want you to realize that there is life outside parties, shopping, and wealthy boyfriends who you seem to change as many times as your wardrobe."

"At least I *have* a life. What do you have? You rarely left the house. You're only social when you have to be, and you dress like someone in the Sears catalogue." I cross my arms over my chest, eyeing her up and down. "No wonder Dad left."

"He left because he's a lying sack of shit and a crook!"

Harlow enters, sniffling. "Could you guys stop!"

"Way to go." I scowl at Mom.

She returns a similar expression.

"I'm sorry, baby." Mom takes my sister into her arms. "I'm

just tired and hungry. It was a long drive." She lifts Harlow's chin. "How about you? Are you hungry too?" She nods her head as she wipes the tears away. "Okay then. How about I start cleaning and you go with Kylie to the store? I'll make a list."

"Sure," I say, holding out a hand to Harlow. "Come on. Let's go check out our new"—I pause, cringing at the thought —"town."

"Here, let me give you some cash." Mom digs in her purse and pulls out her wallet. "And give me a second. I need to make that list." She rummages through the drawers, pulls out a paper and pencil and starts scribbling.

Harlow wraps her arms around my waist. I slide my hand up and down her back while we wait for Mom to finish.

We take the car into town. There's not much to it—a bunch of old brick buildings, housing various businesses, most with names painted on the large windowpanes that face the street. Yeah . . . it doesn't look much better than the last time I saw it.

Finding the grocery store is easy. It's on the corner, with a small parking lot next to it. There was probably a building there at one time. Had to be. All the other buildings on the block are connected, except for this one empty space.

Pushing the door open, I'm blasted by cool air. What a relief. "Harlow, do you want to grab a basket?"

"Sure."

She separates one from the bunch as I review Mom's list, then we start down the first aisle. It occurs to me that I haven't set foot in a grocery store since I was a kid. Boutiques, yes, drugstores occasionally, malls, most definitely, but not a grocery store. "Alright, kiddo, I think this is more your element than mine. How about I take the cart and give you the list."

She laughs. "I guess you are out of your element."

I tweak her nose. "Hush or I'll hide all your books." She looks at the list, her smile suddenly gone. "Bug, I was only kidding."

"No. I know. I was just thinking how I had to leave most of them behind."

I put an arm around her shoulder, wishing I would have filled my bag full of her books instead of my shoes or at least a combination of both. "Didn't you read all of them?"

"Yeah. But they were my favorites, and I like reading them more than once."

"Maybe they have a library here. I've heard they have *loads* of books." I tease. She knows I've never set foot in one. Well, maybe when I was a kid . . .

"Yeah." The corners of her lips edge up a little. "Hopefully."

"If there isn't, we'll tell Mom we are *out of here*."

She hugs me. "Thanks, Kylie."

"No problem. Now get going. As much as I love the cool air in this place, people are staring, and it's starting to piss me off."

"Okay," she says on a giggle.

We load all our stuff on the conveyer in front of a vintage cash register. There's a bell beside it with a sign that says "Ring for service."

Ting, ting!

"Hold your horses!" a gravelly voice says from an open door behind the checkout counter. Looks like an office. "I'll be there in a minute!"

When he finally steps out, he stops and stares at us. His face is etched with age, his ice-blue eyes boring into us with hostility. "What are *you* doing here!" he barks out, as if we have no right to be in the store, the town, or both.

I feel Harlow move behind me. "This *is* a grocery store." *You moron.* "Where people buy things?"

"You've got a smart mouth on you."

I've had the day from hell with my last nerve ready to snap. "Is this how you treat all your customers, or just newcomers? Because as far as that Midwest hospitality I've heard so much about, you *suck*."

He bristles from the onslaught, but his expression readily changes to amusement as he continues to assess me. Harlow pulls at my arm, wanting to leave.

"So your momma's finally came home, huh?"

"What's it to you?" *How does he know who we are?*

"Yep. You got sass just like your great-grandmother."

"I wouldn't know. I've never met her."

"Damn shame. About the only decent person I ever knew in this world. I was sorry to hear she passed away." His face softens. "You look just like her—your mom."

I take that as an insult. "I'd like to pay for this stuff sometime today. So . . ."

"Yep. Lots of sass," he mumbles to himself as he pushes numbered buttons on the register. "Too bad about all that."

"About all what?" *Like could you get any more cryptic?*

"Her parents'."

"Whose?" *Man,* he's irritating

"Your mother's."

"Oh, right." I have no idea what he's talking about. Maybe he's starting to lose it. Whatever, I just want to get out of here.

"That'll be sixty-five dollars and fifty-two cents."

I hand him seventy. "Why are you hiding behind your sister, little girl?"

"None of your business!" I hit him with a glare that would shrivel any normal human being.

Unaffected, he hands me the change, then watches as I pick up a grocery bag and hand it to Harlow. I take the remaining three into my arms and nudge her toward the door. She watches the man over her shoulder as we leave.

"I guess we can tell Mom that he's still terrorizing people," Harlow says when we're near the car.

"Yeah. He's a jerk."

"Hey, little girl." We both turn at the old man's voice. He's holding the door open.

"Just keep walking," I tell her.

"No. It's okay." She turns and runs to him.

I watch as he squats down in front of her. Her back is to me, so I can't tell what's going on, but I'm physically at the ready to rip him a new one if I need to.

Harlow has always been fearless, but this whole thing with Dad has changed her. Watching her confront this . . . *ogre* with that familiar confidence not only adds a bit of sunshine to this totally crappy day, but it fills me up with pride.

The man stands up and Harlow walks toward me, balancing her grocery bag while tearing the wrapper off an ice cream bar.

"He gave that to you?" I ask when she's by my side.

"Yeah. His name is Charles, and he's actually really nice."

I choke. "I didn't think you could be bought with a treat." She shrugs her shoulders as she passes. "How come I didn't get one?"

"I asked him that. He said you were rude and needed to learn some manners."

"Ha! Seriously? *I* need to learn some manners?"

"That's what he said."

"Crazy old man."

Harlow squeezes past me on our way into the house. "Mom, Mom!"

"*Whoa.*" I fumble the bags, almost dropping them.

She whips her head in my direction. "Sorry!" Then runs to the kitchen, dumping the grocery bag on the table. "Mom!" She hollers.

I cringe at the thought of eggs breaking.

"Upstairs," she calls back, her voice muffled.

Harlow races past me, taking the stairs two at a time.

What a cutie.

I set my bags next to hers and rummage through for the eggs. Thankfully, they were in mine. I place all the perishables in the cooler along with a fresh bag of ice, then leave the rest for Mom. I have no idea where she wants all this stuff to go.

All the windows are open now. It's bright and miserably hot.

It's creepy to think about Nana dying in here. Mom mentioned she had lots of friends, so she was discovered the morning after she passed away.

The living room furnishings are fading with age, but they're not as gross as I first thought. Framed photographs and tacky knickknacks are scattered throughout the room.

The only photos I've seen of Mom are after she married Dad. These are when she's younger, and dorky looking, which is crazy considering how beautiful she turned out. Well, I mean, she could be if she worked at it. Her hair is a sandy-blond color in these pictures. It's a lot darker now. We got the light-blond hair and fair skin from our dad.

My favorite picture of Harlow and me from our family trip

to the Caymans is sitting next to one with us on the beach in Santa Barbara. On the wall above are all our school photos, each of us with our own sequence from first grade to present, matted behind small oval circles and framed. It's strange to have someone so interested in our lives and not know them.

I continue through the room and spot a photo of Mom standing next to a pretty, older woman. She's too old to be her mother, so it must be Nana. I take a quick glance around and realize I haven't seen any of Mom with her mother and father. It makes me think of what Charles said. More family drama, I suppose.

After climbing a steep set of stairs, I peek into the first bedroom at the top. It's extremely small with light blue walls. There is a twin-sized bed with a super cool, retro wrought iron bedframe covered with a patchwork quilt of various prints of blue and green material. Next to the bed is a window seat with lots of fluffy pillows. I cozy myself in with my phone and look out at an enormous tree rooted in the middle of the front yard. Its branches remind me of a fountain the way they hang down. I have never seen a tree like that—at least that I've noticed.

"This was my room," Mom says, startling me.

My hand goes to my heart. "You scared the crap out of me!" I get up to leave. "Where do you want me to sleep?"

"No, this is fine. I'll sleep in Nana's room." I settle as she moves to stand over me and look out the window. "I did a lot of daydreaming in this spot."

"Yeah. I guess meeting Dad was a real step up." I don't mean to be bitchy, but it's my habit and our way.

She takes a step back. "Look. I know you're angry with me —usually are for one reason or another—but let's do our best to get along for Harlow's sake, alright?"

"Not a problem for *me*. You're the one who's always harping."

"That's not true."

"Yes, it is."

"I'm just trying to raise you as a level-headed, well-rounded adult." She crosses her arms over her chest, her frustration apparent.

"*Whatever*." I pick up my phone and start scrolling. She stays a moment longer, grumbles something, then leaves.

We got along fine until I turned twelve, then she was constantly on my case for every little thing. I had to fight her just to get a cellphone. All my friends had them since they were, like, seven, but my mom refused. She argued there wasn't a reason for me to have one. So irritating. It was my dad who bought me my first iPhone. Then she started hounding me about my clothes, never letting me buy what I wanted. I told Dad, and he gave me my own credit card. Same with my first car. She wanted to buy a hideous, beat-up piece of crap just because it was my first. I told Dad, and he went out and bought me an Audi.

I can't figure out what her deal is. Regardless, it's all gone now—the house, the car, the clothes, and the social life.

On the bright side, I graduated this year, so I don't have to deal with a new school.

"Dinner," Mom calls out.

I must have dozed off. The light has changed. "Bug," I call out as I step out of my room. "Did you hear Mom?" There's no response. I walk down and peer into the next bedroom. Harlow is just crawling off a bed, looking sleepy. "Hey, did you fall asleep?"

"I guess so." She rubs her eyes, then stumbles toward me as she attempts to smooth her sweaty hair away from her face. "It's so hot."

"Yeah. I don't know how we're going to survive the summer here."

"Do you think we could get a blow-up pool for the backyard?"

"Hey, that's a great idea. Maybe we can find one of those big, soft-sided ones and put a couple floaties in it?"

Her face lights up. "That would be amazing!"

"We can definitely look into it," I say, following her down the stairs.

"Kylie, can you please not be mean to Mom? I hate it."

"I'll try, but you know how she is. It's hard to take."

"I think she's amazing. You just have a burr up your ass most of the time."

I stop on the step. "Burr?" As soon as she reaches the bottom, I chase her into the kitchen, tickling her. "Where did you learn *that* word?"

She's laughing hysterically. "Frank!"

I let out a surprised laugh. "Frank said I have a burr up my ass?"

"Yep."

I look up just as Mom turns her face away, grinning.

Coming from Frank, the insult feels like a compliment. I'm not sure why, but somehow it does. Maybe because he took the time to explain my crabbiness to Harlow. He wouldn't have bothered if he didn't care.

5

WE SPENT the last couple of days cleaning, which was a whole new adventure for me—we've always had a cleaning crew. I did my best for Harlow, but now my nails look like crap.

The electricity was turned on this morning, so I could charge my phone, finally. I missed like a million posts, but nothing from my father.

Mom told me I need to watch my data usage because we can't afford the big phone bills anymore. She asked me to keep it on airplane mode. *Yeah, right. Not happening.* There's no internet in the house. What am I supposed to do? Send smoke signals?

I ask her if I can take the car into town to find a place with WiFi, but she says no, that we need to conserve gas and directs me to a shed in the backyard with a couple of old bicycles. I tell her she must be on crack if she thinks I'm going to ride one of those into town. Hell, I haven't been on one since I was ten. She ignores me and walks away.

Shit.

There is a red one and a blue one—definitely going with the blue; less conspicuous. I swear they're as old as my mother, maybe even older, and completely covered in cobwebs. I shudder at the thought of spiders. I look around for something to clean them off with and find an old broom and a rag.

It's rough going at first—the bike and I battling each other —but I get the hang of it quickly. The ride creates a breeze, which helps because I'm grossly hot and can feel my newly applied makeup oozing down my face.

Wow! A café. Will wonders never cease.

I would kill for an iced latte right now, but Mom would only give me a few dollars. She says we don't have the money to waste on extras.

Just kill me now!

"What can I get you?" the dorky-looking guy with glasses asks when I walk up to the counter.

Uck! Is he seriously wearing a Hulk T-shirt? I mentally cringe.

"Do you have WiFi?" *Priorities.*

"We do."

I refer to the large black chalkboard behind him with a menu scrawled across it. I groan inwardly when I note that even an iced coffee is out of my price range. And there isn't a variety of black coffee's either.

"Okay, can I get a coffee with . . . do you have soy milk?" I can see the humor in his eyes and it pisses me off.

"No. Sorry."

"Coconut milk?"

He grins. "Two percent is the best I can do."

"*Fine*," I respond, irked by the utter backwardness of this establishment. It's worse than I thought. "Leave lots of room for milk."

He salutes. "Yes, ma'am." I glare at him. "Do you want that to stay or go?"

"To stay." *How else am I going to use the WiFi, idiot?*

He pours the coffee in a mug and points me in the direction of the milk. I add it along with a sweetener and look around for a place to sit. I choose a comfy-looking chair facing Main Street —yes, that's its actual name, *so* unoriginal. I take out my phone and check my Instagram while waiting for my drink to cool. I could ask for ice-cubes and dump it in a bigger glass, but then he would wonder why I didn't just order an iced-coffee.

No way am I sharing my financial issues with the barista boy.

Barely anyone has responded to the photos I've posted or returned my texts. Well, they have, but they're slow to respond, and I'm getting one-word answers, like they don't want to talk to me. I know a brush off when I see it. I've perfected the move. It kind of sucks to be on the receiving end.

Maybe the word is out about my dad. Emma lives across the street. Her mom was probably home when the FBI barged in to our house.

Whatever. That's the least of my worries.

I debate whether to text my dad again, but then I figure, what's the point?

It's so weird. If he's worried about getting his calls traced, he could just get a burner phone.

Maybe he *did* get beat up and is in some hospital somewhere with amnesia, or worse . . . dead. I'm running out of excuses.

I test-sip my coffee when my phone pings. *Finally!* Someone's reaching out.

It's a text from my closest friend, Celine, who asks if the rumors about the FBI being at my house and us sneaking away are true.

Great.

I respond by telling her we didn't sneak away, that we are visiting my grandmother and ignore the comment about the FBI.

I'm not telling her the truth. It's none of her damn business.

She responds with, "Oh . . . well." And precedes to tell me all about the party she was at last night, and how I should have been there, along with all the gossip I missed.

Yeah, so maybe she isn't the greatest friend. I mean, other than shopping, going to parties, and staying current and relative, there isn't much depth to the friendship.

It occurs to me that, other than being the brunt of a scandal, I am now irrelevant. With no monetary value and a scandal hanging over my head, I'm of no use to them, therefore I don't exist. *Wow.* Nice.

I test the coffee again.

Whatever. They're all a bunch of leeches anyhow.

I stare out at the street, feeling weirdly disconnected.

"Do you want a refill?" the coffee dork asks from beside me.

I look into my still full coffee. "No. I'm good." And, as is my usual custom with non-essential people, I dismiss him and return to my phone. I decide to stay away from the usual social media. TikTok is always interesting.

"I've never seen you before."

"Nope." I respond without looking up. "I just got here. My family is staying at my nana's house for a while."

"Cool. I'm Otto."

I look up briefly. "Kylie."

"Nice to meet you."

"Yeah." I dismiss him once again, getting back to nothing relevant. You have to be careful giving guys like him false hope. I've had many a geek falling at my feet. It's not only embarrassing but annoying.

I watch funny videos until I'm cell-phoned-out, then pick up a newspaper from a small table next to me and flip through local news I care nothing about.

I'm *sooo* bored.

At home we'd be at the beach or shopping. There's no beach here, and I'm sure the shopping here is heinous.

Who am I kidding? I'm broke. I can't even afford a damn latte.

Now I'm *really* depressed.

I return the paper and look around. The place has some style—not hipster or overly trendy—but lots of warm tones and textures that work well together. The wall behind the counter is all exposed brick lined with natural wood shelves holding small plates, coffee mugs, and glasses. The large front window with "JoJo's Café" painted on it lets in the perfect amount of diffused light so as not to blind you.

I sigh. I am seriously going to go stir-crazy in this town.

With my coffee finished, I find a place to take my mug and approach Otto. "So, what's there to do in this town?"

"I don't know. Not much."

I turn around to the sound of bells jingling as two hot guys come in. I find myself striking a pose.

"Hey, Spaceboy," one of them says to Otto as he walks up to the counter. "Two icecaps to go." He turns his head in my direction, taking me in from head to toe. "Hey. What's up?"

"Not much."

"I haven't seen you around here before."

I give him my you'd-be-so-lucky-to-have-me smile. "My family and I just got into town, and I'm bored out of my mind. I was just asking Otto here what there is to do."

"Spaceboy wouldn't have a clue." He leans in close. "We're just on our way to the lake to go boating. Do you wanna come with us?"

There's a lake?

"I could be into that, but I'll meet you there. I need to stop at home and get my bathing suit."

He leans back, pumping his eyebrows as if to say wearing nothing would be fine with him, then grins. "Alright. We'll wait for you at the pier. Oh, I'm Chase and this is John."

"Kylie."

"Kylie, we'll see you soon."

"You sure will." I wink at him, pleased that my totally dismal day is looking up.

He pays for his drinks then smiles at me. "See you in a bit."

Otto pipes up as soon as they're gone. "Just so you know . . . they're kind of bad news. Total players."

"Nothing I can't handle."

I wait for them to drive away. The *last* thing I want is for them to see me riding my stupid bike home. "I'll see you around," I say to Otto when the coast is clear.

"Sure."

Before I open the door to leave, I turn. "Why did he call you Spaceboy?"

He leans his hip against the counter, wiping his hands on a rag. "I'm into astronomy."

"Like looking at stars and stuff?"

"Yeah . . . stars and stuff," he says in a dry tone.

"*Ah-ha.*" I leave the door closing behind me.

I ride home as fast as I can and rip through my suitcase to find my bathing suits. I choose the hot pink bikini, then throw a sheer, white tank dress over it.

"Mom!" I holler, hurrying down the stairs for shoes. My duffle bag is still by the front door.

"What?" Her voice is far away and muffled, but definitely from upstairs.

I rummage through the bag for appropriate footwear. I don't know where I'm going to put all these. The closet in my room is tiny.

"Where are you?" I call on my way back up the stairs.

"In the attic."

Where's the attic?

I notice an open door leading to a rough set of stairs with a steep incline. "Mom?"

"Yep. Up here."

"What are you doing?" I ask when I reach the top. Harlow is with her. "Hey, Bug."

"Hi," she returns. "Isn't this cool? Look at all this stuff!"

All I see is tons of old junk. "I got invited to go boating. Can you drive me to the pier?"

"With who?"

"I don't know. Two guys."

"Kylie. You can't go off with two strangers on a boat. That's not exactly safe."

"It's fine. They're my age, and it's not their boat. It's their parents'. Super nice people," I say, lying all too easily.

"You met them?"

"Oh yeah. I can't not show. They'll be waiting around for nothing."

"I suppose, but I don't need to drive you. It's just down the street. Take a left out of the house, go three blocks, then turn left again. The pier will be right in front of you."

"Why didn't you tell me there was a lake?"

"Sorry. I've been busy." I turn to leave. "Don't you think you should put on something a little . . . less revealing?"

I look down. "Why?" I stare at her, perplexed. I mean, it's almost a sin to keep this body covered up as it is.

She shakes her head. "So you're going to walk down the street half naked?"

I shrug my shoulders. "What's the big deal? I'm wearing a cover-up."

"That doesn't cover anything. I can see right through it. It's inappropriate."

"Maybe to you."

"Kylie, this isn't Santa Barbara."

"*Obviously.*" I roll my eyes at her. "Okay. Well, I'm heading out." Without giving her a chance to respond, I hurry down the stairs.

"I want you home before dark!" she hollers after me.

"Yeah sure. No problem," I call over my shoulder, with no real intention of heeding her request unless it suits my interests.

I slip my feet into a pair of wedges, swing my bag over my shoulder, and head out on foot. No way I'm showing up on that stupid bike.

I'm soaked with sweat when I get there. Four blocks is a long walk when you're struggling for speed in heels.

Chase waves when he sees me. My shoes are loud on the

wooden boards as I walk down to where the boat is tethered. "Hey, beautiful," he calls out.

"Hey." The craft is half the size of what I'm used to. Oh well. It's a welcome distraction.

He holds out a hand and helps me into the boat, then slides an arm around my waist, pulling me against him before kissing my cheek. Pretty familiar considering I just met him. But he's hot, so I don't mind.

"Kylie, everyone. Everyone, Kylie."

John from the café is there along with another guy and two girls. We're an even threesome. We exchange the typical pleasantries as Chase takes the seat behind the wheel. The engine roars to life, and we pull away from the pier. When we're far enough away he punches it, then John passes out the beers and the fun begins. Now *this* is familiar.

The afternoon is spent wakeboarding. The girls are nice enough. Everyone on the boat besides me has lived in Foxall their entire lives and are either in college or starting in the fall. I'm vague about my situation and only share that I'm visiting for the summer from Santa Barbara.

Chase has his hands all over me every chance he gets. I revel in the acceptance. I don't mind the feel of his body either. He is *ridiculously* hot—tall, blond, tan, and built—my kind of guy.

As the sun dips lower in the sky, we head toward shore. *Uck.* Back to reality.

Chase pulls alongside the pier slow enough for John to jump out with the rope. Once the boat is secure, we all pile out. I say my goodbyes to everyone, then wait for Chase to gather his things.

It only takes a moment, and he's on the pier with me,

pulling me into his arms for a steamy kiss. "I want to see you later," he says when we come up for air.

I'm feeling good right now with the alcohol lending the perfect buzz. "*Mmm*," I lick my lips, tantalizing him, and watch his eyes go big with anticipation. Guys are so easy. "When?"

"Let me think." He kisses a sensitive spot next to my ear, then moves to my cheek, my jaw, then to my neck before pulling away abruptly. "*Crap*. I have a thing with the parents' tomorrow." He takes my hand, linking my fingers with his. "But there's a house party, Saturday. We have it every year. Why don't you go with me?"

"Sounds like fun," I purr as the alcohol tingles my system.

He lowers his arms to my waist, locking our hips together, and begins to sway to a rhythm in his head, grinding out a sultry dance. "Where do you live? I can pick you up."

I hesitate to give him my address. I'm used to being picked up from a mansion, not a teardown. It's kind of embarrassing. Trapped, I do it anyway.

He kisses me again. Throwing myself into it, I sigh against his mouth.

"*Damn*, girl." He pulls away with a look of desire I've become accustomed to. I put a hand on his chest and giggle. He tips my chin up. "You are so hot."

I've been told this a million times from guys better looking and a hundred times wealthier, but I like him well enough to pass the time. When he leans in to kiss me again, I push him away. My lips are swollen and tender from the roughness of his face. "I have to go."

He turns me around and smacks my butt. "Yeah, you better, before I take you on the floor of my boat. Right now, I don't think I'd give a shit who sees us."

I roll my eyes to myself, but smile back at him as I saunter down the street, turn the corner, and he's out of sight.

Sex is such a tool. You can get pretty much anything you want by letting them think they can get some. I'm not sure what I want from him—he's an obvious player. Just need some relief from boredom, I guess.

"Hey," I say to Harlow, kicking my shoes off at the front door. She gets up from the couch and comes over to hug me. "What have you been up to?"

"Nothing. You smell like beer." She steps back, wrinkling her nose.

"I was partying with some friends."

"Well, you should shower. You reek."

"Good plan." I move to the bottom step. "I'll see you in a bit. Where's Mom?"

"She had a job interview."

"This late?"

"I guess it was after closing. She's probably on her way home."

"That must have been a long interview."

"I don't know. I guess. It's only been a couple of hours."

"Okay, I'll be down in a minute." I never thought about where the money would come from. "What day is it?" I ask her on my way up.

"I don't know, Thursday, I think. Why?"

"I've got a party to go to on Saturday." That's pretty sad that I can't remember what day it is. The boredom has muddled my brain.

The shower in this house is not normal. It consists of an old claw-foot tub with an oval curtain ring attached to the ceiling by rods. It's tiny but serves its purpose. I brush out my hair and dry it, which takes a while because it's thick and hangs down to the center of my back. Back in my room, I get dressed and check my phone. I'd left it behind.

There are a million texts from Mom, but none from my friends. Not that I expected any. "Losers."

Realizing I'm hungry, I head to the kitchen in search of leftovers. Mom's on the couch, so I tell her, hey.

She follows me in. "How was boating?"

"Fine." I peruse the contents of the fridge. Not finding anything, I shut the door.

"Only fine?"

I'm sober now—the reality of my life is noticeably tragic. "It was just above totally sucking because it was a lake instead of an ocean, and they were basically nouveau riche wannabes instead of my *real* friends that I've known since kindergarten." *Who now don't give two shits about me and suck, anyway.*

"Sorry I asked," she mutters, leaning against the counter. "Hey. I don't appreciate you not answering my texts. I got a call for an interview, and I had to leave Harlow home alone."

"I was fine," Harlow hollers from the living room. "I'm not a baby!"

"I didn't bring my phone with me."

"You *always* have your phone."

"I didn't want it to get wet. Back off, okay?" I didn't bring it because, what's the point? I've ceased to exist. But I can't tell her that. She wouldn't understand.

"That has never stopped you before." Her voice rises.

"So . . ." Harlow enters and sits at the kitchen. "Did you get the job?"

Mom has a look like she's counting to ten. "Yes, I did." She smiles at Harlow. "Thanks for asking."

Which basically means, *Kylie, you suck. Your little sister is more considerate than you are.* I hate her unspoken guilt trips.

My chin comes up. "I'll bite. What demeaning low-level job will you be doing?"

She ignores the insult. "I will be a receptionist at Dr. Taylor's Office. He's the general practitioner in town."

"Cool," I say before thinking.

She looks just as surprised by my enthusiasm as I am. I *can* be nice occasionally. Besides, it's better than I was expecting. I figured she'd be waitressing at some nasty, local diner. I mean, she doesn't have a college education or anything.

"You know you could help out by getting a job as well," Mom says. "You're eighteen."

"What's *that* got to do with anything?"

"You're old enough to be out on your own. The least you could do is help with costs. Like your cell phone, for example. I told you, it's a major expense and not a necessity."

"Not a necessity? Seriously? I'll die without it!"

"Do you know how sad that sounds?"

Bite me.

"Plus, you'll want money for any extras. I know how important clothes are to you, and I can't afford to keep up with your lifestyle."

Work . . . are you kidding me? It's a horrifying thought. "So you're penalizing me because I'm eighteen?"

"Kylie. Come on, seriously? You're not in high school anymore. There's no reason for you to sit on your butt all day."

"Dad wouldn't make me work." It's summer! Which is

supposed to be about sleeping in late and partying whenever possible. I just graduated for eff sakes.

With one raised eyebrow, I get a look that says, *do you see Dad anywhere?*

"I could get a job," Harlow pipes up. "I want to help too."

"That's very thoughtful, honey, but there is a thing called Child Labor Laws. I'm sorry, you're not old enough to work."

"Well, that's dumb," she grumbles.

Mom directs her attention back to me. "What do you plan to do about university in the fall? You're going to need money for tuition, books, living expenses."

I had decided on the University of Southern California. "Shouldn't you have money set aside for that?"

"Your dad insisted on handling all the money."

"Whatever. He'll have this all straightened out before I need to worry about it." I sound more confident than I feel. My mother ignores me, and I head back upstairs. To do what? I have no idea.

6

MOM STARTED HER NEW JOB, which left me watching my sister.

Harlow needs to get outside more, so we're off on an adventure—at least that's what I told her. Morning temperatures are generally decent if you get going early enough. If not, you're sweaty and gross the moment you walk out the door.

I dusted off the other bike and lowered the seat as far as it would go. She seems to be doing okay, but the bike is too big, and there wasn't a helmet for her. Back when people rode these bikes, helmets weren't a thing. Not that I would be caught dead wearing one—beauty before safety is my motto—although a dented head isn't that attractive either.

There isn't much to the town of Foxall. I'm not sure what keeps this place going. There must be some kind of industry around, maybe farms or something—probably. Ugh, I can't believe I live in Ohio.

Most everything is still closed as we ride down Main Street. We pass a beauty salon I hadn't noticed before. I can only imagine the skill level working there . . . *scary*. At the grocery store from hell, I notice a "Help Wanted" sign in the window as we ride past.

Oh, hell no!

We take a left turn when the stores end and ride alongside a large green field that ends at an elementary school with a playground. We find the bike rack and slide them in. As soon as Harlow's is wedged, she's off running to the swings.

Harlow and I compete to see who can go the highest the fastest. I let her win, claiming my weight as a disadvantage and declare I need to go on a diet. Which of course is bogus—I have a perfect bodyweight to height ratio. I've checked.

Bored with swinging, I move to a bench and take out my phone as Harlow continues to play. Zero message alerts. I realize I didn't exchange numbers with Chase. I'm slipping in the social department. A woman walks up with two young kids, a girl that looks to be about Harlow's age and a little boy who looks to be around five-ish.

"Hello," she says, smiling. The little girl runs over and instantly makes friends with my sister. *Nice.* "You look familiar." She sits beside me on the bench while the little boy, looking unsure, nuzzles into her side.

"I just moved here, so . . ."

"Do you have relations here?"

"Excuse me?"

"Family."

"Oh, um, my nana lived here, but she died."

Her face lights up with recognition. "You're Grace's great-granddaughter. Of course! I see the resemblance now."

"Yeah?"

She pats my leg. "What an amazing woman. The world will

be short an angel with her gone. You know when I had pneumonia, she was over every day helping with the kids, cooking and cleaning? She was like that with everyone, always willing to help. I swear she must have had a hand in raising every one of us kids—set us all straight a time or two, *that's* for sure. Is Sarah here with you? She must be."

I stare a moment, confused. "Oh, Mom. Yeah, right. You know her?"

"We grew up together. We were best friends . . . before she took off without ever looking back." I hear a slight bitterness in her voice. "But anyway . . ." She waves it off. "How old are you? You look about the same age as my son."

"Eighteen."

"Then you just graduated. So did Otto."

"Yeah, I met him at the coffee shop."

She laughs. "Of course. Small town life."

"I guess so." Deciding that I like her, I gift her with a smile.

"Did you all come back to get Grace's affairs in order?" She places her hand over her heart. "I hope Sarah's not selling that beautiful house."

Beautiful? That dump?

"I don't know. We are staying for the summer." No need to share our situation with her. Our life is nobody's business.

"I'm Joanne, by the way."

"Kylie, and my sister's name is Harlow."

"What a fantastic name."

"Thanks."

We watch the girls play and talk about trivial things. I feel my skin frying and remember I didn't put sunscreen on either of us. *Crap.*

Joanne stands. "I think we'll continue our walk. Olivia, come on. It's time to go. The grocery store is probably open by now."

"Awe, *Mom*," she complains from somewhere in the jungle gym. "I'm having fun."

"I'm sure we'll see Harlow again. Besides, I thought you wanted pancakes." She looks over at me conspiratorially. "They wanted pancakes, and I wanted a walk, so I bribed them with a quick trip to the park." She takes up her son's hand as Olivia comes running to her side. "It was nice meeting you, Kylie."

"Thanks, you too. *Um*. Mom's working at some doctor's office in town . . . if you wanted to see her."

"That must be Dr. Taylor. He moved here from Cincinnati to take over his father's practice after he retired. He'd be an outstanding person to work for—not bad to look at either," she says with a wink.

"Oh, good," is my best guess at a response.

"His wife left him—couldn't handle living in a small town."

I can relate, but I need to know this *why*? I guess that's how small-town gossip goes. Everybody sharing everybody else's business. *Yep. Glad I kept our situation to myself.*

She smiles. "Anyway, tell your mother I'll stop by when I get a chance. I'm glad she's home. I missed her."

"Okay, I will."

I watch Harlow swing from rung to rung like a monkey, working her way across the bars to the other side. The playground equipment is new, the setup extensive. I think it's the largest I've ever seen, not that I'm any kind of expert, but it's definitely bigger than the one Harlow had at her old school. Getting up from the bench, I decide to give it a try.

"Hey, kiddo." She swings to the last rung and steps down. "I want to see if I can still do this." I swing my way across, my feet almost scraping along the gravel. When I reach Harlow, I feel like my arms are close to being pulled from their sockets. Height to weight ratio may be there, but weight to strength is lacking.

"Good job," she says.

I rub my palms at the base of my fingers where blisters are already forming. "Thanks. But we should get going. It's getting hot and Mom wants me to stop at the grocery store to pick up something for dinner. She's expecting me to cook."

Harlow scrunches her face. "That's a scary thought."

"*I know*. You can help me pick something out."

"Okay."

People are out and about now, so we walk our bikes on the sidewalk. "Why are they all staring at me?" I ask Harlow while returning a raised eyebrow at a lady whose expression is somewhere between shocked and appalled.

"Your shorts *are* really short and so is your tight half tank."

"So?"

"*Kylie* . . . your butt's hanging out, and I can see your stomach."

"Again, *so*?"

"Do you see anyone else walking around half naked?"

I pull my top lower, but it springs back up. "I'm not half naked! This is the style."

"Maybe where we came from, but not here."

"Oh my god! You sound like Mom." In truth, I don't care what Mom or the general population thinks. But Harlow? "Are you embarrassed?"

"No. I'm used to it. If I have a body like that when I grow up, I'll probably dress like that too."

The thought is oddly disturbing.

The grumpy old man is nowhere to be seen when we enter the store. Maybe he took the day off? I'm relieved at the thought, and I don't know why. It's not like I'm scared of him. I just didn't like the way he looked at me and Harlow when we came in that first day. It was weird. Not like pedophile weird, just . . . I don't know exactly.

I pick up a small basket. "Alright, Bug, what are we going to make?" My range of knowledge in this area is extremely limited. "Maybe if we browse the aisles, something might look interesting."

Coming down the second aisle, Harlow stops, picks up a small box, and holds it out to me. "We can have mac n' cheese and hot dogs."

I make a face. "Gross."

Although the suggestion is far from appealing, I could probably make it without burning the house down. Maybe they'll have tofu-dogs so I can stay away from all the disgusting by-products.

We head to the refrigerated section—no tofu dogs—then make our way to the counter. Once again, no one is there, and I have to ring the bell.

"I'm coming," the man says as he steps out of his evil lair. So much for him taking the day off. "Oh, it's you." He sours, obviously not pleased to see me. "And *you*." A hint of a smile appears at the sight of Harlow.

"Hi, Charles!" She beams up at him.

"Is this dinner?" he asks me, looking slightly appalled.

"What's it to you?"

"It's not healthy to be feeding Harlow this garbage."

"You *sell* it."

He stares at me a second then says, "Wait here. I'll be right back." Harlow and I look at each other as he disappears down an aisle. Returning a moment later, he drops a package of steaks in front of us.

"This is better."

I scoff at him. "One, I have no idea how to cook them, and two . . ." I look down at the price. "I don't have enough money with me to buy them." The words sound foreign coming from my mouth. "Thanks anyway, but we'll stick with the hotdogs."

"Grilling them is best. Got a grill?"

"I don't think so." Did he not hear me?

"Then fry them in a frying pan till they're slightly pink in the middle, about five minutes on each side. And now that you work for me, I'll put it on your tab."

"But I don't—"

And being an employee, you get a"—he pauses, thinking—"a thirty percent discount."

"Work for you?" I almost choke on my disbelief. "Not on your life!"

The corner of his mouth edges up, before dropping back into the stern pinched-mouth expression he usually has. "You need a job, and I need a worker."

"You don't even like me. And how do *you* know I need a job?"

"Are you working somewhere else?"

"No."

"Well then, you need a job. If you're not working, you'll only be getting into trouble."

"How do you know?"

"Years of experience."

"Your kids were hellions, huh?" I tease. The idea of someone else making his life miserable brings great pleasure, but there is pain in his eyes, and I find myself back-peddling. "What would I have to do? You know . . . if I worked for you."

Am I actually considering this?

"Stock shelves, work the register, among other things. I'm getting old. I need a break."

"You're not old—you're *ancient*."

He full out belly laughs, shocking me. "Boy, you sure do remind me of your great-grandmother."

I'm starting to wish I'd known her.

"How about you come in . . . let's say Tuesday around ten. That's four days from now. How does that sound?"

I roll my eyes. "Fabulous." His grin says he's won. "I didn't say I would work for you. I was just wondering what the job would entail."

"Here . . ." He leaves again, coming back with a frozen bag of something. "Just boil these in water until they're hot. No longer, or they'll turn into mush."

"Do you want to come cook dinner for me?"

"Hell no. I *hate* cooking."

After bagging the items, he hands Harlow a lollypop. "Thanks, Charles!" she says with an ear to ear smile.

He hands me the small bag of groceries. "How come I don't get one?" I ask.

"Here." He reaches for a package of Sour Patch Kids. "These are more you."

My lips twitch, fighting a smile. The old man has guts and a sense of humor. "Smart ass."

"Better than a dumb ass."

Harlow covers her mouth to hide a giggle.

I glare at him. "So this is how it's going to be?"

"Suppose so."

"Fine. I'll see you Tuesday."

He nods and we leave.

What did I just do?

"Wow. Look at this!" Mom looks up, surprised as I set a plate in front of her. "I didn't give you enough money to buy steaks."

"Kylie got a job!" Harlow exclaims, nearly vibrating in her seat.

She looks shocked. "Where?"

I set a plate of food in front of Harlow and sit down with mine. "The General's store."

"What?" She looks flabbergasted. "How did you manage *that*?"

"I didn't ask for it. He just gave it to me."

"Yeah, I think he likes her because she's as mean as he is and doesn't take any of his shit."

"*Language*," Mom and I say in unison, provoking her to roll her eyes.

"I'm impressed. Even more so because it's at Fitwald's."

"No big deal." Even though it is. She's never used those words when referring to me. I'm surprised by the warmth it makes me feel.

Mom cuts into her steak, and after taking a bite, looks at me astonished. "You cooked this perfectly."

"I guess I'm full of surprises tonight," I say with more attitude than I mean to. In truth, I'm amazed myself. I looked online how to cook a steak and decided to broil it.

I slice into the meat and take a bite. "*Mmm.*" It *is* good, and the peas don't taste like mush. The mac n' cheese isn't so bad either. I added some fresh grated cheese and pepper, which made a huge difference to the normally bland flavor.

I scoop up a forkful of peas. "We ran into an old friend of yours at the park."

"Really? Who?"

"Joanne." She moves the peas around on her plate with her fork. "Yeah. She seemed a bit peeved that you took off and never talked to her again."

"She said that?"

"More like implied." Mom's face falls. "But said she was glad you were home." I think she said that. Whatever. I want to keep the positive vibe going. "So what's the story?"

"Another time, okay?" She looks over at Harlow as if to say *not in front of her*.

"Sure."

Harlow looks up. "I played with her daughter, Olivia. She's the same age as me."

"Is that right?" Mom says, attempting a smile.

"Yeah, and she's really nice. Can I play with her again sometime?"

"We'll see. Probably. I need to talk to her mom first."

"Do it soon. I want a friend to play with."

"*Hey.*" I pretend to take offense. "What's wrong with me?"

She rolls her eyes. "A younger friend."

"What are we going to do with Harlow if we're both working?" I ask.

"I don't need a babysitter." Harlow looks horrified at the idea. Mom or I have always been home—she's never needed one.

"I don't know." Mom takes another bite of steak. "I'll have to think about it."

"I'll just tell Charles that I can only work after you get home. Which is better for me, anyway. That way I still have a summer to enjoy."

"Do you think he'll be okay with that?"

"What choice does he have? He's the one who forced me to take the job."

Mom laughs. I forgot how pretty it sounds. Catching a true smile is a rarity, let alone a genuine laugh.

"He wants me to start Tuesday. I'll stop by next time I go to JoJo's and tell him I can't work till . . . You work till five every weekday?"

"Yes, but if you want to start at four, I'm sure Harlow would be okay by herself for an hour."

"I'd be fine by myself for *the whole day*." She stares us both down, her arms crossed over her chest.

"I'll see what he says. He likes Harlow."

"Yeah?" Mom's eyes widen in surprise.

"He gives me treats," Harlow says around a mouthful of food.

Mom gets up, opens the fridge, and brings a pitcher of iced tea to the table. "That means he's sweet on you."

"I don't understand?" Harlow looks confused.

"It's an old-fashioned saying."

She takes another bite of noodles, looks like she's contemplating while chewing, then says, "Oh, right. I get it. Hey, I found a Scrabble board in my closet. Can we play later?"

"Not me." I put down my fork. "I've got plans."

"I'm in. That sounds like fun."

"Hey, Mom. Since I cooked, will you clean?" I want to go get ready for the party. Chase never said what time he'd pick me up and since we didn't exchange numbers, well . . . At least I'll be ready when he shows up.

"Sounds fair. Where are you going?"

"Out." I'm up the stairs before she can ask any more questions.

7

I TAKE the stairs down to the living room in my Jimmy Choo wedges, short shorts, and an off-the-shoulder, lace crop-tank.

"Where are you going?" Mom asks with the usual scornful undertones as she comes out of the kitchen, drying her hand on a rag. "It's almost ten o'clock."

"I told you . . . out."

"Where?"

"To a party."

"With who?"

"What is this, twenty questions?" She gives me a look. "*Fine.* The guy I went boating with."

"You didn't ask."

"As you pointed out earlier, I'm eighteen, an adult, and therefore shouldn't have to."

"You're still living under my roof."

"That I will be helping pay for."

"Oh . . . well," she stammers at a loss for words.

"Can't have it both ways, Mom," I say, enjoying the win.

I'm kind of liking this. Contributing gives me certain rights and freedoms she never gave me before—though I took them, regardless.

"Kylie . . . You might be giving the wrong impression if you go out looking like that."

I glower at her. "What impression would that be?"

"Well, that you're looking to party."

"*Perfect*, then I've hit the mark."

"You know what I mean."

"Mom, this is how I always dress." Why has the fashion police suddenly stepped up her vigil?

"But we're not in California, we're in small-town Ohio. People around here might get the wrong idea—that you're . . . well, loose."

"Are you saying I look like a slut?"

"No, I . . . well, sort of."

"*Seriously?*" I gape at her. She's accused me of being lots of things, but never that. "Oh my god! I can't believe you're calling me a slut!"

"Kylie, don't be so dramatic. I'm just saying the way you're dressed could be perceived as inappropriate. This is a conservative town."

"You *dragged* me to this god-forsaken place," I yell at her, my anger spiking. "This is the way I always dress. It's not my fault if the people here are fashionably stunted."

A horn sounds. *Finally.* I need to get the hell out of here. I look out the screen door at a shiny, black Dodge Charger. Figures. I doubt you'd find a Lexus or Maserati here, just Midwest American muscle—at least it's new.

"I gotta go."

"Kylie, just be careful. I worry."

"Don't. I get it. I'll try not to embarrass you." With that, I leave, the screen door slamming behind me.

Chase leans over and opens the car door from the inside. Classy . . . *not*. He grips my chin after I climb in and gives me a slightly better-than-average kiss. I think the alcohol from the other night may have exaggerated his worth. *Very disappointing.*

"How's it going, baby?"

"Good. You . . . *baby*?" *Ugh*. I'm feeling like the lead in a hillbilly movie.

He laughs and hands me a flask. "Let's get this party started!"

I unscrew the top and take a swig. "*Whoo!*" I shudder, then take another before replacing the lid and handing it back to him.

"You hold on to that. I'll catch up when we get there."

I'm glad he's smart enough not to drink and drive. I'd hate to dump his ass before we'd even left.

The party is packed with people spilling out onto the lawn. Chase takes my hand and leads me toward the house. The music is blaring. A party like this would be shut down in minutes in Cali, but we're in Ohio on a farm in the middle of nowhere. He relieves me of the flask, takes several huge pulls then looks me over. "Damn girl, you look hot. *Yes, sir*."

"Damn right I do." *And you're beyond lucky to be in my presence.* I don't know what I was thinking. The guy's a total knob. Back home, he wouldn't have received more than an over the shoulder glance before I moved on to more serious interests.

People are dancing in the living room, hanging out by the

keg in the kitchen, or playing beer pong on the dining room table. *Yep*. This looks like every other house party I've been to, other than the size and quality of the house, the people, *and* the booze. I grab the flask back, taking three huge gulps. *There. That'll make things look better.* I giggle to myself.

He introduces me to several people, but we settle around the ones I met on the boat. A girl leans in and says, "Gemma is totally jealous of you. She's had the hots for Chase since kindergarten, but every summer since he discovered girls, he's hooked up with whatever hot, new girl blew in looking to party."

"She can *have* him," I say, meaning it. "The guy is a loser."

She lifts a quizzical brow. "Then why are you with him?"

"Boredom."

She laughs good and hard, then with a conspiratorial gleam in her eyes leans in and whispers, "I think Chase has met his match,"

Chase must think I've said something witty on his behalf because he squeezes me into his side affectionately.

Idiot.

The evening drones on. I chugged the beer Chase put in my hand when we arrived, along with many others, before reaching the blissfully numb state, where life is good and nothing else matters.

The music has a good electronic beat, and my body finds a subtle match to the rhythm. I think it's Martin Garrix or Zeds Dead. They were both amazing at Coachella.

Gemma grabs my hand and pulls me toward the living room. "Let's *daaance!*"

"Hell yeah!" We pass by Otto in route. "Hey, there, Spaceboy," I stumble, stopping our advance. "Your mom and mine were bestest . . ." I giggle. "I mean, besties, growing up."

"I heard that!" he yells over the bass. "You okay?"

"Yep. Freakin' awesome!"

"Come on!" The girl yanks on my arm, pulling me away.

"Gotta *daaance!*" I shout. Gemma copies the sentiment and adds a "*whoo hoo!*"

I dance my way into the mosh of bodies and lose myself in the music. Closing my eyes, I pretend everything is as it was, and I'm in Cali with my friends at a beach house. A body presses up against me from behind, matching my rhythm. I open my eyes and turn my head. Chase is grinning at me. *Alright . . . the boy can move, I'll give him that.* Maybe he's not completely useless after all, but that could be the alcohol talking. *Who cares!* I just want to lose myself and feel normal—my normal—at least for tonight.

8

I WAKE up to the sun blinding me. *What the hell?*

I crack an eye open. I'm on my front porch laying on the beat-up wicker loveseat. My head pounds as I sit up. A jacket slides off my body, landing on the decaying wooden planks.

How did I get here?

I force both eyes to focus and look around. Barista boy is asleep in one of the chairs, his head cranked at an odd angle. I stand up and stumble a little, waking him, before sitting back down and praying the earth will stop spinning.

"Oh, hey." He sits up, stretching. "Ow!" He grabs his neck then rolls it side to side.

"What are *you* doing here? What happened? Where's Chase?" I take deep breaths, trying to center my world. It helps.

He rubs his eyes under his glasses, then blinks several times. "Well, let's see . . . he pulled you off the dining room table around midnight after you stripped down to your bra and underwear"—I drop my face into my hands and stare at him through my fingers—"and threw you over his shoulder, then took you to a bedroom."

I groan.

"Don't worry, your virtue is still intact."

"My virtue? Who talks like that?" He looks at me like, *screw you*, which has me straightening. "And how would *you* know?"

He shrugs a shoulder. "I kept walking in on you two."

"Oh my god! *Perv*."

He fixes me with a bored stare. "It wasn't like that." He stands, stretching his arms high, clasping them, then moving side to side, arching forward then backward to stretch out his back. "I was looking out for you."

"*Why?*"

"Because you were over-the-top inebriated and Chase is a pig."

"You don't even know me."

"Maybe not, but I know Chase, and I didn't want anything bad happening to you."

"So what did happen?" Actually, I'm not sure I want to know.

"Nothing. After he carried you into the bedroom, I kept walking in, like I said. He was just as wasted, and with me constantly interrupting, he passed out—you both did. I tried to wake you up and get you out of there, but you were too out of it. So I stayed close, checking in on you." Otto sits back in the chair. "Around one, you came stumbling out. I helped you find your clothes and brought you here."

Oh, hell. I rub the spot between my eyes. "Thanks." I owe him *big* time.

"You're welcome."

"Why are we on my front porch?"

"You kept giving me numbers and telling me to punch in a code."

"The security system passcode at my old house."

"Yeah, well, anyway. I tried the door, but it was locked, which was weird. People don't lock their doors around here, so I stayed."

"You didn't have to do that."

"I wasn't just going to leave you here. You were barely conscious."

I move my tongue over my teeth. "*Uck*. I feel like I have hair growing in my mouth." Otto watches me, probably judging. "I didn't even like the guy," I say, feeling the need to clarify for some reason.

"Then why were you with him?"

"I don't know. Something to do?"

"Why would you put yourself at risk for something so mundane?"

"What are you, my mother?"

"It just seems stupid."

I hand him his jacket. It's time for him to go, and I need water. I don't care that he's played guardian angel. I don't need a lecture. "Okay. Well, bye."

"Yeah, sure." He stands and takes the steps off the porch.

"So . . . were you creeping on me all night or what?"

He turns. "Not at all. You were the loudest person there, so . . . pretty hard to miss."

I thought he was going to admit he had a thing for me. "*Ugh*. Kill me now!"

"You'll survive."

Hardly. I've never drank to the point of embarrassing myself —lots of my friends have, and I've always hated how obnoxious they were. Now I'm *that* girl. "I hope my mom doesn't hear about this."

"Who's she going to hear it from? No one's going to admit they were drinking illegally at a party."

"I guess." I run my tongue over my teeth again, but my mouth is still dry as a desert.

"There's a hose on the side of the house."

I give him a look like, *seriously?* "What time is it, anyway?"

He checks his phone. "Seven."

"Harlow should be up." I stand, gripping my head as everything spins. "Thanks for taking care of me." He nods. "*Really* . . . thank you." I could have had sex with Chase without knowing it. I shudder at the thought.

"No problem. I should get home."

"Sorry you had to sleep in a chair all night. I hope you're not too kinked up."

"I'll be fine. It's not the first time I've fallen asleep in a chair."

"So you make it a habit of rescuing drunk girls at parties and sleeping on their porches?"

He laughs. "No. This is a first for me. I've stayed up late waiting for celestial events and accidentally fallen asleep."

"Got it. Are you going to get in trouble?"

"No. I texted my mom and told her I had to take care of a drunk friend."

"I thought no one wants to admit to drinking illegally?"

"Mom and I are close—I can be honest with her, plus I wasn't drinking."

"Must be nice."

"Not drinking or being close to my mom?"

"Being close."

"You're not?"

"We've never exactly seen eye to eye."

"That's too bad."

"It is what it is."

"Okay. Well . . . I'll see you at the coffee shop?"

"Yeah, sure."

I watch him get into his battered truck and drive away. *Ahhh*, my head. I open the screen door and knock softly on the inner door. I see Harlow through the glass, walking toward me with a baffled expression on her face.

She pulls the door open. "What are you doing out here?"

"Long story." I step past her. "I'll tell you when you're older."

She eyes me warily. "You smell gross."

"I smell like bad decisions."

"You were drinking again?"

"Don't worry. It's the last time till I'm eighty. *Promise*." I look around. Luckily, Mom's nowhere in sight. "Look, Bug, I'm going to crawl in bed and die. Don't let Mom wake me up. Tell her I'm sick."

"Okay. I guess . . ." She seems put off by me asking her to lie.

"Don't worry. It's the truth. *Believe* me. I just need some water, then I might throw up. Actually, I think I'll just throw up." I run upstairs to the washroom and lift the lid just in time. I'm going to die. And from what Otto told me, I deserve it.

Opening my eyes, I glance out my window. It looks around mid-afternoon, being that the sun is high, and it's like a hundred degrees in my room. Normally, I shut the window in the morning to keep the cool air in, but in this case, the priority was fresh air.

Soaked with sweat and still queasy, I head to the shower. *Cold shower.* That's what I need, but a huge glass of water first. I flap my sticky shirt away from my body, attempting relief. *Uck.* I feel so gross right now.

The water is heaven as it hits my back and trickles down my body. The old plumbing is lacking in water pressure, but right now I couldn't care less. It's my saving grace.

Thoroughly cooled, I step out and dry off, catching my reflection in the mirror. It's going to take lots of makeup to make me look human again. Hopefully, Mom won't be able to smell the alcohol that I'm sure is permeating from my skin.

I can't believe I did this to myself.

No, I can. My life is shit right now, who could blame me?

I shake my head at the person staring back. There's no excuse.

After using gobs of makeup and brushing my teeth several times, I make my way downstairs, feeling marginally human.

"Are you feeling better?" Mom asks when I reach the bottom step.

"Yeah, sort of." I move to the kitchen.

She gets up from the couch, following me. "Harlow said you were throwing up this morning." She eyes me, knowingly. "Maybe you had something that disagreed with your system or maybe too much of it?"

"Nothing you can say is worse than what I've already said to myself, so leave me alone." I move to the fridge for some orange juice. Definitely more appealing than a lecture.

"Of all the irresponsible—"

"Mom! Back off, okay? *Uuh...*" I groan. I need some pain meds.

"No. I won't back off. Were you alone? Did you sleep with anyone?"

"Mom! *No.* Otto took care of me. And would you stop yelling?" I chug the first bit of orange juice straight out of the carton and sigh in relief. Whoever invented this stuff should be sainted. Knighted. Made a king!

"Would you *please* use a glass?"

I ignore her, focusing on my next priority. I rifle through the cupboards, looking for something to subdue the hammering in my head.

"Is that the boy you left with last night? What if you're pregnant?"

I whip around on her, instantly regretting it, then wince. "Oh my god! I didn't sleep with anyone. Otto is Joanne's son. You know, the best friend you haven't talked to in a million years? He watched over me."

"Well, thank god," she says, sounding relieved . . . and quieter. "This time you got lucky. Cupboard, left of the sink, second shelf."

Grateful for cutting down the search time, I dump out two Ibuprofen into my hand, pour the orange juice in a glass to get her off my back, pop the pills in my mouth, and chase them with big gulps of heaven. I briefly close my eyes. Let the healing begin.

"Can I get you something to eat?"

I'm surprised by the generosity, considering. "Really?"

She smiles a little. "*Really.*"

"Like what?"

"Anything—well, anything I have available to me."

I think about the possibilities, trying to come up with something that sounds good in my condition. "French toast?" Yeah . . . That sounds *sooo* good right now.

"I can do that. Just one more thing."

I huff out a breath, annoyed. "What?"

"Please, Kylie, it's hard to make good decisions when you're drunk. Please don't put yourself in that situation again."

"I already told you I wouldn't. Can we drop it now?" I sit down at the little table. "Where's Harlow?"

"Joanne came by while you were sleeping and we had a nice visit while the kids played out back, then she offered to take her to the beach."

"Nice. There's a beach?"

"A small one, yes."

"So you two made up?" She stares at me a moment. Probably wondering if I care or if I'm just being snarky.

"Yes, actually . . . It was like I never left." She smiles a little before she turns and gathers the ingredients.

I watch her while she works. "So, what didn't you want to tell me in front of Harlow?"

"I'm not sure if now's the time. It's a long story and you're not all that well."

"I'm well enough."

She looks out the window. "There's a lot about my past you don't know." She moves to the counter, takes three eggs from the carton, cracks them open one at a time, letting the contents slide out into the bowl, then whisks them with a fork. "My parents were dirt poor, and what money they did have, they spent on alcohol. My father was abusive when he drank, which was most of the time—my mother took the brunt of it, but I got my fair share."

I watch as she lights the gas burner under a frying pan. I'm not sure how to respond to this revelation. The thought of anyone being abused gets my blood roiling, let alone family.

"It escalated to the point where Nana took me in and told my parents to never set foot in her house unless they were sober. She saved me." She dips three slices of bread into the egg batter and places them into the pan. "My mother tried to sober up and would come by now and then. She wasn't a bad person. But the alcohol controlled her life.

"I hated my father for many reasons, but I believe he was the cause of her drinking. It was her way of surviving in his world, allowing her to keep her sanity, even if it was through a drunken haze. Then she couldn't stop." There's a sizzling sound as she flips the egg-battered squares over. "I don't know for sure why she was the way she was, why she tolerated him. I can only guess. Maybe it's easier to think of him being the cause than believing the alcohol was more important to her than I was."

I can't imagine what that would be like—to never feel safe. "So is that why you took off and never looked back?"

"Partially. I loved living with Nana and Gramps, but my parents were still a problem. Because of them, I was a social pariah. Everyone either looked at me with disgust or pity. I had a lot to give, to contribute, but I also knew no one would ever get past their perception of me to find out. It was lonely, and I wanted to make something of myself. I decided the only way to accomplish my goals was to leave.

"So when your father came into town all charming and handsome, in his red convertible Corvette, I was bowled over. I thought for sure, once he was here for a while, the talk of my family would get to him and he'd back off. But he didn't." She pulls a plate out of the cupboard, then pauses, lost in her story a moment before continuing. "He was visiting relatives for the summer because of some trouble he'd gotten into back home. He understood what it was like being an outcast. He told me he was the black sheep of his family, and, for me, having someone to relate to for the first time was powerful." She scoops the French toast from the frying pan onto a plate. "So . . . I fell for him. Your father was several years older than me and personified everything I was looking for—independence, freedom, a new life."

She sets the plate in front of me, along with the syrup. "When the summer was over, he asked me to leave with him. I was only sixteen and desperate to get away, so yeah . . . I packed up, said goodbye to Nana and Gramps, and never looked back. Do you want butter?"

Butter? I don't usually do butter. "Um . . . Yes, please." I also don't have French toast—all those carbs. "You said your parents died before I was born. Is that true or are they still alive?"

"No. They died in a car crash a year after I left—my dad was driving drunk and drove them into a tree. I was sad, but not surprised."

"Why didn't you ever tell me any of this before?"

"I suppose I didn't want to relive it. With them gone, my life had moved on. Plus, you've never cared about anyone but yourself, so what would have been the point?" I glare at her, not liking being called out. "Sorry. I'm sorry. That was uncalled for."

"*Whatever.*" I pick up my phone and scroll randomly. Disgusted with the lack of social communication, I return it face down on the plastic tablecloth, slather some butter on my breakfast, slice off a corner, and pop it into my mouth. *Mmmm!* This is good.

"Kylie . . ." I eye her suspiciously. "I'm sorry for what I said.

And thank you for listening. It means a lot to share my life with you."

"Yeah. Okay." I dismiss her apology readily—mostly because of the insult, but also being uncomfortable with the intimacy.

I feel for her though. She must have been scared a lot growing up. I have friends, or did, whose parents liked to party. They've said it can get embarrassing, but as far as I know, they were never abused. Then again, no one shared personal stuff like that with me.

The screen door in the front of the house creaks open. "I'm home!" Harlow calls out. She runs into the kitchen with her new friend Olivia trailing behind. "We're going out to play," she says without stopping, then disappears out the side door, the screen door slamming closed behind her.

My damn head. Man, I hate this.

"*Ooh*, French toast," Joanne says, sounding way too chipper as she enters the kitchen with Otto behind her. "Lucky you."

"Yeah. Lucky me." I force a smile, hating being on display while feeling like a bag of poo.

"Let's all go sit out back," Mom says as if reading my unease. "It's beautiful out. Kylie, come join us when you're done, if you're up to it."

"Sure. Um . . . thanks for breakfast. It was delicious," I say awkwardly, uncomfortable giving the compliment. *Whatever. She's such a bitch most of the time*, I tell myself, justifying.

Everyone exits out the back door, except Otto, who makes himself comfortable in the chair across from me. "How are you feeling?"

Man! Leave me alone already. I'm *so* not up for being face-to-face social.

He did save my ass though.

"Not too bad," I respond, eventually. "Better than I deserve."

"Yeah, you were pounding them last night."

Do we really have to rehash this? "It's been a tough couple of weeks, okay?" Otto opens his mouth, probably to lecture me. "That's not an excuse," I add quickly, not wanting to hear it. "What I did was stupid. I just wanted it to all go away for a while. But when I sobered up . . . it was still there, compounded with a massive hangover—totally not worth it. And to be clear, I'm not one of those girls that gets drunk to get attention."

Why am I justifying myself? He's insignificant.

"I believe you. Alcohol makes people do stupid things. So what's your story? I already know about your dad."

I'm taken by surprise. I can't believe my mother would go blabbing about it. "What did she say?" My words sound clipped.

"Sorry." He looks confused by my hostility. "Just that there were some issues with work and he had to stay behind for an extended period to sort them out. Um, and you guys came here to figure out what to do with your Nana's place."

"Oh." I retreat.

"That isn't what's happening?"

"Yeah. There's more, but I don't want to talk about it." I take another bite. "So tell me something about astronomy?" Anything to get him off my back. He reminds me of my mother, always prying for information.

"What do you want to know?"

I swallow before responding. "I don't know . . . what are you into, like, what's your drive? Do you just like looking through telescopes and seeing what's out there, or is it more than that?"

"Are you asking me because you're interested or to change the subject?"

"Both."

He grins. "Fair enough."

I like his smile, and he's kind of cute in a studious sort of way. His dark-brown hair is buzzed short on the sides, wavy on top. His eyes are a light shade of brown, which I hadn't noticed before. It's hard to make out the exact color through his glasses.

"When I look through a telescope, I'm transported to something beyond our basic existence. What we know is considerably limited, and I want to be a part of the discovery process. The whole concept is mind-boggling!" His face lights up with enthusiasm over the topic. "Did you know there are over one hundred billion galaxies in the observable universe? I can't fathom how people are self-centered enough to believe that, with a universe this large, we're the only life forms. It's *ludicrous*. I mean . . . there's methane on Mars. Did you know that?" I shake my head. "There are only two ways methane can be made, by anaerobic decay of organic matter or a geochemical process called volcanism or hydrothermal activity, so there is an indisputable possibility of life on Mars. I'm not proposing there are three-eyed Martians, but . . ." I rub the spot between my eyes. "Sorry. I get carried away sometimes."

"It's okay. The pain is self-inflicted, therefore deserved, but it's getting better. Do you want to be like an astrophysicist or a rocket scientist or something?"

"Astrophysicist actually." He looks surprised that I would even know the word.

"That's a lot of school," I say, letting the insult go.

"It is. But I'm brilliant at math, and I love to learn."

"You're not conceited at all."

He laughs. "Hardly, just a fact."

"I could have used your help in school, being that I only had a *ninety-two percent* in physics." I grin as his mouth gapes open. *Yeah, looks can be deceiving, Spaceboy.*

"Wow, beautiful and smart—that's a deadly combination."

The boy's flirting, not that I'm surprised. "So, I've been told." My father used to say that all the time. He's the only one besides my mother that knows how smart I am. With my looks, no one cares if I'm intelligent. Besides, I liked the anonymity of that particular trait. "So, do you think I'll have any problems with Chase?"

Otto thrums his fingers on the table. "Hard to say. His dad owns a lot of the properties in town and he has this entitlement attitude which makes him a real prick. Let's just hope he's not *really* into you, because if he is and you turn him down . . . Yeah, you could have problems."

"*Great.*" I stand up with my empty plate, rinse it, and place it in the sink to deal with later. "Do you want to go outside?" I need some fresh air.

"Sure."

Gnawing at the inside of my lip, I consider the Chase dilemma as I follow Otto out the back door. Is he seriously wearing cargo shorts? *Uck!* Whatever. I need to figure out how to play Mr. Small-town Big-shot, so I stay on his good side, while keeping my distance. I definitely don't need any more complications in my life.

"SO . . . I'M HERE," I say, walking up to Charles. I've caught him in the middle of stocking cereal boxes.

He looks me over. "Did you bring a change of clothes?"

"No, it's hot out." I'm wearing a T-shirt, cut-off shorts, and wedges. No body parts are hanging out.

"Well it's cool in here, so I suggest long pants, and since you will be standing a lot, comfortable shoes."

"*Whatever*," I say with a flick of my wrist. "What do you want me to do? And this better not suck."

He snorts. "Nice attitude."

"Hey. *You* wanted me."

"God knows why."

I make a turn to leave.

"As long as you're here," he quickly adds, "let me show you how to use the cash register."

He shows me more than that. By nine o'clock, when we close, my head is spinning and my feet are killing me. He was right about the shoes, and did it not occur to him to ease me in slowly? The worst part is the hideous green grocer's apron he made me wear. Green is totally not my color—makes me look sallow. My friends would fall over themselves laughing.

Or not. Because I have no friends.

"You can work from twelve to six—those are the busiest hours," he says, locking the front door behind him. It's nice that the store only stays open till nine, but crazy in the modern world of twenty-four-hour convenience.

"Slave driver." He gives me his surliest look. "I can't start till later. My mom works till five, and I have to look after Harlow."

"Oh." His face softens at the mention of her name. "Yeah. That wouldn't do."

"My mother said she'd be okay with Harlow being home by herself for an hour if you want me to come in at four."

"No. I wouldn't feel right. Why don't you bring her with you and your mom can pick her up on her way home from work? She's working for the Doc, right?"

"How did you know?" He opens his mouth to speak but I answer for him. "No wait . . . let me guess. You heard it over coffee at JoJo's." I bet the gossip in this town is worse than all my ex-Cali crew put together. And that's *including* their social media.

"Why would I go there?" He scowls. "I can make my own damn coffee."

"The coffee you make is probably swill."

"Load of crap if you ask me."

"Don't knock it till you try it."

"We got a deal, or what? You bring Harlow and come at four?"

"Let me make sure it's okay with her first. How many days do I have to work?"

"Don't make it sound like it's community service! You get paid for your time, ya know?"

"Whatever. Let's start with four days and see how it goes." I do have financial needs now. No way am I losing my phone. I wonder how much my plan costs?

"Sounds fair."

I hear a whistle—a cat-call—and turn. A group of guys on the other side of the street are pointing at me. "Next time take it all off!" one of them says, laughing.

"*Great*," I say, mortified.

"Jared McKay!" Charles bellows. "You want me to have a talk with your mother the next time she's in the store?"

"No, sir. Sorry, sir," he sputters. "I didn't see you there!"

"And that makes your actions okay?"

"No, sir. Absolutely not, sir."

Charles shakes his head as they quicken their pace down the street. "What's that about?" he asks.

"Did you raise fear in *all* the kids in town?"

"Don't change the subject."

"Bad choices."

"It involve alcohol?"

"Yes."

He shakes his head again. "Devil's brew, I say. More stupid things done in the name of alcohol than anything else in this world, except maybe religion. I'm pretty sure that's a fact. Is this a problem for you?"

"Drinking? Not usually."

"Glad to hear it. Don't want no drunken Jezebel working in my store."

"Excuse me?" My hands instinctively plant themselves on

my hips as I pin him with a glare. "You got some nerve! I don't need advice from some bitter old man thinking—"

"If you ain't got a problem, then you got no cause to get all sore about it."

"*Whatever.*" I turn away abruptly, pulling my bike from the bike rack. No need for a lock. Who would want to steal this prehistoric piece of crap? "I've gotta go."

"Fine. See you tomorrow?"

"Yeah. I don't know . . . maybe." I swing my leg over the bike and begin peddling toward home.

I knew I'd catch some flak from my drunken escapade, but hopefully the small little minds in this small little town will get over it soon. I don't know . . . If my mom's story is any indication, reputations have a way of sticking in a place like this. Hopefully, I won't be around long enough to find out.

The sun has set, but there's enough of an afterglow to make all the colors pop. I never thought I'd be someone who'd love old houses, but the ones on or near Main Street aren't just old, they're historic—some of them enormous—with rich family histories left in marks and cuts, each with a story to tell. When you live among mansions, there is no such thing as quaint, majestic, or historical. Just ostentatious, extravagant, and sometimes gaudy.

The work that families have put into the landscaping is breathtaking. Each yard is more beautiful than the next, like a silent competition, each family attempting to outdo the other. I can't help being impressed every time I pass. How do they arrange them to flow and not have them looking like a tumultuous mess?

I lean my bike against the shed and walk to the front of the house to inspect our front yard. *Yeesh!* What an embarrassment.

There are definite borders, outlining the beat-up old porch where the flowerbeds used to be, but they're overrun with weeds. I use my foot to move scrubby-looking greens around to see what's what. I'm surprised to see pink flowers underneath. Squatting down, I push through the mess.

"*Ow!*" Something poked me.

I stand up, checking out the pinprick of blood on my finger. I'm tempted to say screw it, but the thought of the flowers fighting against the tenacious weeds as they threaten to smother them out completely makes me sad.

Next thing I know, I'm on my knees pulling everything out that isn't prickly or flowering.

I hear the screen door slam shut. They're spring-loaded—the side one too. It's kind of annoying.

Mom walks down the steps and comes up beside me. "I thought I heard someone out here. What are you doing?"

I'm too intent on my task to look up. "Getting rid of this scraggly shit."

"It used to be so beautiful. Nana's yard was her pride and joy . . ." Her voice trails off, making me look up. She's staring at the mess, looking sad, but attempts a smile when our eyes meet. "She would be pleased to see you caring for it."

"No big deal." I brush off the intended compliment, not wanting her to think I care about something so stupid. Why I do is still a mystery to me, but here I am.

"Do you mind if I help?"

"No."

She disappears and comes back with a box of gardening tools. Setting it down, she hands me a pair of gloves. "Easier on the hands."

I slide them on. "Thanks." I notice she doesn't have any. "What about you?"

"I'm good."

Next, she hands me a small shovel. I watch as she digs around a plant with prickly leaves, like the one that bit me. She loosens the surrounding dirt before gripping it at the base and pulling it out.

"That looks a lot easier than how I was doing it."

"How was your first day at work?"

"Fine. Kind of boring."

"Well, I appreciate you making an effort to help out."

"I'm not doing it for you. There's no way I can survive without a phone."

"Right," she says, as if reminding herself of my true nature.

Whatever. It's not just about the phone. I need money to spend, and I know I can't depend on her. And I guess a small part of me feels the need to help—*maybe*, I don't know. I just don't want my sister to suffer in any way.

Harlow bursts through the door. *Slam*. "What are you doing?"

"Weeding," Mom says.

Harlow comes to the edge of the step and gives me a funny look. "And you're helping?"

"Hey, it was my idea!"

Harlow looks at Mom for confirmation. "It's true."

She takes another step down. "It's dark out."

It's getting there. There's still a little light left, but not much. "Bug, can you flip the outside light on?"

"Can I help?"

"Sure," Mom says.

She runs up the steps and flips the switch. Mom and I both

squint at the sudden brightness. Now we can really see. It's worse than I thought.

"Make sure you don't leave the roots behind," Harlow instructs us.

"How do you know that?" It amazes me, all the random stuff she knows.

"Home and Garden channel."

"Is there anything you don't know?"

She smiles. "Duh, Kylie. I'm only nine."

"Could have fooled me." I throw a dirt clod at her leg.

"Hey!" She laughs, picks it up, and throws it back at me.

When I duck, it hits Mom in the side of the head. "Ow!" She turns in our direction, looking stunned.

"Nice look, Mom." I laugh.

Harlow runs to her, brushing her off. "I'm so sorry. Are you okay? I was aiming for Kylie."

"Oh?" She laughs. "In that case . . ." Mom grabs her and takes her over her legs, hugging and tickling her.

I reach for my little shovel and a clod of dirt hits my chest. I stare at Harlow, then at Mom. They point at each other. The fight is on.

It's dark now, except for the light of the moon and the ones coming from inside the house as we hose off in the backyard. The water feels amazing—perfect temperature, refreshing. We should build an outside shower someday, if we stick around.

I watch Mom as she holds the hose for Harlow and helps her scrub the dirt out of her hair, accidentally spraying me. When she smirks, I realize it was intentional.

I've never seen a playful side to my mother before. I like it.

· · ·

I listen to the rain as I try to sleep. The air smells so clean and fragrant, totally different from what I'm used to.

I don't remember having the windows open at our old house. I never thought about it before, but I like all the fresh air, especially at night when the scents are the most potent. It seems silly now that we would have kept the house closed up with all that fresh ocean air.

Ever since Mom told me the story of her life growing up, things feel different between us. I feel like I understand her better. She grew up with nothing. Me having everything I wanted must have seemed wrong to her. I don't know . . . I just never saw it other than her not liking me for some reason. Dad was always the one who gave me what I wanted. And since he did, it was like he understood me better, cared more. Now I don't know.

10

"Are you sure you're okay coming to work with me?" I pass Harlow a plate dripping with water. She dries it and places it in the cupboard next to her head.

It's fallen on me to cook dinner. If I didn't, I wouldn't get anything to eat until after work. As much as I like to watch my intake, I'm not into starving myself.

The crazy thing is, I don't mind cooking. I found an amazing recipe app. It's kind of addicting scrolling through all the mouth-watering photos. But the cleaning part, blows.

"No, I don't mind. It sounds like fun." Harlow dries the last pot and puts it away.

I give her an odd look. "Fun is hardly the word I would use for what I'm doing."

"Look at it this way." She addresses me like she's going on thirty. "You're being a Good Samaritan by helping an old man who might not be able to run his business by himself anymore."

"Good Samaritan? You reading the dictionary again?"

"Ha. Ha."

"I'll be right back." I run upstairs to check my makeup, then back down, throw my phone into my purse, and hike the strap over my shoulder. "You ready?"

"Yep."

"Wait." Remembering, I run back up the stairs and grab a pair of jeans, then I'm down again, jamming them into my purse. "*Whew*. I'm out of breath. I need to exercise more."

"Kylie, you've *never* exercised."

"Oh, yeah, right." I tap her gently on the nose. "I guess it's time to start."

She shakes her head at me while pulling on her shoes. I slide on some comfortable flip-flops and we head out. I lock the door behind us. I don't care how friendly Otto thinks this place is. Where I come from, you lock your doors.

I'm surprised at all the color as we take the steps from the porch. Because of the dark, it was hard to tell how everything looked when we finished last night. There are more flowers than I expected.

"How pretty," Harlow says.

"Yeah." We stop to admire them. I know it was a team effort, but I'm filled with pride, anyway. I realize it's a feeling I'm not too familiar with.

I'm totally going to kick ass with the rest of the neighborhood. Maybe not this year, but next year.

Ugh! I'm losing it. I probably won't even be here.

Harlow walks beside me as I push my bike to the store. Mom will drive Harlow home when she's done work, and the other bike won't fit in her dinky car. Besides, it's too big for Harlow. It's not safe.

I'm soaked with sweat by the time we reach the coffee shop. "Hey, Otto." I sigh, relieved by the air-conditioning.

He smiles at me, then at my sister. "How's it going, Harlow?"

"Good. I get to go to work with my sister."

Otto directs his gaze to me. "You're working?"

"Yeah. So?" I glare at him.

"Where?"

"The General's store." *As if it's any of your business.*

His eyebrows lift in surprise. "Really?"

I huff out a breath. "I wish everybody would stop making such a big deal about it. Yes, I can work. I'm not completely useless."

"I never said you were. I'm just surprised. It's hard to find work around here, and I'm stunned that Mr. Fitzwald hired someone. He's . . . well. He's *always* worked alone."

"He's nice," Harlow says, jumping to his defense. "He gives me treats."

"What?" Otto laughs. "Charles hates kids—he hates everybody."

"Well, he seems to really like Harlow. I don't know. Maybe he's changing or something."

"Or *dying.*"

Harlow picks up my hand, visibly distressed. I give Otto a stern look.

"Sorry, Harlow. I was just being . . . um . . . I was just joking." He turns back to me.

"Can I get an iced coffee and plain black coffee to go?" I talked mom into giving me the extra money. I explained it was for a good cause.

He looks at Harlow, then at me. "You let Harlow drink coffee?"

"No. I'm proving a point."

He furrows his brows at me.

"Don't worry about it."

We say our goodbyes and walk quickly to the General's store. Air-conditioning, I need air-conditioning. A bell over the door rings as we walk in.

Is that new?

"Did you just add that bell?" Charles is sitting at his desk with lots of papers in front of him.

"Yeah, I got sick of not hearing customers enter my store. My ears aren't what they used to be. Don't want to get ripped off." He turns to Harlow and smiles. "Hey there, sweat pea."

Every time he smiles, I expect a cracking sound from lack of use.

Harlow waves. "Hi, Charles."

The guy may be a total prick, but if he's nice to Harlow, then he's okay with me.

"So you came to help?" he asks her.

"Really? I can help out?" She looks thrilled by the idea.

"Sure you can." He leans back in his chair. "I'll teach you all about the grocery business."

"Oh, yay," I respond in my driest tone. "Free labor."

"Don't sass me, girl."

"Or what?" I respond, crossing my arms over my chest. I have to admit, he's fun to spar with.

"It's okay. You don't have to pay me," Harlow says, looking earnest. "I'll do it for free."

"No you won't." Charles points a finger at her. "An hour a day, four days a week is worth something."

"*Wow* . . ." Harlow beams, clearly astonished by her good fortune.

Charles smiles at her then looks at me, his expression

souring as he looks at my feet. "You need to wear closed-toed shoes."

"Who says?"

"The law. You'll be thanking me if you drop a box cutter on your toe, and what's wrong with you that you need two coffees?"

I hold out the plain coffee. "One's for you. Although, why I bothered, I'll never know. All you do is harp on me."

He stands up. "I told you. I can make my own stupid coffee."

"Just shut up and try it."

Harlow looks between us, concerned.

Grumbling something, he takes the cup. "Fine." He blows on it first, then sips, then blows a couple more times, and sips again before his eyebrows go up.

"So? What's the verdict?"

"I haven't had a cup of coffee this good, since . . . well, since my Mary died."

"Was that your wife?" Harlow asks.

"Yes, she was."

"I'm sorry." She places a hand on his shoulder. "Did she just die?"

"No," he says a bit wistfully. "She died forty years ago."

I choke on my drink. "You've been depriving yourself of a decent cup of coffee for forty years? Are you crazy?" At his expression, I'm reminded that tact has never been one of my strong suits. "Sorry," I mumble.

He takes another sip. "*Mmm.*" He closes his eyes, savoring the flavor. "I had no idea."

"Glad I could enlighten you."

"Is this from JoJo's?"

"Is there another café in town?"

He gives me a look, clearly irked by my sarcasm.

Maybe if someone would have given him a decent cup of coffee sooner, he might not have been such a grump all the time.

I smile inwardly. I *love* being right.

The front doorbell chimes.

"No more lollygagging." Charles gets up out of his chair. "Come on, Harlow. I'll show you how to bag the *right* way." He gives me a direct look.

"*What?* It's not rocket science."

"That's what *you* think. There's a technique in doing it right, but you seem to have trouble following directions."

"You're too picky."

He ignores me.

When the customer finishes her shopping, I ring up her sales while Charles makes a production of showing Harlow the "right way" to bag groceries.

The lady watches with her mouth hanging open as Charles patiently works with Harlow. By her expression, you'd think someone excised the demons out of him. It'll be all over town in the next hour.

When Mom stops in, Harlow begs to stay, until she's reminded of her sleepover at Olivia's house, then it's a quick goodbye, and she's out the door.

"So how come you're nice to Harlow and mean to everyone else?"

"I don't know what you're talking about." he growls. The irritable, sour old man is back.

"So you never had any kids?"

He turns away. "I lost both my wife and daughter in childbirth." His voice is filled with anguish. I tell him I'm sorry right before he retreats into his office, shutting the door behind him. I'm not sure if he heard me or not.

Now what do I do? No one is in the store, and my phone is in the office.

I walk out from behind the counter and look around. The place could use some help. I zero in on the snack, gum, and candy display at the checkout aisle. It's a wreck. Deciding to start there, I organize it according to product—color whenever possible—then size, placing the larger items at the bottom.

I stand back to admire my work. It looks a hundred times better.

Now, I'm *really* bored. I stare at the closed office door, debating whether I want to deal with grouchy to get at my phone or leave it. I decide against it. I walk up and down aisles, straightening shelves. I loathe messy stores. It's such a turnoff.

I manage to stay busy most of the day and see little of Charles, which irks me. It's *his* damn store.

Chase surprises me, coming in right before we close. I figured I'd be seeing him at some point. I'm surprised it wasn't sooner.

"Hey there, gorgeous," he says, flashing a brilliant smile.

It's too bad he's such an ass—he really is cute. I finish wiping off the conveyer belt and return the cloth and a bottle of cleaner under the cash register.

Tilting my head to the side, I twirl the ends of my hair around my fingers while giving him a flirtatious, eager smile. "Backatcha, handsome." This isn't my usual brush-off tactic. I've had to put some thought into it. "I was wondering when you would come find me." My expression switches to a full pout. "I thought maybe you didn't like me anymore because I got a little . . . *wild*," I whisper the last part, sounding remorseful, weak. *Uck.* So not me.

"Oh, no, baby. I loved it." *Of course you did, you lowlife.* "But next time"—he leans in conspiratorially—"let's make it a private dance, okay?"

"Yeah, right," I pump my eyebrows with over-the-top enthusiasm, making the action look disturbing. "How about tonight?" I plead, adding a touch of needy.

"*Uhhh . . .*" He stares at me, looking confused. "Yeah . . . Okay. Oh, ah, actually . . . sorry, I can't. Um . . . I just remembered I have plans with the boys."

I smile to myself. This will be easier than I thought. I cross my arms over my chest and plaster a pissed-off, dejected look on my face. "That's not fair," I whine, stomping a foot, adding to the effect. "You'd rather spend the evening with your smelly old buddies instead of me?"

"*Aw*, now don't be like that."

"*Fine*," I huff. "What about tomorrow?"

He hesitates. "*Ahhh* . . . I can maybe get together with you sometime next week?"

"Next week!" He cringes at the high-pitched screech. "I see how it is. You just use me, then you're too busy." I work up a few tears.

He looks around, obviously concerned with potential bystanders. "No, baby. It's not like that. I'll tell you what . . ." He pulls out his phone. "I'll text you."

Dumb ass. "Okay." I bubble. "Let me have your phone." He looks concerned but unlocks it and hands it over obediently. Under contacts, I type 'Beautiful New Girlfriend' and a phone number that's one digit off. That way, if he comments about it, I can play the dumb blond card.

He looks at his phone after I hand it back to him, then at me. I plaster on a bashful, hopeful expression, willing him to agree with what I've typed. "We can text all night, okay?" He gapes at me. "There's so much about you I want to know." I'm probably laying it on a bit thick now, but I'm having too much fun to quit.

"Yeah, sure I will," he says, eyeing his escape route. I stifle a laugh. "O-okay, now." He inches toward the exit. "I'll talk to you later."

"You better. And text me as soon as you leave. You know what? We should get together with your family." Ha! Final nail in the coffin.

"Uh, sure, yeah." His feet are moving fast now. "Got to go."

And he's gone.

"See ya." I give a dismissive wave as the door closes behind him. What a moron.

"Not bad," Charles says, wiping the lid off a dusty can of peas with his pocket rag. "Should I applaud?"

"If you must." I grin, feeling satisfied with my ruse.

"I assume that had something to do with that bad choice you were telling me about?"

"Could be."

"You're pretty good. Scary—but good. Ever thought of getting into theatre?"

I laugh. "No. Think I should?"

"You'd be up for an Academy Award in no time." He chuckles to himself as he moves to the front door and flips the sign to Closed.

I close down the register like Charles showed me, gather up

the receipts, the zipper bag full of cash, and lay it on the desk next to him.

"You know, you should have a display of weekly sale items in the front of the store. You'd probably generate more revenue. People have a tendency to buy what they don't need if it's on sale. And you could add a basic necessities display near the register. You know, things people forget but always need—lip stuff, batteries, tissue, stuff like that—along with the gum and candy."

He scowls at me a moment, then says, "That's smart."

"I can be when I want to be." Although, it's in every other grocery store. He obviously doesn't get out much.

"You got a smart mouth, *that* I'm sure of. You go ahead with your display ideas." He gestures at the store with a dismissive flick of his wrist. "And anything else you want to change."

"You trust me . . . just like that?"

"I got no problem saying you got good ideas."

I choke. "Did you just give me a compliment?"

"It's possible."

I clutch my shirt over my heart. "I'm in shock."

"Don't sass me, girl."

I smile sweetly at him. "See you, old man."

"Bye, brat."

I laugh and head out, feeling surprisingly cheerful.

11

"YOU CAN COME over tomorrow when it gets dark." Otto presses the button to get the espresso started for my iced latte.

I stopped into the café to use the internet and treat myself. I have a little money in my pocket since Charles believes in paying cash at the end of every week.

"That's quite a proposition," I say, winking. I get perverse enjoyment out of watching geeks squirm.

His eyebrows shoot up in surprise, then narrow into what looks like resentment before scooping ice into a tall glass. "You're the one who asked to look through my telescope."

I stare at him a second, thrown off my game. "I know. Um . . . but I have to work tomorrow. What about tonight?"

"I have to close." He pours the espresso over ice, then adds the milk. "I won't be done until ten."

"So? It needs to be dark, right?"

He dumps my latte from a glass into a to-go cup, then sets it down in front of me.

Wow! Seriously? A to-go cup? He knows I'm staying to use

the internet. I look from the cup back to Otto. "Come on, I was only teasing." He continues to stare at me like I'm an irritant he wants gone. "Can't you see I'm in a good mood?" I pick up the latte and smile sweetly at him. His sour expression doesn't change. "I'm *so* bored. I could use some intellectual stimulation."

"Yeah, among other things."

I let out a long, exaggerated sigh. "Okay. I'm sorry. I'm perpetually on."

He regards me warily. "I've noticed."

I ignore the dig. "Where do you live?"

His expression is like, *fine, whatever.* "I guess I can swing by and get you after work."

What am I? Some desperate female he's doing a favor for. *Please.* I don't want to look at the cosmos *that* badly.

"Never mind. Don't worry about it." I pick up my drink to leave.

"Kylie. Hey. Sorry. I'd love to show you, okay?" The corner of his mouth tugs up in an attempt at a smile. "I just . . . Never mind."

I pause a moment, debating if dealing with his moodiness outweighs my need for staving off boredom. I have *definitely* hit rock bottom if my idea of a thrill is looking through a telescope with doofus here.

"What do you think?" His smile's more sincere this time. "It's supposed to be a clear night."

I'd say that was a sufficient attempt at sucking up. "I'm sure I can ride my bike over. I mean, nothing in this town is *that* far. Where's your phone? I'll give you my number and you can text me the address."

He reaches below the counter, swipes to unlock it, then hands it to me. "Just put it in."

I open up his contacts and pause, tempted to enter something like "Hot Babe" in light of what I did to Chase, but nix the idea and type in the essentials since he seems to be lacking in the sense of humor department.

A few seconds later, some guys come through the door, looking me up and down like I'm a tasty treat. They were probably at the party. *Assholes.* I'm so over it.

I hand him back his phone. "I'll see you later."

"Sure thing."

So much for the internet. I don't feel like dealing with whatever those guys think they're entitled to throw at me.

As soon as I'm out the door, I take a long-awaited sip. "Heaven." I've missed this more than anything else I left behind. I take another sip. *Well, maybe not the Audi.* I climb on my bike, balancing my latte in one hand, and start peddling. *Or the pool, the beach, the shopping.* The list rambles on in my mind as I peddle to the pier.

I rest my bike against a tree, then walk down the wood planks to the end. Kicking off my flip-flops, I sit down and drop my feet into the water. The coolness is a welcomed relief.

It's funny, not too long ago I'd have stressed about getting dirty. Now I'm digging in gardens and sitting on filthy wooden boards. I'd like to think Frank would be impressed. I wish they didn't live so far away. It would be nice to see him and June again. We only spent the day with them, but I don't know . . . They're like how grandparents *should* be.

I swirl my toes in the water, watching as a boat slowly comes toward me. It's sleek, sporty, and expensive, not exactly the high-end craft I would expect to see around here. Definitely didn't notice it when I was out with Chase and his buddies.

It pulls up alongside the pier. A guy jumps out and tethers it. The sight of him has me sitting up straighter and shielding my eyes for a clearer view.

Holy shit! He's muscular, bronzed and shirtless, with shorts that hang low on narrow hips. His sandy-colored hair is a little long for my taste, but it's windblown sexy—totally acceptable.

Not taking my eyes off him, I stand and make my way toward him. He's busy doing something in the front of the boat. "Hi," I call out, getting his attention.

He stands up and brushes his hair away from his face before shielding his eyes, squinting up at me. "How's it going?"

"Good. Your boat?"

"Family's." He reaches for his sunglasses and slides them on. "I'm the only one that uses it, though."

"It's beautiful."

He looks it over. "She is."

"She?"

"The *Anna Marie*."

"Named after your mother?" I joke.

He snorts. "Yeah, actually. The first Mrs. Stafford."

"How many were there?"

"I believe the old man is on number four, or is it five? I've lost count."

"I can relate to family dysfunction. What's your name?"

"Tristan."

Sexy name. "I'm Kylie."

"I'm just coming in to grab a few things from the store, but if you want to go for a ride, I'll take you out."

I can feel myself slipping into seduction mode, but stop for some reason. "Actually, I have to go. Another time, maybe."

What am I saying? Mr. Hottie just asked me out on his boat. And I have to do what, exactly?

He smiles. "I'm sure I'll see you around town."

"I'm sure you will." *You're an idiot*, I chastise myself as I turn away.

"Hey," he calls out, stopping me. "I haven't seen you around here before."

"No." I turn, thrilled at being called back. "I'm just here for the summer. You know . . . family drama."

"Yeah. Me too. But I was banished here. Not that it's a hardship. I'd rather be here with my grandparents than anywhere else. But my parents don't know that, so I let them think otherwise, leading me to exactly where I want to be."

I smile, impressed. "Smart."

He grins, flashing me his dimples. "Survival."

"I know that word all too well. But here? *Uck!*"

"No way. It's perfect. No crowds, clean fresh air, the lake."

"Where's your home?"

"Manhattan."

"And you'd rather be here? Are you nuts?"

He laughs. "Maybe. But this is where I've always been the happiest."

"A little odd, but okay."

His smile is laid-back. Status pours off him in a way that only people who are born with it can carry.

What was I thinking going for Chase? Lost my head, I guess. Stupidity under duress.

"So . . . what did you do?" I know it's prying, but maybe he has an issue with drugs. I'd rather know sooner than later. Wouldn't be the first rich boy I've come across that did.

He grins. "Let's just say I have a bit of a temper with ignorant people." He turns his back to me and starts fiddling with something.

"Fair enough." I take his busyness as my cue to leave. *Damn.* "Well, I'm going to head out. It was nice meeting you."

He doesn't look up, but waves. "You too."

I return to my bike, pushing off toward home, mentally kicking myself the whole way.

12

I TEXT Otto when I arrive. I don't want to disturb his family by knocking on the front door this late at night. After greeting me, he leads me up a flight of stairs to the second floor of a creaky old house similar to my own, except his has been updated.

He opens a door that leads to more steps. They must have an attic as well. The stairwell is narrow, opening into a tiny room, which Otto calls a widow's peak. It's sparsely furnished and not much larger than an eight by eight space with floor to ceiling windows and French doors that lead out onto a tiny balcony where he has his telescope set up.

"This is beautiful . . . and very high," I say, looking over the low railing. I'm not usually afraid of heights, but this is unnerving even for me.

"Yeah. Late at night, it's quiet, except for the crickets and frogs. It's easy to imagine I'm the last person on the planet."

I lean back against the house, putting distance between me and falling to my death. "Would you want to be?"

"Sometimes. You?"

"No way. I *like* people." There's an awkward silence as we stare at each other. I can't imagine he's used to having a hot girl in his space. I decide to make it easy on him. "So teach me something."

"What do you want to know?"

"Don't have a clue," I say, feigning ignorance. "Tell me something I don't know." As if *that* line hasn't been used a million times.

He eyes me suspiciously, probably remembering that I'm smarter than I let on.

"You know . . ." I point at the telescope. "Some fun facts."

He clears his throat, like he just swallowed a sour pill. "Fun facts?"

"Oh, whatever." I wave it off. "You know what I mean."

"Okay, well there are eight planets and five dwarf planets in our solar system, but NASA believes that there are hundreds more waiting discovery so . . ."

I roll my eyes and look at him like, *no duh*.

"What?"

"Try top private schools." The words sound bitchy. *Ugh*. It's sad how natural it comes.

He looks away and shakes his head, grumbling, "Figures." Then turns back, crossing his arms over his chest. "I'm not sure what you want me to tell you."

I try to think of an appropriate question. "What's your favorite area of study?"

He doesn't answer right away but stares at me, assessing, then shrugs. "I guess exoplanets. There have been over four-thousand discovered and some with a real possibility . . ." His voice trails off.

"What?"

"I don't know. Waiting for a smart-ass comment?"

I grin, placing a hand on my chest. "Me?"

"You're making me uncomfortable. I'm not even sure why you're here."

I sigh, feeling a slight twinge of guilt for being a jerk. He's a nice guy. "I told you. I'm bored."

"I'm sure there are a lot of other things you can do to fill your time."

"Well I haven't been able to come up with any, so . . ." This normal conversation shit is new to me. I wrack my brain trying to think of another topic. "I always thought black holes were interesting."

He brightens. "Yes. Especially the recent discovery of the eighty-three quasars powered by super-massive black holes."

Okay? "Interesting."

"It is."

"What do you think is on the other side of one? I mean, everything gets sucked in. Where does it all go?"

"The theory out there is that matter is condensed into its simplest form and then added to the mass. So if a person could actually jump in to a black hole, they would be stripped down to an atomic level and slapped to its side, in essence becoming a part of it."

I look out into the night, enjoying the breeze. "It's weird to think of it that way. I mean, if the gravity is so strong that light can't escape, you'd think it would pull you somewhere, not just vaporize you."

"That's why science fiction movies are so good."

"True. Can I look?" I motion to the telescope.

"Sure."

I tentatively push away from the wall and peer through the lens. "Wow!" I turn, staring at him. "That's a galaxy! Which one is it?" I turn back, squinting one eye so the other might see more clearly.

"Andromeda. It's the closest galaxy to our own. Here." From behind, he reaches around me to adjust a knob, his chest briefly touching my back. The heat that rushes through me has me taking a step to the side.

What the hell?

I stare at him, slightly unnerved by my reaction. Unaware, he peers into the telescope, making more adjustments before stepping back. "There. Have a look. I've locked it on Saturn." When I don't move, he stares at me, looking puzzled. "What's wrong?"

I pause for a minute, giving my head a shake. "Nothing." I return to the telescope. "Oh wow, the rings are amazing. I've seen the planet in photos, but nothing compares to seeing it in real-time."

I see him smile proudly in my periphery.

"Here, I'll show you some other cool things."

I step out of his way, not wanting to test my reaction to him again. "So, what's it like living here?"

I could be here for a while. Who knows what's happening to my trust fund slash education fund? I might have to get a student loan and go to a community college. *Uh.* I can't even imagine . . . The humiliation.

"I don't know. It's home, so . . ."

"Yeah, but like there's nothing to do, right? No nightlife. Galleries. How do you stand it?"

He looks at me and shrugs. "You don't miss what you don't have?"

I drop my face in my hands. "I'm going to die."

"People sometimes drive to Cincinnati when they want to do the big city thing."

"Really?" I get excited. "How far away is that?"

"About two hours."

My body slumps.

"You act like it's Siberia."

"It might as well be when you don't have your own car." No way Mom is going to let me drive the car that far. "Too much gas," she'd say. I need to do some shopping, and while I hate to admit it, I need to tone down the wardrobe. Harlow's comment the other day bothered me. I need to save my money though. I want to make sure we have enough to get by.

Did that thought seriously just come from me?

"Um . . ." He breaks me away from my thoughts. "Here, have a look. It's Jupiter."

I look into the lens. "It's so big!"

"Yeah, she's a big one."

"So do you use this thing to spy on people in their bedrooms?"

"Not lately."

I crinkle my nose, repulsed. "Gross!"

"I'm kidding."

"Oh, right." How can I tell? He never acts like I expect him to.

"Do you miss your friends?"

I rub my arms, feeling the sting of rejection.

"Are you cold? We can go in if you want."

"Sure."

Once inside, I sit on a small Victorian lounger while Otto

stretches out on the floor in front of me, leaning back on his hands. His legs seem excessively long in such a small space.

"So?" he asks.

I try to think back to the last question. "Oh, yeah. My friends?"

"You were obviously part of the 'in-crowd' and must have tons of friends. It must be hard being away from everyone."

"Not as much as you might think. They ousted me from the group."

"They *ousted* you?" He seems genuinely surprised.

"Yeah. Out of sight, out of mind. I've ceased to exist."

"That doesn't seem right."

"No. It's not. They were my best friends when my dad let us party on the yacht and now . . ." I shrug my shoulders.

"I'm sorry."

"Don't be. They're not worth it." Saying those words feels good. They're *not* worth it.

"So you were loaded?"

"Lifestyles of the Rich and Shameless, baby."

"Do you miss it?"

"Of course I miss it! Who wouldn't?"

He shrugs his shoulders. "Sounds all fake to me."

"What would you know?" I snap. That was my life. He has no right to insult me.

He looks around. "Nothing, obviously."

"Yeah . . . well . . . It's not all like that. There are wealthy people that lead a down-to-earth lifestyle." *I just don't know any.* "Sorry I got snippy. Things are complicated at the moment." I sigh, thinking of the depths of it and the fact that it is totally out of my control.

He leans forward and picks at the carpet. "Do you want to talk about it?"

"I don't know." I moan dramatically as I slide to the floor, resting my back against the lounger. I stretch my legs out next to his. "I just feel so lost and out of place. Everything that I thought was, wasn't, and I'm not sure I like who I am all that much." I'm surprised by my easy response and wish I could take it back. It's not like we're friends. I don't know . . . we did sort of bond over my drunken mistake at the party, but still . . .

He returns to leaning on his hands, his expression thoughtful. "It sounds like your existence has been flipped upside down, and you've been thrust into a complete culture shock. Feeling out-of-sorts is understandable."

"Thanks," I say, meaning it.

"No problem. So if you're so rich, why are you working? I can't imagine it's your first choice in how you'd like to spend your summer holiday."

The question takes me off guard. I'm not sure why. It's a simple deduction. "Things are a little messed up right now."

"You don't have to talk about it if you don't want to."

"Yeah. I'd rather not."

"No problem. So, a friend of mine just came in for the summer and invited me out on his boat. Do you want to come with us? It's not a yacht, but . . ." He grins.

"Why, Otto . . . are you asking me on a date?"

He blushes, then skewers me with a glare.

I hold my hands up in defense, completely taken aback. "Can't you take a joke?"

He stands up. "Look. Never mind."

"Hold on. What did I say?" I push myself up off the floor.

He runs his hands through his hair, then starts to pace. "I'm sorry. I don't like being teased, okay? I got enough of it growing up, and I'm not putting up with it anymore." He stops, his expression determined and direct. "I need to know. Is everything a game to you? A way for you to get your kicks? Because if it is, I'm just not interested in being around you."

I laugh nervously. I've never been talked to like this before. "Lighten up. It was just a joke."

"Jokes can hurt."

I think I've been schooled by a . . . I want to call him a dork, but realize he's not even close to one, and I falter for a lack of a smart-ass comeback. "I'll do my best to tone it down. I've been like this for a long time," I say, attempting to lighten the mood. "It's not going to be easy." I jab him in the ribs with my elbow.

He smiles a little. "Fair."

"So about this friend. Should you maybe ask him first if it's okay if I come?"

"He won't mind."

"Do *you* still want me to come?"

He takes his time as he considers. "Sure."

"Seriously? Don't do me any favors, alright? Look. I need to go. Thanks for"—I wave my arm indicating the space —"everything." I walk to the stairs. The guy is so sensitive. It's exhausting.

"Kylie, I'm sorry, I'll let it go." I stop my descent. "I just . . . This didn't end the way I would have liked." His smile is sheepish. "Come boating. It'll be fun."

I contemplate for a moment, then decide to give the kid a break. "Okay. Sure. What day are you going?"

"Sunday?"

"That works."

"Just meet us down at the pier. I think at twelve, but I'll text you."

"*Sure.*"

I finish my way down the steps, then the next set, and then I'm out into the night. Definitely the strangest evening of my life.

13

ON THE WAY TO WORK, I pass a sales rack outside a clothing store. I've never noticed this place before, probably because I've never come this way. Harlow needed me to walk with her to Olivia's, and from there I rode my bike into town.

As I comb through the items, I realize I've never looked through a sales rack before. I find three T-shirts in colors I like —all inexpensive and conservative—and take them into the store to purchase. Yesterday was payday.

At a quick glance, I notice a lot of other cute items, and I'm forced to stop and look. Although the clothes aren't expensive by my previous standards, they are way out of my budget now. The bitterness of being reduced to this meager existence boils in my gut.

In the beginning, I told myself that I was just slumming it for the summer. Nothing wrong with seeing how the other half live—it was probably even good for me—but now I'm fearful it's permanent. We haven't heard anything about my dad or our financial situation, and he certainly hasn't been in touch.

I bring the T-shirts up to the counter, doing my best to squash the sense of humiliation.

"If you like these, we have some other shirts you might like over here on the wall." She points, coming from behind the counter.

I know she's only doing her job—salespeople are trained to upsell—but it pisses me off, anyway. "It's okay," I say icily, stopping her. "I'll come back when I have more time."

She stops, her smile dissolving. "Sure."

"It's just that I'm in a hurry." I feel bad for being bitchy.

"How would you like to pay for that?" Her smile is strained.

I pay in cash. A first for me. Credit cards have always been my go-to.

She places the shirts in the bag and tells me to have a nice day, though I know she doesn't mean it. I thank her anyway and give one last look around before I leave, the fury at my situation continuing to build. *This is ridiculous.* I'm living in this tiny hellhole of a town, and I can't even afford what's on the racks at a stupid boutique in bum-friggin-nowhere.

I stomp into the grocery store and throw my stuff on the floor of the office.

"Got somethin' stuck in your craw, girl?" Charles asks in his usual surly tone.

"What the frick is a craw?"

"Never mind. What's eatin' you?"

"Nothing!"

I head to the back and change into my jeans. There aren't any customers in the store, so I look for boxes to unpack. The stack is a mile high. "Great."

I have an incredible urge to punch and kick the tower of goods until they lie at my feet in a mangled heap. "Eff my life!"

I heft a large box of paper towels out to the appropriate aisle, rip open the top, and start stacking them on the shelves. In my current state, towels are safer than eggs.

Where the hell is my dad? I've gone through all the possible scenarios in my head, trying to justify what's happened, and nothing helps. I'm starting to wonder if what the Feds accused him of is true. If so, that means he bailed on me, making me suffer—making *us* suffer. I don't know what to believe. Grabbing the last roll, I bash it against the edge of the shelf several times, containing the scream that's bubbling to the surface, then throw it as hard as I can against the shelf.

"What the heck's going on?" Charles yells from somewhere in the store.

How did he hear that? "Nothing!"

Surprisingly, I feel a lot better. I place the battered roll on the shelf behind the others.

The bells on the door chime. I quickly take the empty box to the back, break it down, then move to the cash register. A lady stops at my sale display and loads her cart. I look over my shoulder at Charles, who's just left his office. He shrugs at my silent remark, but I know he's happy. Eventually, she comes through the checkout with her cart.

"That will be thirty-seven, fifty-two. Plastic or paper?" I can't believe that's still a thing. Charles says that everyone got all over him to use paper bags because they're biodegradable. I said okay . . . but they're killing the forests by cutting down all the trees to make the paper. He growled at me and disappeared into his office for more than an hour.

"Have a nice day," I say, sort of meaning it.

I work in retail as a grocery store clerk. *Uuk!* I go into the office and grab my phone to kill time, then park myself at the register.

"Hey, you work here?"

Tristan places a small carton in front of me. I don't know if it's being caught in a menial position by an equal, or the demeaning experience at the clothing store, but his question rubs me raw. "Bite me."

"Excuse me?" His eyebrows shoot up, looking stunned by the attack.

"So what? I work! Most people do."

"*Sorry*. It's just Charles has never had anyone work in his store before. It surprised me."

"Oh." My cheeks suddenly feel hot. "Yeah. I hear that a lot. For some reason the old buzzard likes me."

"Kylie, quit your yammering. We've got shelves to stock."

"Oh, leave me alone, old man! I'm talking. It's called customer service. Ever hear of it? *No*. Because you're mean as sin."

I hear him mumble something like, "Didn't sound like no customer service to me."

"I can see why he likes you." Tristan's crystal-blue eyes sparkle with humor.

I hadn't noticed the color of his eyes before—he'd had sunglasses on. Now my body is all a buzz. He's the entire package and heart-stoppingly beautiful.

"I'm sorry. I didn't mean to snap at you." I pick at an invisible piece of lint off the conveyer belt, feeling ridiculous in my grocer's apron.

"It's okay. No one likes being cooped up inside on such a beautiful day."

I appreciate his tact. "Thanks. That will be one seventy-five."

He hands me two dollars.

"I'll see you around, okay?" he says when I hand him his change. "I've got to get this to my grandmother. She's baking a strawberry-apple pie, and we're out of whipping cream."

"Do you need a bag?"

"No, I'm good." He takes the carton.

"Enjoy."

"Oh, I will. Her pies are the best," he says emphatically.

I groan as the door closes behind him. Why did I snap at him like that? He's the only person in this town that understands the lifestyle I'm accustom to, and he's freaking hot. How do I keep messing this up?

"That boy, Tristan, is trouble," Charles says from his office.

I find him hunched over his paperwork as per usual. "How would you know? Everyone's trouble to you." He narrows his eyes at me. "Do you know him personally?" I wouldn't mind some details. "No wait. You don't talk to people—you just grump at them."

"I talk to people. That boy just gets in trouble a lot, from what I've heard."

"Yeah, well, what do they say about me?"

"They're all a bunch of idiots."

"Exactly."

He grunts and starts punching numbers into his ancient calculator that makes a crunching noise as numbers print across a tiny slip of paper.

I take a drink from my water bottle and notice a framed photo on his desk that I hadn't seen before. It's a young man and woman all dressed up. I lean over him for a clearer view. By the clothes, I'd say it was taken in the fifties.

"Hey," Charles says. "Do you mind?"

"Chill, old man. Is this you?" I pick up the frame.

"None of your business." He snatches it back and returns it to its previous position.

"Stop being mean. Is that your wife?"

"Yes." He blows out a loud, irritated breath. "That's Mary."

"Then why are you being such an ass about it?"

"Didn't anyone ever tell you you're supposed to respect your elders?"

"No. Is it because she died?" He doesn't respond. "You can't be a dick to everyone because your wife and child passed away. It was eons ago."

"What the hell would you know about it?"

"I know I wouldn't be miserable for the rest of my life over it. What would your wife have said?"

"She'd tell you that you were nosey and to mind your own business."

"I doubt that. You know I'm right."

"What I know is that you've got a lot of sass."

"So you've told me." I hear the front door chime, so I turn to leave.

"Maybe you should try to get rid of that chip on your shoulder," he calls out to me. "Just because you lost your daddy's millions doesn't mean everyone around you needs to suffer."

I whip around. "How dare you! You don't know what you're talking about."

He gives me a highhanded look. "It doesn't take a genius to figure it out."

Does this mean everyone knows? Mom must have opened her

big mouth. "My dad just needs to sort some things out." I fix him with a vicious glare.

"You might want to be careful. Expressions like that can cause some nasty lines."

"Is that why you look the way you do?"

"Nothing but sass," he grumbles, returning to his papers.

An elderly woman comes to the register with a nervous smile on her face.

"It's okay." Her concern has my anger subsiding. "He's just being his usual irritating self."

She covers her mouth, stifling a laugh and winks. "Young lady, I think you are good for him."

"I heard that, Bertha!" Charles calls out.

"I'll see you next week," she says to me, ignoring him.

"Sounds good. Do you need a hand with this bag? Charles could use the exercise."

She giggles. "No. I think I've got it."

"Yup. Nothing but sass."

As she leaves the store, I go back to stocking shelves and think about Tristan and his grandmother's strawberry-apple pie. I wonder how mine would measure up? I shake my head at where my mind has wandered.

I've been baking lately. Mom said it was the best pie she's ever tasted. I couldn't believe how good the crust was. Weaving strips of dough for the top was fun, and the three of us ate it in like two days. I don't know why you'd put whipped cream on pie, though. Vanilla ice cream is a hundred times better. Maybe it's a Midwest thing.

Oh my god! I can't believe I'm even thinking this kind of shit.

14

I DECIDE on my turquoise bikini since it's not as skimpy as the pink one I wore boating with Chase. Why get a couple of guys all drooly when I have no interest in them? It'll only make the day awkward and weird. I pull the tags off on one of my new T-shirts and put it on along with a pair of cut-off jean shorts and stand in front of my mirror, feeling an odd mixture of disgust and pride. Disgust because my shirt is from the sales rack and pride because I bought it with my own money. *Whatever.* I happily lift my twelve-hundred-dollar beach bag filled with essentials over my shoulder and all feels right in the world again.

"Where are you going?" Harlow asks as I slide my feet into my flip-flops. She's on the couch with one of her new books we picked up at the library.

"Boating with Otto and a friend of his."

"Can I come?"

"I don't think so, Bug. I've never met this guy. I wasn't exactly invited myself. Otto just told me to come."

"Oh." She looks at her book, then back at me. "I'm so *booored*," she moans, looking miserable and frustrated.

I get where she's coming from. School's out, and she only has the one friend as far as I know, she hangs with me a lot when Mom's at work, and reads constantly. That would get old fast, and Otto's friend is probably harmless—some geeky guy from astronomy club or something.

"Okay, sure. And if the guy doesn't like it—*tough*."

"Yay!" She jumps up and wraps her arms around my waist.

"Go get your bathing suit on and grab a towel. I've already got sunscreen. I'll text Mom and tell her what's up." She said she'd be right back, but I don't want to keep Otto and his friend waiting.

"*Whoo hoo!*" she shouts, running up the steps.

The walk goes quick with Harlow bouncing along beside me, rambling on about the characters in her latest book. We turn the final corner and see Otto standing on the pier next to a boat I suddenly recognize.

That's the friend? Tristan? Now I wish I'd left Harlow at home. And worn the pink bikini.

"Hey, Kylie," they both say as we walk up.

Otto looks at Tristan, surprised. "You two know each other?"

I answer for him. "Yes. We met here, actually. I was enjoying one of your amazing iced lattes when his boat pulled up." My insides are jumping with glee at the opportunity to connect with him again, especially since I bungled things up the last couple of times.

Tristan climbs out of the boat to stand with us. He looks down at my sister. "And who's this?"

"Oh, hey." Otto directs his attention to Harlow. "Sorry. I didn't even say hi. How's it going?"

"Good."

"I hope it's okay. She was stuck at home, bored."

Tristan squats down to her level. "Do you know how to wakeboard?"

"No," she responds, looking a little shy.

A big smile crosses his face. "Then today is your lucky day, because I'm going to teach you."

Bonus points for being nice to my sister and super bonus points for his jaw-dropping smile.

"Wow!" she says, brightening. "Really?"

"Absolutely."

"That's nice of you." I'm so in love.

"No problem. I'm glad you brought her." He makes his way back in the boat. "Climb aboard."

Tristan holds out a hand to Harlow, helping her onto the boat. After getting her situated, he presents his hand to me. I stare into his eyes as I slide my hand along his palm before grasping it, making the seductive act seem unintentional. Just one of my many premeditated moves to get a guy's mind on possibilities if he's interested.

Who am I kidding? What guy isn't?

Once on board, I turn and catch Otto rolling his eyes and feel something twist uncomfortably inside. Embarrassment?

What do I have to be embarrassed about? I know what I want and I go for it. Is that so wrong?

"You want to take my hand too?" Otto says to Tristan.

"Dude, I was brought up to be a gentleman."

Otto barks out a laugh, making me feel even more off.

Jackass.

I sit next to Harlow, who snuggles into my side. I wrap my arm around her and give her a squeeze. The familiar connection grounds me instantly, and I find myself wanting to stick my tongue out at Otto like a petulant child.

Tristan takes his position behind the wheel. Once again, I'm taken in by his bronzed, muscular torso—a beautiful sight to behold. He turns to me, smiling in a way that makes me think he can read my mind. I return it with a sly, sultry grin. He acknowledges me with a nod, then returns his focus forward.

Yeah. *This is more like it.* I'm in the game.

I don't want to look, but I can't help it. Yep, Otto is watching me, not looking too pleased. I smile at him innocently, flipping my hair back. He turns away, staring straight ahead. The dismissal stings.

Eventually, I strip to my bikini and enjoy the feel of sun on my body. I love being on the water—sea or lake. I realize now, it doesn't matter. It's the varying shades of blue, the fluidity of it, even the mysteries it holds below. I close my eyes and lift my face into the wind and listen to the sound of the spray hitting the sides of the boat as it cuts through the water.

"Kylie." Harlow taps on my arm. "Can you put sunscreen on me? I feel like I'm burning."

Oh, hell. Great chaperone I am. "Sorry, Bug. I better get some on as well."

I lather her up and place some on my shoulders, chest, and arms as we continue our tour of the lake. The bright-green trees are dense around the perimeter, except for an occasional house near the water's edge—some rather large, which I find surprising. Must be summer homes.

Tristan brings the boat to a crawl, then turns to Harlow. "Alright. Are you ready?"

She looks at me apprehensively.

"It's okay," I say, flashing her an encouraging smile. "It's easy. You got this!"

The boat comes to a stop and gently rocks side to side as Tristan retrieves the towrope from a bin up front. He steps past us and leans over to tie the rope to the lead pole, then unstraps the wakeboard from the side of the boat and sets it on the floor in front of Harlow.

"Okay," Tristan says. "Come over and slide your feet into these bindings." I watch intently as he gives her detailed instructions. He's an excellent teacher and oh-so-sexy.

"Ready?" Tristan asks her when he finishes.

She looks panicked. "Now?"

Tristan laughs. "You'll be fine. Otto will get in the water with you and help you get situated." He looks at Otto for confirmation.

"Sure." Otto places a hand on her shoulder. "It's a lot of fun." He takes off his glasses, pulls his shirt over his head, and throws it on the bench. I expected scrawny, not sinewy and muscular. "Here." He hands me his glasses. "Hold these."

Still confused by the fact that he should be a twiglette, I look up into strong, angled features while reaching for his glasses. He's like Clark Kent when he becomes total-hottie Superman. I'm shaken from my trance when I hear the glasses hit the floor.

Otto gives me an odd look before picking them up and setting them in my hand, then turns and dives off the end of the boat. He comes up flipping his hair out of his eyes. I continue to stare at him, astonished.

What the eff? Did the world just flip on its axis?

"Can you move over for a second?" Tristan asks, snapping me to attention.

I step to the side. "Oh, sorry."

"No problem." He lifts the seat, digging out a life vest, and hands it to me. "Here. This should fit Harlow."

My brain is jumbled. "Right. Harlow?" I hold the vest open so she can slide her arms through, turn her around, adjust the straps, buckle her in, then give her an affectionate smack on the butt, sending her toward the back of the boat.

Tristan helps her in to the water, then turns to me. "She can swim, right? I didn't think to ask."

"Since she could walk." Having a pool in the back and the ocean a stone's throw away, Mom made it a priority growing up. "Do you have a little sister?"

"No. Three older ones. Lots of nieces, though." He flashes his dimples. "I'm the baby of the family—a late, unexpected oops."

"They must have been happy to finally have a boy. You know . . . to carry on the family name and all."

He barks out a laugh. "Yeah. Right."

I'm confused by his reaction, but I laugh along anyway.

He turns to Harlow bobbing in the water next to Otto. "Okay, like I showed you." He waits a beat. "You good?"

She nods her head vigorously. She is definitely nervous, and I begin to worry.

Otto hands her the rope and steadies her in the water while giving her some last-minute instructions.

Tristan walks past me to sit at the wheel. "Okay, here we go!" he calls to Harlow.

"Okay!" she hollers back.

My brave, little Bug.

"Give me a thumbs up when you're ready."

"You'll do great," I hear Otto say.

Tristan watches over his shoulder, waiting for the signal. Harlow gives him the thumbs up, then quickly re-grasps the rope handle. He pushes up on the throttle gently. Suddenly she's out of the water and balancing perfectly. He doesn't go fast, just enough to keep her above water without struggling.

"*Way to go!*" I shout, genuinely proud.

She stays up for a couple of minutes, then releases the rope. We circle around to her.

I lean over as the boat drifts slowly alongside her. "Why did you let go?"

"I didn't want Otto to stay out in the water all by himself."

What a sweetie. I step to the back and reach out as she swims over and hands me the board, then I pull her in. "You did awesome!"

"Thanks. I thought we could get Otto, and I could try by myself?"

I look over at Tristan. "Sounds good to me."

We circle back and pick up Otto. He'd positioned himself closer to shore. "Thanks for taking the time with her," I say when he pulls himself into the boat.

"No problem." He grabs a towel and smiles. "She's an awesome kid."

I beam a proud smile. She is definitely the better of the two of us.

The sudden reality hits me. What kind of role model have I been? Shitty at best. In fact, she's been more of a role model than I have. I suck.

· · ·

Later in the afternoon, Tristan and Otto switch it up and wake surf. Both are equally athletic. Watching them interact reminds me of brothers the way they hassle and tease each other.

"Have you guys known each other a long time?" I ask while we take a break, letting the boat drift silently in the water.

Tristan is the first to respond. "I've spent most of my summers here with my grandparents. So, yeah, since we were eight or so."

A huge wave splashes into the boat, dousing us, catching us all off guard.

"What the hell?" I scream, wiping wet hair and water out of my eyes. I look around trying to get a sense of what happened and see Chase on a Sea-Doo, circling before coming full stop alongside our boat.

"You okay?" I ask Harlow.

She grabs a towel and wipes her face. "Yeah." Then hands it to me.

"You dick!" I yell at him, blotting my eyes. "My little sister's on board!"

"She got a little wet, big deal." He smirks. "Hey. You guys better watch out for this one." He jerks his head in my direction. "She's a hellcat."

Tristan turns to Harlow. "Cover your ears." You can hear the retrained temper in his voice. She immediately does as she's told.

He leans over the side of the boat, getting as close to Chase as possible. "The only reason I haven't tackled you off that machine and ripped your head off is because there is a kid on board," he says, seething. "And if you *ever* try to swamp my boat again . . . you won't know what hit you, you piece of shit!"

"*Whoa.*" Chase's hands shoot up in mock defense, a grin

plastered on his face. "Dial it back, dude. I was just cooling you all down."

Tristan makes a move to jump at him. Chase guns the motor, taking off like the chicken shit he is. "I can't stand that guy," he snarls and kicks at the life vest lying on the floor.

I take Harlow's hands away from her ears. "It's okay now."

She looks over at Tristan who looks like he could kill someone. "Are you sure?" she whispers to me, looking doubtful.

Tristan breathes deep, his calm, happy-go-lucky expression returning. "Sorry about that, Harlow. I don't deal well with bullies."

"I guess that's a good thing," she says, giving him a tiny smile. "I don't like them either."

"Alright," Otto claps his hands together, looking like he's dealt with this situation before. "Who wants to go next?"

"Me!" Harlow jumps up, her uneasiness forgotten.

"Awesome," Tristan says. "And after, I can pull you all on the raft."

"Can we do that instead?"

"Sure."

"*Eeee!*" she squeals. "Can you go really fast?"

"Till you're screaming in fear."

"Yay!"

Tristan opens another compartment and pulls out the deflated raft, followed by an electric pump. Little by little it unfolds, then expands until we all have to duck underneath as it fills the boat. When it's full size, we all help throw it out the back.

Otto jumps in the water and steadies it while Harlow and I step in. Once we're settled, Otto pulls himself in, accidentally sliding on top of me.

We stare at each other for an awkward moment. "Sorry about that," he says, before squishing in beside me.

"It's okay." Not my usual response to a dork invading my space. Smacking the hell out of him and telling him to get the eff off would have been more like it. I smile at him instead, catching how his eyes turn from light brown to gold in the sunlight.

Oh my god! Why am I noticing this shit? He's totally not my type.

I shake it off, focusing on Tristan who *is* my type—and boy is he ever. I look at him behind the wheel. He should be in a magazine ad or on a billboard, modeling Calvin Klein underwear—he's that kind of sexy.

Tristan guns it, and we're flying across the lake. He does figure eights, crossing over his wake, jumbling and popping us around in the raft. I can't remember the last time I laughed this hard.

Harlow is vibrating with excitement as she gives Mom a full description of our day. I don't know how she still has this much energy. I'm wiped.

The day was good, surprisingly fun actually, but on the flipside, I've now added my completely ridiculous reaction to Otto to the weirdness that has become my life.

Crap! I forgot to get Tristan's number. What's wrong with me?

We were dropped off on the dock, and I didn't think of it. It would have been weird timing, anyway, with Harlow there . . . and Otto. Then he was gone.

I shower the lake water off my body, change, and realize I'm starving. I start down the stairs but notice the attic door open. I flip on the light and work my way up the steep stairs.

What a mess. It looks like Mom and Harlow tried to tidy things up, but I don't think Nana ever threw anything away. It will take a while to organize and get rid of stuff.

I wander through furniture with styles that span over several decades, when a large steamer trunk catches my eye. I remove the boxes, cluttering the top, flip the latch, and lift the lid.

I don't know exactly what I was hoping for, but it definitely wasn't linens. I rummage through it anyway, hoping something better is waiting to be discovered in the layers. Near the bottom, I am rewarded with the feel of hard edges. Reaching in, I pull out an old photo album. *Nice.*

I sit cross-legged on the floor, using the trunk as a back support, and open the cover. There is an old, black and white, stoic family photo of a mother and father and two young children.

The next couple of pages are of the same family on an outing as they sit on a blanket with their picnic basket at the water's edge, and a few with them in front of . . . That's our house!

That must be Nana as a little girl. *She had an older brother? I wonder if he's still alive?* I'm sure Mom would have told me if he was.

I look closer at the house. It was beautiful in its glory days. The trees were a lot smaller than they are now, obviously. But the flowers . . . Wow! Even in black and white, they're beautiful.

I have a lot of work to do.

I wonder if any of the perennials are the same as the ones still growing out in the garden? That would be amazing if I helped bring something back that has been part of this house for generations. I sure wish fixing up the house was as easy as the flowers.

I continue to flip through the pages. I see Nana as a young teenager, her brother dwarfing her as he stands with a protective arm around her. In the next picture she's a little older, maybe late teens or early twenties, standing next to an extremely good-looking guy.

"Way to go, Nana."

He looks familiar somehow. There are more with the two of them together, laughing and having fun. The following page shows them standing rigid side by side. The man is dressed in military garb, and Nana looks sad, her smile forced. I've seen that same smile on my mother so many times.

I flip the page, but there are no more photos. I look at the last one more closely. I can't help feeling that I know this man.

Then it hits me. "Holy shit!" I yell to no one. "It's Charles!" *No frigging way!* "Mom! Mom, come here!"

I hear her running up the first flight of stairs. "Kylie, where are you? Are you all right?" She sounds frightened.

"Up here. Sorry, I'm fine. Just come here."

She's out of breath by the time she reaches me. Harlow's behind her. "What is it? Did you hurt yourself?"

I stand up and hold the book out to her so she can see the page I'm on. "Did you know that Nana and Charles were a thing?"

Her eyes widen in disbelief. "What?" She looks down at the book, peering closely, trying to make the connection. "Oh, my." Her hand goes to her mouth. "That *is* Charles." She looks at me, stunned, then takes the book from my hands, flipping the pages back and forth. "She never said anything about this to me. Ever."

"Let me see, let me see," Harlow says. Mom lowers the book to her. "He's so good looking. What happened?"

Mom and I laugh. "Yeah, no kidding," I say. "I guess that's what years of being an angry jackass will do to you."

"*Kylie*." Mom jerks her head in Harlow's direction.

I roll my eyes. As if she hasn't heard worse. "Do you remember him that way?"

"Surly?" she asks.

"I think we already determined that." I laugh. "*No*. Good looking."

"I don't know. It wasn't something I thought about. He was always just mean."

"He is not mean!" Harlow jumps to his defense. She's become his self-proclaimed champion.

"Sorry, Harlow, but he was when I was growing up."

"Well . . . he isn't now," she mutters.

"I wonder what the story is, or was?"

She turns the page. "That's the last picture."

"I know. And now I'm *really* curious."

Mom places her hand on the blank page, then looks at me. "Kylie, I wouldn't go asking Charles about it."

I nod in agreement. *At least not right away.*

"*Whoo*." Mom breathes out the sound. "This is wild. I can't believe she never said anything." She hands the book over to me. "Well, I better get back to dinner before it burns. That's an amazing find."

"Definitely. The plot thickens. Is it okay if I stay up here and see what else I can find?"

Mom looks taken aback. Understanding, I laugh. When have I ever asked her permission to do anything?

"Sure." She smiles. "You cooked all week, anyway. Harlow, are you coming down with me?"

"I think I'll stay up here."

"Okay."

When Mom disappears down the stairs, Harlow turns to me "Can you believe it?"

"That our Nana had a fling with the neighborhood grouch? No, I can't." Her immediate glare has me shrugging my shoulders.

"Can I see the book?"

"Sure." I hand it to her and look over her shoulder as she starts at the beginning.

"I wonder if he broke her heart?" Harlow asks when she reaches the last photo. "Maybe he came back from the war really mean or something—like in the movies?"

"What movies have you been watching?"

"Not just movies." She shakes her head at me. "A lot of military personnel come back with Post Traumatic Stress Disorder. PTSD for short. It wasn't talked about during the first couple of wars, but a lot of relationships and marriages suffered because of it." She sets the book down and moves to a dresser. "I wonder what else we can find?"

I gawk at her "Hey. Back up. Where are you learning this stuff?"

She gives me a confused look and throws a hand in the air. "It's everywhere, Kylie."

"I know, but where are you hearing about it?" I'm a little concerned that she's watching shows that are inappropriate and possibly disturbing to a nine-year-old.

She starts opening and closing drawers. "I don't know . . . Discovery Channel, History Channel, the Life Network, take your pick."

"Shouldn't you be watching the Disney, Family, Nickelodeon . . . stuff like that?"

"Why would I want to watch *that* garbage?"

"It's not garbage. It's age appropriate."

She rolls her eyes. "I'm going to go read till dinner. It's too hot up here."

"What are you reading?"

"A book about a teenage girl growing up in the 80s."

"Sounds interesting."

"I'll give it to you when I'm done."

I laugh. "Sure. Why not? I need something to do since I don't have internet, a TV, or a social life."

"*Poor* Kylie," she teases.

"Brat!" I grab her and tickle until she begs to be released. She falls to the floor when I do, pushing her hair out of her face. Her smile fades, and her expression turns serious.

"Kylie, what do you think happened to Dad?"

I shake my head, finding it hard to meet her childlike stare. "I don't know, Bug."

She gets up and walks to the top of the steps. "I think maybe someone is framing him and he knows it, and he's hiding until he can clear his name."

My eyebrows shoot up in surprise. "I was thinking the same thing."

"Yeah?"

"*Yeah.*"

"Do you think he'll be okay?"

"I don't know. I hope so."

"Me too." Harlow looks down the stairs then back at me. "Dinner's probably almost ready."

"I'll be down in a minute."

"Okay."

I hate that she has to worry about him. It's not right. He could have used a disposable phone and called me and explained everything. It pisses me off that he's putting us through this worry unnecessarily.

I place the book back into the trunk and start to close it, but change my mind. "I wonder." I start pulling out linens piece by piece. On the very bottom, I feel a hardness wrapped in something lacey. I unravel it to find a book. I open the cover and see that the contents are handwritten.

It's a diary.

Maybe I should take it to Mom and see what she thinks? Or read it, then take it to Mom? Or maybe I shouldn't tell her at all, put it back and pretend it doesn't exist, because diaries are sacred.

Who am I kidding . . .

I read the first page.

March 5, 1938

I have never kept a diary before. I'm not sure what to write. So here goes. I hate that Ray is such a protective brother. All Charles did was ask me to go for a walk. What does it matter that he's a little older? I am not a child. I'll be seventeen in six months, and it's not his job to tell me what I can and cannot do. It's Father's and Mother's. Charles is such a dreamboat. Why he is interested in me, I will never know. I complained to Mom about Ray, but she said she would discuss it with Father. Life is so unfair.

"Kylie!" Mom calls. "Dinner."

I close the book. Deciding I'm taking it with me, I put all the linens back in the trunk and close the lid. I'm still undecided on who I'm sharing this with, or whether I will continue reading it. I leave the attic, run to my bedroom, and place it under my pillow before heading down to eat.

After dinner, I lay down and crash from carb overload. I need to talk to Mom about her obsession with pasta. I know it's inexpensive but *uhhh*, I'm so bloated.

I wake up in the night confused and look at my phone. It's one-thirty. I roll on to my stomach and go to scrunch up my pillow, but my hand hits the diary. I must have been out of it not to feel the hardness when my head hit the pillow. I move it to my nightstand.

It felt good to be out on the water today. Harlow had so much fun. An image of Otto, climbing into the boat, water dripping from his lean muscular body, pops into my head. I mentally shake the image away. Tristan is who I'm hot after. We have a lot in common. Now *there's* a body.

But Otto's eyes glowing gold as he looks down on me in the raft sneaks into my thoughts, making my stomach flutter. "*Ugh*," I groan, pulling the pillow over my head.

Why am I reacting to him like this? It's doesn't make sense. I guess he does have a lot of interesting things to say, but still . . . This is crazy.

I do like that I can be myself around him. I have no desire to be "on", and it feels like what a friend should feel like. At least, I think it does. But what would *I* know? It took my life falling apart to realize my so-called friends were as good as cardboard cut-outs—total fakes.

Memories of Cali slide in and out of focus—random moments, snippets in time, and I'm suddenly embarrassed at how I've treated people. Why did I not notice before? I guess the sparkly world I lived in blinded me to what was really happening.

I'm sweating and pull the pillow away to slide it under my head as I roll onto my back. I watch the curtains billow with the breeze and take in the evening scents of dew and greens mixed with flowers. I feel myself drift. My final thoughts are of Otto and an overwhelming realization of wanting to be more— more than just a hollow shell of a person I've been living in.

15

THE NEXT MORNING, I find my mom lounging in an old metal chair in the backyard, drinking coffee. "Hey." I sit in the mismatched chair next to her. "It's nice out."

She lifts her face to the sun. "It's beautiful."

I look around the backyard, noticing all the overgrowth. "I guess we have a lot of yard work to do back here."

She looks over at me with a curious expression. "I suppose we do."

"Do you want to do some of it today . . . with me? Neither of us have to work."

"Sure." She continues to assess me, like *where's the punchline?*

I smile, enjoying that my offer has baffled her. "I'll go get the gardening stuff." I stand. "Where's Harlow? She might want to help."

"Reading. I'll go see if she wants to come out." She stands up next to me and pauses a moment, frowning, then shakes her head.

"What?" I ask defensively, wondering what she could possibly find to criticize.

"Nothing. I'm just not sure who replaced you with my daughter, because there is no way *my* Kylie would offer to do yard work." She chuckles.

"What can I say? It turns out I kind of like it. Not the getting dirty and sweaty part, just how things look after."

"*Huh.*"

I shrug my shoulders. "I know, right?"

I bring out the gardening tools and kneepads, dropping them at random locations for us to start, then pull on my gloves, ready to get down to business.

"She said she will be out soon," Mom says, walking toward me. "She's at a good part in her book."

"Okay." I dig around a deep-rooted dandelion, wiggling it loose before giving it a pull.

Mom moves the kneepad next to me, kneels down. "Hey, you found an extra pair of gloves. Thanks."

"Yeah, it was dark in the shed when you were in there last time. Must have been hard to see."

We work silently for a while, my thoughts eventually drifting to my dad—the life we had, my relationship with him, and how he was with my mother.

"Do you love Dad?"

She stiffens. "It's complicated, Kylie."

I jab the earth with my spade. Leaving it there, I sit back. "What's complicated about it? You either do or you don't." I'm not sure why I'm snapping at her.

"There is a lot involved—things you know nothing about. Why do you care so much, anyway?"

Yeah, why would I care? I'm selfish. She's made that clear my whole life. I feel like getting up and walking away, but questions are eating at me and I need answers. I calm myself and ask, "So tell me what I don't know—what I should know?"

"Kylie, I don't think—"

"Come on! You know more than you're telling me. I feel like I have a right to know who my father really was. *Please.* I need you to help me understand."

She remains quiet, working the dirt, not making any actual progress.

"Finish your story. What happened after you ran away with Dad?"

She groans. "I don't know, Kylie. It wasn't good."

I want to scream at her to stop being so cryptic. "Mom, just tell me!"

"Alright." She sits on her knee pad, crossing her legs, and faces me. "Jared thought his parents would love me because of how beautiful I was, but that's not what happened. They were repulsed that I came from what they deemed "white trash." They didn't say that directly to me, but it was expressed loud and clear to your father. Jared thought they were being ignorant and in time would change.

"When I got pregnant about two months after we were back, they were appalled. They called me a gold digger and threatened to disown your father if he didn't get rid of the child and me."

"Seriously?" I pull my knees up to my chest.

"I know, it was despicable. But your father didn't believe them. He said I was everything he wanted, and once we were married, they would see things differently. So, we went to the courthouse a week later, and when we confronted them with the happy news, they asked him to remove me from the house, like I was some sort of mongrel, and told us to never return."

"That's . . . harsh."

"You have to understand, Kylie, to people like your grandparents, status is everything."

"Did Dad stand up for you?"

"Your dad doesn't like anyone telling him what to do. He seemed more upset that they didn't respect his choice than how they treated me. I think it was my first insight into what I'd gotten myself into. But at the time, I wasn't concerned about anything other than how hurt Jared was by his parents' anger.

"Eventually he shook it off and said that they would just have to accept me and the baby. You were born, he got on with a reputable investment firm, and was making excellent money. Things were good, other than the silent treatment from his parents."

"Wow."

"I hope their lack of attention didn't hurt you. I know we've never discussed it before."

"I never took it personally because I figured it had something to do with Dad, being that he never spoke to them or about them. But now . . . knowing they wanted me gone, like I was some terrible mistake? Yeah, that hurts a bit."

"I should have discussed this with you when you were old enough to understand. I'm sorry for that. I guess I was avoiding it because if I had to explain *their* issues, the rest might come to light, and I wasn't comfortable confiding in you given our relationship. But know that they disliked you because of me— no other reason."

"It's not your fault they were snobs."

"Yeah. But still."

Mom and I both turn when the screen door slams shut. Harlow is dragging Otto out by the hand.

Seeing Otto in dorky chino shorts and an Avengers T-shirt makes my thoughts of him last night seem ridiculous.

"Hi, Otto," Mom greets him, standing up.

"Hey." Otto gives me a crooked smile. "I just came by to see what you were up to."

I take my gloves off and push off the ground. "Um, just doing some gardening."

"I see that."

"Here." Mom hands him her gloves. "I'll let you take over."

"Sure. What guy doesn't like digging in the dirt?"

"Come on, Harlow." Mom wraps an arm around her shoulder. "Let's go make some lemonade."

That she looks relieved to be leaving, makes me think there is more she's not telling me. It might give me a clue to where my dad is. Who knows, maybe there's more to his disappearance than just him embezzling the money?

"Did you just wake up?" Otto asks, shaking me from my thoughts.

"What?"

"Did you just get up? You look a little . . ." I glare at him. "What?" He leans away, pretending to look fearful before releasing a toothy grin. "You look beautiful as always!"

I haven't showered yet, no makeup, and I'm dressed like a scrub. This is a new low, even for me. "Of course, I do. What's with all the super hero T-shirts? They remind me of something Harlow's little boy friends would wear."

"Hey, don't knock the duds. They're 80s classics I found at various vintage stores online."

Dork. "You really don't have to help."

"I don't mind."

"Do you know what you're doing?"

"Yep. I help Mom every year."

"Then you know more than I do."

Otto starts in with one of his celestial updates, and our chatter is comfortable—perfect for a lazy sunny day. We go to town on the weeds, and by the time he finishes rambling on about the latest telescopic innovations, we have a massive pile of crabgrass, dandelions, and thistles beside us.

"Hey, I almost forgot." Otto stops mid-dig. "Mom wants me to ask if you all want to come to dinner tonight. I told her you would be off work, so, unless you all have other plans . . ."

"No plans. Hold on. I'll go ask." I run to the back door. "Mom! Joanne wants to know if we can go to their house for dinner tonight."

"Sure!" she yells back.

"Looks like we're coming." I pick up my kneepad and move to Otto's other side.

We work in silence for a bit. My mind wanders to the lake and the need to cool off, then to boating with Tristan and the realization I don't know much about the latest love of my life.

"So what's Tristan's story?"

Otto stiffens. "What do you mean, his story?"

"I don't know . . . Does he have a girlfriend?" I catch Otto shaking his head. "What?"

"You and every other girl."

I take immediate offense. "Me and every other girl what?"

"It's always the same. Girls are drawn to him for his looks, but there's more to a guy than that."

"*I know.*" I point the tip of my spade at him. "You're just jealous."

He smirks. "Hardly. It's just an observation. I've known him a long time."

Hardly? Of course, he's jealous. He's just in denial. I'm hot, he's not. It's the way of it. *Moving on.* "He told me why he's here. He made it sound like he's a bit of a hothead, but he doesn't seem that way to me." I let out a small laugh. "Well, other than getting pissed at Chase, but that was totally understandable."

"Yeah. Tristan is definitely one of the good guys."

"He is, and we have a lot in common, we both come from the same people." Otto bristles. "Oh, come on, you know what I mean."

"You mean the snobby, self-centered, closed-minded jackasses that like to think they're better than everyone else?" His words are like a slap in the face. "Because, you know . . . that's how *he* sees them. He rebels against everything his parents stand for. So, *no*, I don't think you would have a lot in common."

"Oh. Um, okay." His assessment stings, hitting me in a way I never thought possible. I return to weeding, not knowing what else to do. I should be taking him down for talking to me like that, but for some reason, I can't raise the anger. I feel about two inches tall.

He takes his gloves off and rests a hand on my arm. "Kylie, I'm sorry. I shouldn't have said that."

His touch is oddly soothing, considering. "You wouldn't have said it if you didn't think it was true."

"It's just . . . you have a way of making people feel beneath you."

I shrug a shoulder. "I've had years of rich-bitch training."

"Is that a course they teach in your fancy private schools?" The corner of his lip edges up.

I let out a weak laugh. "No, it's a socially acquired lesson."

"Do you think you could avoid unleashing it when you're around me?"

"I can try."

We go back to clearing out the garden, this time working in silence.

In the bathroom, I do a double take when passing the mirror. "Oh . . . my god!" I'm all sweaty, my hair is sticking out in all directions from a hair-tie that's ceased to do its job, and I have dirt smudges all over my face. *I look hideous!* I shake my head at my reflection, mortified that anyone saw me like this.

I step into the shower, letting the water run cold over my shoulders as it washes off all the hot, sticky grime. I feel a little hollowed out after Otto's attack. But he was right. That was my world. I still don't like being called out on it. I'm kind of dreading going over to his house tonight—things were awkward when he left.

I step out and dry off. Maybe I'll take over one of the pies I made yesterday—maybe the strawberry apple one?

Really? A pie? Who am I? Martha friggin' Stewart?

After drying my hair and getting dressed, I decide to read more of Nana's diary. I shut my door and settle myself comfortably in the window seat.

March 28, 1938

I am so in love. Father let me walk with Charles today. He is incredibly smart. He is basically running his father's grocery store.

When he held my hand on our walk, I thought I was going to die. I know it was forward of him, but he was just so cute. How could I resist? When he did it, he said that he had been waiting forever for the chance to touch me. Can you imagine? When he looked at me with those sincere, beautiful blue eyes, I thought I would melt right there on the sidewalk. We talked about all kinds of things. I can't wait to tell Marge tomorrow. She will faint dead away.

I read through several entries. She mostly talks about day-to-day life and wishes that she could spend more time alone with Charles. There is a lot about school and friends, her parents and her brother, her fears and insecurities. She talks a lot about Charles and the things he makes her feel. Apparently, he was quite the romantic. He brought her flowers and wrote her poetry. He loved to read the classics. They both did and discussed literature regularly.

April 13, 1938
Charles asked me to be his girl today. Of course, I said yes! And he kissed me! My first kiss. His lips were soft, and my insides went hot and tingly and my heart pounded like I'd just seen a bear. I could have kissed him all day. I wonder if it is wrong to feel that way? I've never had a beau before, so I wouldn't know. Father has really taken to him. They talk business and politics when we sit on the front porch after dinner. I find the subjects boring, but listening to Charles talk, whatever the topic, makes me melt.

June 20, 1938
All anyone seems to talk about these days is war with Germany. I got angry with Charles today because he said he would enlist as soon as war was declared. How could he want to leave? He has a great job!

Why would he want to go and fight? He could get killed, and I would die if that happened. He says it is his duty to fight for his country, but what about his duty to me? He said that it is not the same thing and that he would be a coward if he didn't go. I thought that was the most ridiculous thing I have ever heard.

"This pie is unreal," Joanne says to me after dessert is served. "Girl, you are a natural."

Dinner went well, but I still feel off from the verbal smackdown I received this afternoon. "It's no big deal. I just followed a recipe."

"It's more than that. I follow recipes all the time and my pies aren't remotely this good."

"That's for sure," Otto mutters to himself, then looks up when he realizes it's gone quiet. "What? I was just agreeing with you." His face is now bright red.

"Well, anyway," Joanne turns to me. "You should bake for the café. It would be a great addition. I've been getting my bakery items frozen from a place over in Chatwell, but this is just as good if not better. Definitely fresher."

"Wait . . . You own Jojo's?"

"Well, yeah."

"How come no one said anything to me?" I look directly at Otto.

He shrugs his shoulders. "Everyone knows. I guess it didn't cross my mind."

"It's a nice place."

Joanne smiles, sitting up a little straighter. "Thank you. We like it." She moves her fork onto her plate. "So? What do you think . . . about baking for me?"

"You should taste her brownies," Mom interjects. "Oh, and her mixed berry tortes."

"I love the Nanaimo bars," Harlow jumps in.

I guess I've been going a little overboard with the baking lately, but I'm bored and looking for things to do with Harlow besides visiting the library—which is her favorite pastime next to playing with Olivia. And okay . . . I *really* enjoy it.

"I'll take anything you want to give me." Joanne takes another bite of pie. "We can see what sells best and go from there."

"*Uhhh,*" I draw out, not knowing what to say. This is crazy.

"It would mean a little extra money and you would be doing me a big favor, but no pressure. Just bring in what you make. I have a feeling once people get a taste the treats will be gone by noon."

"I guess so. It's really no big deal. The recipes are just from an app. I'm not a professional."

"Who cares when they taste *this* good."

"Yeah . . . Sure. Okay." There are several other desserts I've been wanting to make, but our little family will become obese if I keep baking just for us. "Cool," I say mostly to myself, since the conversation has moved on.

"Hello?" a male voice calls out from the living room.

"Hi Jason," Joanna replies, then turns to the rest of us when he enters. "Everyone, this is my husband."

After introductions, he walks over and kisses Joanne on the cheek. "Hi, hon. Nice to see you again, Sarah."

"Hi," Mom says with a warm smile, leading me to believe they were friends growing up.

"Sorry I'm late. I had a showing that took forever. Lots of questions."

"Are the Chesney's at it again?" Joanne asks as he loosens his tie, then begins loading his plate.

"*Uh-huh.* Man, I'm starved." He walks into the kitchen and puts his plate in the microwave.

Joanne leans in. "These people have looked at, I swear, every house for sale like three times and still haven't made up their minds."

Jason sits down with his plate. He eyeballs the pie before reaching across the table and picking up a loose piece of apple, popping it into his mouth.

"Jason!" Joanne scolds, looking embarrassed.

"*Mmm,*" he says appreciatively. "Who made the pie? It's definitely not Joanne's." She smacks him on the arm. "Ow!" He laughs.

"Kylie made it," Joanne says. "She's going to start baking for JoJo's."

"Make sure she gives you a fair price." Jason winks at me.

I smile, not knowing how else to respond. This whole family scene is new to me.

The conversation shifts to other things—thankfully. I have always loved being the center of attention, but this is a different kind, and I don't know how to take it.

After dinner, Olivia and Harlow take off to a park across the street. The rest of us help clear the table, then Joanne shoos everyone out of the kitchen except Mom.

Otto turns to me. "Do you want to go for a walk or watch a movie or something?"

I shrug. "Whatever you want. It doesn't matter to me."

"Let's go for a walk," he says.

"Okay."

I follow him to the front door. "Mom," Otto calls out.

Her head pops out from the kitchen. "Yes?"

"We're going to get some air."

"Sounds good. Maybe check on the girls?"

"Sure thing."

We cross to the park and watch Harlow and Olivia play for a bit, then continue down the street. I feel vulnerable, an unfamiliar emotion, and I don't like it. Suddenly, I wish I'd agreed to a movie. At least then I wouldn't be dealing with this awkwardness.

"Kylie, I've been thinking a lot about this afternoon," Otto says, breaking the silence.

"It's okay. Forget it."

"Yeah. But I can't. I feel like a total asshat for snapping at you. I'm just so tired of how Chase and his friends treat me. Just because they have money doesn't give them the right to treat me like shit. Tristan has never been that way toward me, he's the complete opposite of them. And you, just, well . . ."

"It's okay." I stop him, in case more insults were coming. "I understand, and for what it's worth . . . Chase is a total dick and has nothing on you."

"Thanks. It means a lot to me that you recognize it. And just to be clear, you may have been that kind of person in the past, but you're not one of them anymore. Well, at least not as much as you used to be."

"Is that supposed to make me feel better?"

"Sorry. But you have changed from when I first met you."

Hearing him say it makes me feel a little lighter, and sort of honored in a weird way. "Thanks."

"No problem."

And just like that, we're good again. Honesty without the drama. Who knew?

16

"Why do you keep staring at me like that," Charles grumbles.

"Sorry. No reason." Nana's diary has been in the forefront of my mind, but I can't tell *him* that—at least not yet. I want to finish reading it first—find out the whole story. But even then . . . It's a diary.

"Charles. Did you start this store on your own?"

He looks up from his desk with his usual surly expression. "Why would you ask that?"

I lean against the doorjamb. "Just wondering." I know his father had it before him—Nana wrote it in her diary—but it was the only opening I could think of. I want details about the past.

"My great-grandfather started it, but I worked for my grandfather and then my dad after school, from when I was Harlow's age. Started with bagging groceries and helping customers out to their cars when they needed me to."

"So your dad was a General?" He looks at me, suspicion in his eyes. "The name of the store?"

"Oh, right. Dad was in the Spanish American War and World War I, but my grandfather was the General. My great-grandfather called the store Fitzwald's Mercantile."

"Did you go to war?" I think about what Harlow said about PTSD and wonder if Charles had to deal with that.

"Yes, I did, like every other man that could enlist."

"How well did you know my great-grandmother?"

His brow furrows. "You're asking a lot of questions. You got something to say? Say it." His expression is hard, his words harsher than usual.

"Jeez, back off. Nothing. I was just . . ." *Think, think, think.* "You mentioned that I remind you of her, and . . . I never got to know her . . . *sooo*, I was just wondering."

He sighs. "Listen, there's a history there that I'm not too keen on digging up."

Finally, an opening. "Oh, really? Do tell."

His eyes flare. "I just got done tellin' you . . ." He stops, calms himself. "As far as being like her, she was brave, strong-willed, and didn't take crap from nobody. She was also the first person to help out when someone needed it." He turns away. "I need to get back to these books."

I want to tell him he's wrong. Other than having a strong personality, Nana and I are nothing alike. I don't have a selfless bone in my body—that trait skipped right over me and into Harlow.

The front entrance door jingles. I peer out from the office as Tristan walks in. "Whipping cream again?" I step behind the checkout counter and give him a flirty smile.

"Nope. Gran says she has a hankering for peach cobbler— her words not mine—so it's peaches and vanilla ice cream this time." He comes over to the snack display, contemplating before deciding on a bag of chips. "You know, I think I'm addicted to your brownies. Otto insisted I try one, and I'm already craving another."

"From Jojo's?" Stupid question. I dropped some off on my way to work today. I swear the guy makes me addled half the time.

"Yep. I'm definitely going to have to get another one before heading home—one doesn't crush the craving. I hope they aren't all gone."

I laugh. "I'm glad you like them."

"Just a second. I need to grab this stuff." He disappears down an aisle and returns shortly, dumping his bounty on the conveyor in front of me. "Do you want to go to the movies with me?"

I do a mental happy dance. It's about time he got around to asking me out.

"Otto doesn't like dramas. Only action, sci-fi, and end of the world type stuff."

"There's a theatre here?"

"No. We'll drive over to Chatwell. There's a decent one there."

"How far is that?"

"About twenty minutes?"

"Sounds fun. When do you want to go?"

"Do you work next Saturday? I know with your mom working, you have Harlow during the week."

He must have been asking Otto about me. *Nice.* I lean backward, looking into the office. "Hey! Grumpy pants! Do I work next Saturday?"

Charles snorts. "I don't know why you're asking me. You seem to make your own hours."

I face Tristan again. "No, I'm good. Is there a mall there?"

"It's not big, but yeah."

"Would you mind if we left early-ish, like eleven, so I can look for a few things?" I ring his purchases through and bag them.

"Yeah. Sure. I love to shop." He eyes the grocery bag. "How much?"

"You do?" Guys hate shopping.

"Well. Yeah. Sometimes. It's more that I love to blow my parents' money. I'm a bit of a shit that way. Besides, I need some new shoes for running—mine are done for."

"That will be eight seventy-five." Tristan pulls out a wallet, fishes out some bills, and hands them to me. "So I'll see you at eleven?"

"That works. We can have lunch before we shop. My treat. Like I said . . . I like to keep my parent's credit card active."

Sounds familiar. "It's a date." I give him one of my sexy, you're-in-for-a-treat grins.

He laughs and shakes his head. "Right."

Right? What's that supposed to mean?

He pulls out his phone. "What's your number? I'll text you when I'm on my way."

Finally. Digits. I've already been creeping him on social media, now I can move on to the more intimate texting phase of the relationship. I give him my number. "Do you know where I live?"

"Everyone knows where Grace's house is. The woman was like the matriarch of Foxall. I didn't realize you were her granddaughter until Otto told me. I sure do miss her."

"Yeah." I feel a little guilty since I can't say the same.

"Well, I'm off to get another brownie. See you Saturday or

sooner if Gran gets another craving." He waves before the door shuts behind him.

I hear a grunt behind me. I turn to see Charles leaning against the shelving with his arms crossed over his chest.

"What's *your* problem?"

He shakes his head. "We have a shipment in the back. I want to show you how to check it against the invoices to make sure what they say they sent is what we got, then where to enter it in the books before filing it. I like to pay the bills right away. I'll show you how I do that as well, and where to—"

"Hey. All that boring stuff is *your* job."

"It's good to learn how a business works. You never know when it might come in handy. I'll give you a raise."

I brighten. "You will?"

"Sure. More responsibility means you're more valuable."

"Okay." I like his logic. "Lead the way."

"So, do I get some brownies too?" he asks, sounding like a little kid who was refused a lollypop.

For the first time, I can picture him as the handsome man with bright-blue eyes and blond hair that Nana fell in love with. My heart softens.

He turns, looking cross. "Or are you going to make me go to that silly coffee place to get one?"

I shake my head. "What was I thinking?" *Grouchy old coot.*

"About what?"

"Nothing." I shake my head.

He grumbles something before cutting open a box and pulling out the packing slip.

. . .

My head throbs on the ride home. It was the brain-splitting tutorial on running a grocery store that did it. But it's Sunday, I'm off early, and I have an upcoming date with Tristan, so all's well. A couple of Advil would be nice, though.

There is an unfamiliar female voice coming through the screen door as I walk up the steps to the house. When I enter, I see my mother standing near a tall, broad-shouldered woman, dressed in a navy-blue pantsuit.

"Kylie. Good. You're home." Mom twists her hands nervously. "This is Special Agent Sherice Walker of the FBI. She stopped by with some information about your father."

My nerves shoot into hyper-drive. "Where's Harlow?" I can't imagine it's good news, being that we still haven't heard from him.

"She's at Olivia's house. Agent Walker called me a couple of hours ago and asked if we could meet. I thought it best to bring your sister to her friends."

"Sarah, why don't we all take a seat?" The agent's calm, gentle demeanor is the complete opposite to those jerks that barged in and trashed our house.

My stomach twists into knots as Mom and I sit side by side on the couch, and Sherice sits in the recliner across from us. I want to grip Mom's hand for support, but that's never been our relationship. Right now, I'm wishing it was.

"Your mother asked that I wait until you got home before giving my update, and since I believe in being efficient, I agreed."

"Thanks. I appreciate that." I look between my mother and the agent, anxiously awaiting the bomb that's about to be dropped.

Sherice reaches into a briefcase and pulls out a file folder. All I can think is, *oh shit . . . he's dead.*

"So we tracked him to Mexico."

Eyes wide, I stare at her, stunned. "Mexico?"

"We're not sure how he slipped past us, but he did. He must have had an escape plan in place—forged documents, a car with counterfeit plates stashed away near by."

"Wait what?" I'm still reeling. "Why would he be in Mexico?"

"It's an easy country to get lost in," she says.

"But wouldn't it be way easier to prove his innocence if he was in the U.S.?"

"Innocence?" Sherice looks confused.

"Well, yeah. Someone obviously framed him. Maybe that's why he had to go to Mexico, because the mob was after him."

"Kylie . . ." Mom shakes her head. "What are you talking about?"

"Come on. There's no way he would steal money. We had shit-tons. Why would he?"

"Sarah, Kylie, maybe if I lay out the facts, all of this would make more sense."

"Yes. That would be helpful." Mom's expression shows her concern for me.

"Your father's company has an annual audit. This year, several discrepancies were found and because of that, a forensic accountant was called in. What she discovered was clients' funds were being invested into dummy corporations, and from there, the money would disappear—on the surface making it look like bad investments. The FBI was brought in to investigate. Our tech guys discovered that the money was being manipulated from an IP address linked to Jared's work account.

He covered his tracks exceedingly well—that's why it hadn't been discovered before—but our hackers are the best."

"That sounds circumstantial to me." I dismiss the explanation with a flick of my wrist. "Anyone could have used his computer to cover their tracks." I sound flippant, but I'm anything but. This is my life we're talking about. What she's saying can't be true.

"Your father only makes two-hundred and twenty-five thousand a year according to his taxes—I'm rounding of course—but there is no way he could live the kind of lifestyle he did on that income."

I process this. "He's an investor. I'm sure he's diversified, maybe owns some properties, invested in some start-up companies. He's a smart man."

"If he did, he would have reported them on his taxes. There would have been a money trail."

"Well, maybe he was hiding it? That doesn't mean he did what you are accusing him of."

"Kylie. I know this is a lot to take in, but the facts are there. And he didn't stick around to defend himself. He ran."

"Somebody had to have framed him!" I can't accept her explanations—I won't.

"Why?" Sherice asks calmly. "You're obviously a smart girl. Why do you think someone would frame him? What's the motive?"

"Maybe someone had it in for him."

"That's an extreme way to enact vengeance, don't you think?"

My mind frantically searches for another answer, but all I see are the truths in her logic, and the fear I've been trying to suppress, verified. He abandoned us. *That selfish asshole!* How could he do this to us? To me?

"How much?" I ask, barely able to contain my anger.

"We don't have exact numbers."

"How much did he take? *Roughly*."

She looks at Mom, who gives her a nod of approval. "Close to a billion, give or take a few-hundred million. It could be more, if he had another scam going that has yet to be realized."

I gape at her. "Is all the money gone?"

"We don't know for sure, but we suspect he has off-shore accounts somewhere. Look. I'm sorry to bring you this news, but there's more. Recently, a police officer reported a man matching your father's description lurking around your previous residence. They gave chase but lost him in the neighborhood. The officer could not make a positive ID but feels confident it was him."

"Why would he be at our old house?" Mom asks. "I'm sure it's empty by now."

"We believe he had money stashed in the house. Some homeowners with—shall we say, trust issues—have secret compartments throughout their homes. The wealthy don't like to part with their valuables easily."

"But if he has off-shore accounts . . ." I say.

"Our theory is that he hasn't been able to access them. Maybe the account information was on his work computer, although our tech guys haven't been able to uncover any. He would have had to be desperate to leave the anonymity he had in Mexico and return to the house. We could use your help, Kylie."

"But I don't know anything. I swear."

Sherice leans forward, placing her forearms on her knees

and clasping her hands in front of her. "I believe you, but your mother shared with me the special bond you two had." The truth of that statement makes me feel sick. "He may try to contact you." She reaches inside her blazer and passes me her business card. I take it, stare at it a moment. "Kylie, if you need anything, anything at all—have questions, get a funny feeling, get lonely and need someone to talk to—I'm here for you twenty-four-seven, okay?"

Too much reality is hitting me at once. "Okay. Thanks," I say, struggling to hold it together. This cannot be happening.

She stands up. "Sarah, you already have my information. If there is anything you need, you be sure to contact me as well." We follow her to the front door. "Look," she says to my mom, "I truly believe that you had no part in this. I know the bureau questioned you extensively—that couldn't have been easy." I look at my mother. She never mentioned it. "Anyway, for what it's worth, we appreciate all your cooperation. I should be going."

"Thank you for coming." My mother, always polite.

"You bet. I will be in touch." Sherice nods her head to me and is gone.

"Are you okay?" Mom asks as soon the door is closed.

The care and concern in her eyes are enough to snap what's left of my restraint. "N-no," I choke out.

"Oh, baby." She opens her arms, and for the first time in forever, I go to her. She holds me tight while I unleash. "Come over to the couch, baby. Let's sit down."

I stumble along next to her, feeling incredibly betrayed. "Why, Mom?"

"Greed, baby."

"But didn't he make lots of money?"

"He never shared his finances with me."

I pull back and look at her, wiping my eyes. "How could you accept that?"

"I accepted everything in the beginning. I was enamored and believed everything he told me. Then, after a while, I wasn't sure what to believe. He was smooth and praised as easily as he insulted. I never knew which way was up half the time."

I filter through memories. He treated her like she was stupid, chastising her in front of Harlow and me. "He manipulated me against you, didn't he?"

"Oh, I don't know . . ."

I wonder if making excuses, justifying his actions, is second nature, even now.

"*Mom.*"

She's silent a moment before continuing, "Yes. It seems so. He did it to everyone. He was also narcissistic, controlling, vicious, and mean." I feel myself trying not to bristle at her description, even with all that's come to light. "He had to be the best, the smartest, the most loved and adored." Her truths flow like a tidal wave.

"Is *that* all," I say on top of nervous laughter, not knowing how to react to all the unwanted information. It's a lot to take in. "It's not how I saw him, but now the blinders are off . . . It's hard. It will take a while to sink in."

"I know." She sighs. "This isn't how I dreamed my life would turn out."

"Why didn't you fight back? I mean, if he was so horrible—"

"I didn't realize how bad things were until I didn't have enough strength to stand up to him. It became easier to ignore it."

"You could have left."

"I tried once, but he threatened to have me thrown in jail for child abduction and drug possession."

"You did drugs?"

"Of course not! But he had his ways, Kylie. I couldn't risk losing you."

I can't believe this was the man I idolized—my father, the man who gave me everything I ever wanted. She went through all this, and I did nothing but defend him. That must have hurt her terribly.

"I'm sorry, Mom."

"It's not your fault, honey." She brushes a strand of hair behind my ear. Her touch is foreign, and it's all my fault. "He raised you to be what you are. I tried to teach you kindness, compassion, appreciation, but he undermined everything I did and said."

"I feel so stupid for not knowing—for not seeing."

"Don't. You were brought up and schooled to see things his way. *I'm* ashamed that I let it happen."

"You did the best you could."

"I wish I could believe that, but it doesn't matter now. I will never let myself be in that situation again."

The mental control he has over me is so obvious now. I still want to defend him, to dig for excuses, even after all that I know. I hate him for that. But, more than anything, I hate that he used me.

"Are you okay?" Mom asks.

"Not really, but I'll figure it out. How do you think he got away with stealing all that money?"

"I don't know, but he has a talent for making people believe whatever lie he's selling, and he is ruthless when it comes to getting what he wants."

"Is this all because his parent's cut him off?"

"I think it has a lot to do with it. His need to prove to them he was more than they ever could be—it drove him for sure. But honestly? I think his priorities may have always been a bit off."

"Is that a nice way of saying you think he's warped?"

"Misguided."

A sickening thought grips me, "Did he even love me?"

"Honey." She touches my arm. "In his way, I'm sure he thinks he does. But I don't know if he's capable of the real thing. I think he loved the idea of you loving and adoring him."

"I don't want to be like him," I say, my voice breaking

"You aren't! You're *nothing* like him." She grips my hands firmly in hers. "He may have tried to make you into his image, but deep down that's not who you are."

"I'm still selfish though."

"Most teenagers are."

"Otto isn't." *Where did that come from?*

"He's special."

I think about it. "Yeah. I guess he kind of is." He's definitely different.

She smiles at me. "You know you can talk to him about this. It might help to have someone to share it with."

"We're not like super close or anything." Besides, he'd probably have a field day with *that* bit of juicy gossip. *'Oh, Otto, by the way, my dad's an accused felon on the run.'*

No. Thinking on it more, he wouldn't say anything. But whatever. It already didn't go well when my friends in Cali found out. And even though Otto and I are only sort of friends, I'd hate for him to look at me differently.

Tristan. Now *he'd* understand. He's used to absurd family drama.

"Mom, have you told anyone? What about Joanne?"

"Yes. I did fill her in."

"Why would you do that? Now the entire town knows!"

"She wouldn't say anything. She knows how protective I am of you and Harlow."

"Well, *Charles* knows."

"What did he say?"

"He mentioned us losing all of Dad's money."

"I think he's just making logical assumptions. Did he say anything about the FBI?"

"No."

"Do you think if he knew the whole story, he would have remained silent about such a crucial detail?"

I laugh a little. "No. That man holds nothing back."

"Sounds like someone else I know." Her lips twitch as she fights a smile.

I give her the victory. She's right, after all.

17

"I'M GOING to the movies with Tristan this Saturday." I set my strawberry-rhubarb pie into Otto's waiting hands.

"Really?" He looks surprised.

"Why is that so shocking? I'm hot, he's amazingly good looking—I'm fun, and he's"—I start to say rich, then remember the blasting I got the other day—"a decent guy."

He angles his head, giving me a hard look.

"*What?*" I ignore the silent accusation. "He *is*. He's sweet, and I like that he is nice to Harlow. Plus, the boy likes to shop!" Which is all true.

"Never mind." He turns his back to me.

Picking up a large knife, he begins cutting the pie into slices then rounds on me, knife in hand, mouth open to say something. Instead, he closes it, trades the knife for the pie, and places it in the glass display case.

"Seriously! *What?*"

"Nothing. It's fine." He scribbles something on a card and places it in front of the pie. "I hope you have a great time".

Oh. I get it. Poor guy has it bad. See? That's what I thought. He just can't admit it. "Otto . . . you and I . . . We're just friends. You know that, right?" He regards me with a curious expression. "Please, don't make this awkward, okay? I like hanging out with you."

He gives me a lopsided smile, almost a smirk. "No. Really." He chuckles. "It's fine."

"What's so damn funny?" I fire back. He *has* to have a thing for me. If he doesn't there's something wrong with him.

"Nothing."

"*Whatever*. Harlow's outside petting someone's dog." I turn to leave.

"Hold up. Mom told me to give you this next time you came in." He hands me two twenty-dollar bills.

"What's this for?" I want to get out of here. The guy makes me batty.

"The baking you've dropped off so far. We're keeping a tally and will pay based on what we sell, which has been all of it. She also told me to tell you that your coffees are on the house from now on."

Hell, I'd do it for the coffee alone. "Tell her thanks."

"Sure. Do you want me to make you something before you go?"

"No. I need to get to work. I'll get one next time."

"When will you be back? With more desserts," he clarifies. "They go fast, and people are requesting them now."

"I don't know. I was thinking of making some blueberry muffins or maybe banana chocolate chip with walnuts. I can't decide. Possibly white-chocolate raspberry."

"*Oh, man* . . . that would be awesome—make all of them! Make tons. That way I won't feel bad eating any."

Despite feeling out of sorts, I laugh at his enthusiasm. "Sure."

I'll get the ingredients from the store today. Charles offered to give me the items at cost if I sell my baking at the store. I told him I'd think about it because I wasn't sure if I could keep up with making items for two locations.

"Hello, baby girl," Charles says the moment he sees Harlow. "What have you been up to today?"

"We made pies!"

Charles looks at my empty hands and frowns. "Where's mine?"

"You think you deserve one?" I tease.

He folds his arms across his chest. "*Hrmph*."

"Oh, quit your grouching. I decided to take you up on your offer and sell my baking at the store. You can sample *one* item"—I hold up a finger—"one, each time I bring some in." He looks at me, ready to lecture. "That sweet stuff can't be good at your age."

He puffs out his chest. "I'm as healthy as a horse! Come on Harlow, let's go pick us out some ice cream."

I watch as he leads her to a vintage deep freezer next to the front door. Charles slides back the cover and lets Harlow reach in and pick out her favorite: a red, white, and blue Rocket Pop. He pulls out a Fudgsicle for himself and slides the door closed.

"Hey. Don't I get one?" I ask.

"You think you deserve one?" he asks, walking away.

"Watch out, old man. You wouldn't want to throw your body into shock with that unprecedented humor." I walk over, slide back the lid, and pull out an ice cream sandwich.

The bell chimes as a customer opens the door. "Hi, Mrs. Merriweather," Harlow says.

"Hi, Harlow. How are you today?"

"I'm great. What can I help you find?"

Charles and I look at each other with raised eyebrows. My sister could teach us both a thing or two.

Something flashes in my periphery. The brightness of it has me turning toward the wall of windows that face Main Street. A silver convertible Mercedes, exactly like my father's, drives past the store, sending my heart pounding against my chest.

"That's Chase's father," Charles says from behind me, possibly registering my shock.

"Oh." I catch the license plate. Ohio. Definitely not my father's car, but my adrenalin's still going haywire. According to Sherice, he could be anywhere. Before she came, I would have been running out the door after the car, excited to see him. Now, understanding the government's case against him and Mom sharing all that she went through, my thoughts are jumbled.

"Have you had any more trouble from that boy, Chase?" he asks, breaking me from my thoughts.

"No." I breathe deep, trying to calm myself. "I think I scared him off."

"Glad to hear it." He places a hand on my shoulder. "Are you okay?"

"Yeah. Why?" I smile, attempting to hide the residual panic.

Charles eyes me. "You look . . . shaken."

"I'm good."

"Okay." He turns away. "Well, come on with me then. I want to give you the combination to the safe."

"Are you crazy?" I chase after him. "Why would you do that? I could rob you blind."

"Yeah. But you wouldn't. I was thinking it would be nice to take a night off once in a while. And this way you could close up for me."

"You *are* older than dirt, so I guess taking a night off now and then would be a good idea."

"Sass."

Harlow and Mrs. Merriweather load the groceries on the conveyer. "I'll be there in a minute," I say to Charles.

I run the purchases through the register. Harlow bags them with veteran skill while Charles oversees from the doorway behind us.

"That was just right," Charles pats Harlow on the shoulder when the woman leaves.

She smiles up at him. "Thanks, Charles."

"What about me?" I ask, a hand mounted on my hip.

"Yeah . . . you know what you're doing too."

I slap a hand on my chest. "Oh, be still my beating heart. I get a half-assed attempt at a compliment. Lucky me."

Charles grins. "There's that Academy Award performance again."

"Careful. I warned you about that face cracking." I put a hand next to my ear. "Is that a fissure I hear opening up?"

Harlow covers her mouth and giggles.

"Smart ass. Now get in here so I can teach you how to open this damn safe."

"Yes, your bossiness."

He shakes his head as I follow him into the office.

Mom comes in about twenty minutes later, looking happier than I've ever seen her.

"Hi, baby. How was work?" she asks Harlow.

"Awesome as usual."

"How was your day?" I ask, still amazed by her glow.

Charles walks up. "Hello, Sarah."

"Hello, Mr. Fitzwald."

"Call me Charles. You're not a little girl anymore."

She looks a little bowled over. "No, I guess I'm not."

"Your girls sure have been a fine help."

"Thank you. I'm glad." Still looking dazed by the civility, Mom turns her attention to Harlow. "Are you ready?"

"Can I stay . . . *please?*"

Mom looks to Charles.

"Sure she can. I've been meaning to organize my paperwork in the office. I bet you'd be a great help."

"Really?" she says, eyes twinkling. "That would be amazing."

"Mom, are you sure she wasn't adopted? We're nothing alike."

She grins. "Positive."

"Harlow, how about I come and get you after I eat dinner? That will give you another hour or so."

A little pout forms. "Okay. I guess so."

I'm pretty sure she would stay all day, every day, if it was up to her. Crazy kid.

I walk Mom toward the door, my nosiness getting the best of me. "You look pretty . . . and happy."

"Thank you, baby. How sweet of you to say so."

"Don't take this the wrong way, but . . . how come?"

Her face lights up. "Talking to you the other day, being open about the past, was a huge relief. I don't feel so alone. Thanks for listening and not judging me to harshly."

"Why would I judge you? I was there and did nothing. Thanks for not hating me."

"Oh, baby. I could never hate you. What happened wasn't you fault."

I surprise myself by reaching out and hugging her. I know what he did wasn't my fault, but the fact that I didn't stand up to him . . . And how mean I was to her. It made it so much worse.

"Oh," she says, hugging me back.

July 4th, 1938

Charles and I went to the July 4th celebration picnic today. It was a scorcher. These days, all I seem to do is wait for the next time I can be with him. There was barely a moment during the day when we were not touching each other. After the fireworks, he told me he loved me, and I him. I know he is the one that I want to spend the rest of my life with. It's crazy, it's only been three months since our first walk together, but I've never been happier or surer of anything in my life. I am worried though, everyone is saying that war could be declared any day. I can't imagine him leaving. It frightens me deeply.

I pull on a pair of cut-off jean shorts, a loose-fitting baby-doll tank, and my Jack Rogers wedges. It's a bit of a Daisy Duke look, which should fit right into the whole "Midwest" scene. I curl my hair and pull it back into a ponytail and give a little extra attention to my makeup.

"You look amazing," Tristan raves when I open the door and step out.

"Why thank you," I gush, pleased by his reaction.

"I brought the convertible. I hope that's okay. It's so nice out."

I walk toward the Porsche Boxster parked in front of the house. "More than okay." I'm glad I pulled my hair back. He opens the door for me, and I slide into the soft leather seats. *Ahh, I missed this.* "Is it yours?"

"No, my grandfather's. He loves his toys."

"He has great taste."

He grins as he pulls away from the curb. "This mall is relatively limited compared to what you're used to, so don't be too disappointed."

"No, it's fine. I just need to build a more functional wardrobe—maybe a little more conservative."

He looks me over and grins.

I can't tell if he's admiring me or making a statement about my clothing choice. I'm about to comment when he says, "So, Otto's been filling me in on your particulars."

"You've been talking to Otto about me?" I flirt shamelessly.

Wait. What does he mean by *particulars*? Should I be concerned?

"You may have come up a time or two." He gives me a sideways glance. "I love Santa Barbara. We vacationed there several times when I was younger. You must miss it."

"Some parts."

"Will your dad be joining you soon?"

"Probably not. I think him and my mom are done." Wow. *That* came out easily.

"Are you okay with that?"

"Yeah. I think it's for the best." I don't want to talk about this right now. I'm still reeling from all that I've learned. "Does this thing go any faster?"

He grins and tilts his head like, *you're joking, right?* Then floors it.

I throw my hands in the air. "Yeah!" I yell into the wind.

I look over at Tristan—one hand on the steering wheel, Ray-Ban's on, hair whipping back, flashing sun-bleached layers. Without thinking, I reach over, sliding my fingers into his hair.

He slows down. "I need a haircut, don't I?"

My fingers make another pass through the thick mane. It's so soft. "Yes, you do."

I take my hand away as he turns to me. "Maybe there's a place in the mall to cut it."

"No way you're getting a mall haircut."

"Why not?"

"You're such a guy. Malls aren't exactly known for hair artistry."

"Yeah, you're probably right."

I pull out my phone and Google salons in Chatwell. I peruse several websites, find one that looks acceptable, and call them. "You're all set," I say after disconnecting. "Now we can get some shape into that shag."

He pulls into a trendy little restaurant. From what I've seen of the town so far, it's up and coming. I order my usual safety food—a salad. I mean, who needs the extra calories?

I grill him about his life while we eat. I want to know more about the guy I'm hot after.

It's not a surprise that he's been in private schools from the beginning. He said he didn't mind being shipped off to boarding school at fourteen, since he barely tolerated his parents. He wasn't into the social scene at school, stayed on the outside of it as much as possible. That part is hard for me to relate to, but he said it was a definite choice. We've seen a lot of the same Broadway shows and frequented some of the same trendy hotspots. My father took me to Manhattan several times when he had business to attend to. I had to beg, but it was worth it. The shopping is unparalleled. His family life is even more messed up than mine, if that's possible. I know I could confide in him about my father—he would totally get it—but I'm not up to sharing yet. Probably fear of being judged, not for my father's crimes, but for how I treated my mother. I feel like he would think less of me. He has a good head on his shoulders, whereas mine needs a lot of work. I don't want him knowing that yet.

It's been a great day so far. Tristan's, polite, engaging . . . but it's weird. I can't tell if he's into me—something I've never experienced before. *All* guys are into me. I've been throwing all my moves at him, but he ignores them and has none of his own. With Otto, it's different. We're friends, but Tristan should be all over me. We're perfect for each other. And he's been a great help with my new toned-down look. Apparently I needed more help than I thought. My initial attempt at conforming to midwestern norms has resulted in gawking stares from men and glares from wives and girlfriends. *Ridiculous.*

"Hey, there's a party tonight," he says, combing through a section of shirts in his size. He stops and pulls one out, putting it against his chest for my approval. The shake of my head has him returning it. "Do you want to go with me? Maybe Otto will want to come too." I pull a baby-blue one from the rack and hand it to him instead. "Nice."

"I don't know. Last party I went to I got wasted and kind of lost my shit."

"Who cares? There won't be any locals there, well . . . except for Otto if he comes. My friend and his family have a house on the lake and come out on weekends. Same with the other people that'll be there."

"Why would anyone want a lake house in Foxall? I'm sure there are better places to build?"

He laughs. "Most of them grew up there. It's a nice lake, Kylie."

I make a sound of indifference. "What's your waist size?"

"Thirty-two."

I pull out a pair of shorts that are a perfect match to the shirt I found him. "Otto was there . . . at the party. He saved me from that jackass, Chase."

"What? *Uck!*" He looks at me like I grew horns and a devil's tail. "You went out with him?"

I cringe. This is what I was afraid of. The guy has principles, standards. "It was a confusing time in my life."

"Didn't you just move here a few weeks ago?"

"Hey, don't judge. A lot has happened. I was lashing out, having an identity crisis, a teenage meltdown—whatever you want to call it."

"How did Otto save you?"

"He didn't tell you?"

"No."

I reluctantly fill him in. He could easily find out on his own, but I'd rather him hear it from me.

He looks disgusted and angry when I finish, his attitude stinging my pride. "*What?* I was hurting." I look up through my lashes with injured puppy-dog eyes. The hurt is real, the dramatics are just a normal extension of myself.

"Sorry, I'm not judging. It's Chase. Guys like that piss me

off, the way they take advantage of drunk girls. You were lucky." He looks at me pointedly. "Really lucky."

"I know." I move to another rack, intent on hiding my shame.

He follows behind me. "Your life must have been shit if you were compelled to go out with *that* idiot."

"Yeah, well, it's better. Still . . . going out with him was a severe lack in judgment. Now can we drop it?" I peer over my shoulder with a fake smile plastered on my face.

"Absolutely."

He grabs a couple more shirts. "I'm going to try these on. Wait for me?"

"Sure. Unless you want me to come with you. You know . . . hang up the stuff you don't want, advise you on your decisions, help you in and out of your clothes." I pump my eyebrows suggestively. "You know . . . a dressing room personal assistant."

He rolls his eyes before disappearing into the change room.

That one always works! I throw my hands up in the air. "I give up."

"What's that?" a girl behind me asks. "Can I get you another size?"

"Sorry. No. Not right now. Thanks."

I plop my body down in a chair, dropping my bags at my feet. *This is so unfair.* What am I doing wrong?

"You have great taste in clothes," Tristan says, coming out. "I like what you picked out."

"You should. I have years of shopping experience."

He laughs. "No shortage of confidence in you, is there?"

"Oh, you'd be surprised." A recent development, one I'm not too thrilled about.

. . .

We watch the latest chick flick—Tristan's the first guy ever to watch one with me. I reach for his hand during a heart-wrenching scene where the girl dies with her newfound love standing over her. I hate sad endings. But it was worth it when his fingers entwined with mine.

When we get home, I lean over to kiss him on the cheek. A G-rated kiss is not my usual course of action after a date with a hot guy, but nothing about this day has been normal.

"Thanks. I had a lot of fun," I say, opening the car door.

"Me too. Here." He climbs out of the car without opening his door, reaches behind the back seat for my bags, then brings them around to me. "I'll pick you up for the party around nine?"

"Okay, sounds good."

With a deep sigh of frustration, I watch as the car pulls away from the curb. I am so . . . infatuated, frustrated, confused, enamored? In love? Definitely halfway there. *Ahhh.* What's his deal? Or mine? He should be falling at my feet.

When I enter the house, Mom's sitting on the couch, reading a magazine. "Hey." I drop my bags at the door. "How was your day?"

"Good. Just taking a break after cleaning the kitchen. Did you have fun? Looks like shopping was successful?"

"Do you want to see what I got?"

She looks surprised by the offer. "Sure, I'd love to."

"Sweet." The novelty of having her as a friend is growing on me. "I found some excellent deals." She lifts an eyebrow. "Well, I am on a limited budget." We both laugh.

"Oh, and I got this for you." I reach into the last bag.

"You got me something?" She flattens her hand over her heart, looking touched and shocked at the same time.

I pull out two soft, crew-neck T-shirts, one a coral pink and the other a bluey-greenish color. "I wasn't sure what colors you'd like, but I know these would look good with your skin tone, so . . ."

"Oh, Kylie, I love them. They feel so nice." Tears glisten in her eyes.

"I know you didn't bring much with you and you've hardly had a chance to shop."

"That's so thoughtful, baby, thank you." She stands up and hugs me.

"No problem." Giving feels good. Surprise, surprise.

"I got a couple of things for Harlow too. I'm just going to run up and show her. She's upstairs?"

"Yes. Are you hungry? There are leftovers."

"Maybe in a bit."

Harlow loved the shorts and shirt I got her. After hanging with her for a while, I put my new clothes away then decide to read some more of Nana's diary. I throw on the comfortable sundress I bought and sit in the window seat.

August 11, 1941

All anyone talks about is this damn war. I'm sick of it. It scares me so much. Charles says there's nothing to worry about. He says that as soon as the Americans jump into the fight, it will be over before it's started, that I have nothing to worry about. Charles and his friends are acting like a bunch of boisterous young boys. War is never that easy.

December 7, 1941

We just received word that the Japanese bombed Pearl Harbor. All those people. It's heartbreaking. My father says the U.S. will go to war for sure now. I'm scared what it will mean for Charles and me. I know it's petty, when so many people have lost their lives, but I can't help thinking it.

December 9, 1941
Yesterday the U.S. declared war on Japan. I knew by the expression on Charles's face when he came to the house this evening that he had already enlisted. He and his friends drove all the way to Chatwell to do it. He said they waited in line for six hours. Fools! I can't seem to stop crying. I feel like if I let him go, he will never come back to me. I know able men need to enlist. It's for the survival of our nation. They could attack here at any time, but why can't it be someone else's beau?

December 11, 1941
Charles and his friends left today for boot camp. It's about four hours north of here. I don't know if I will see him before they ship overseas. I gave him a picture I took of myself at the photo booth in the drugstore. I told him I didn't want him forgetting me. He said I was crazy and that "who could forget someone like you?" The real reason for the photo was I wanted to remind him why he needed to stay alive. He asked me to wait for him and to please write. I told him of course I would, he's the love of my life. I can hear the radio from downstairs as I'm writing. They just announced that Germany and Italy have declared war on the USA. I'm so scared. This war just got a lot bigger.

January 3, 1942
Charles wasn't able to come home for Christmas. He recently wrote that they are sending him to Kentucky for specialized training. He didn't say what kind, but that he would be there for a few weeks. He wrote that he hopes he will be able to come home before they ship him somewhere else. I hope so, too.

February 5, 1942

I got a letter from Charles today. They are shipping his unit to Germany. I won't get to see him before he leaves. I feel like someone has stabbed me in the heart.

June 12, 1942

I don't know what to do with myself. He's been in Germany for four months and we hear nothing but bad news on the radio. He was wrong about it being an easy war. It's horrible what the Nazis are doing, and I doubt we're even getting the entire story. Usually, Charles writes like his days are easy and mundane, like a visit to the country club. I know he doesn't want me worrying, but today his letter is different. His writing is monotone, cold, almost mechanical, like a completely different person. I don't know what to do.

I realize this is all in the past and Charles came home, but I feel her fear, her pain, her sadness. It's like watching a sad movie with a happy ending for the second time. You know the ending's okay, but the middle is painfully sad and stabs you in the heart, regardless.

I grab a bite to eat then pick up the book again, wanting to find out what happens, but I'm so tired I can barely keep my eyes open. I've got that party tonight. I decide to just close my eyes for a minute.

"Kylie!" I hear Harlow's voice through a sleep-induced haze.

"What is it?" I rub my eyes, sitting up in the dark. "What's the matter?"

"Tristan's at the door. He said he's picking you up for a party?"

"Shit!" I jump out of bed. "What time is it?"

"Nine."

"Crap! Tell him I fell asleep, and I'll be ready as soon as I can." I run into the bathroom and look at my disheveled reflection. "Shit, shit, shit!" I take off all my old makeup and quickly reapply it. When finished, I reassess my appearance. *Frick.* I still look like I just woke up. Oh, well, it's the best I can do.

I run to my room and throw on something cute and casual, then rip off the tags from my new sandals and run down the stairs.

"I'm so sorry," I say to Tristan as he stands up from the couch. I swear every time I see him, he takes my breath away.

"It's okay. Your mom and Harlow were keeping me company."

I hope they weren't boring him to death.

"Okay, Mom, *um,* I'm not sure what time I'll be home." I stumble over my words. Things are so different between us.

"Be safe," she says, I'm sure referencing my previous party fiasco.

"I will."

"Don't worry," Tristan says to her. "It's not a big party. Just a small group of friends having a bonfire at a lake house."

"Good to know." Mom smiles at him, looking appreciative.

I look over Harlow's head, while she gives me a goodbye hug. "Is Otto coming?"

"Yeah. We're picking him up on the way."

I kiss the top of her head. "Bye, Bug."

She squeezes me one more time before letting go. "Have fun."

We hop in an SUV and minutes later we're stopped in front of Otto's house. Tristan honks. He's driving an Escalade this time.

"What took you so long?" Otto asks, climbing into the back seat.

"Sorry," I say. "My fault. I fell asleep."

He stares at me in appreciation. "You look amazing for just waking up."

"How sweet." There are no pretenses with Otto. He's not flirting. He's honest, genuine. I like that about him.

It's a good-sized house, about five-thousand square feet of beauty layered into three stories overlooking the lake. I enjoy the familiarity as we walk through the professionally decorated rooms that ultimately lead us out to a massive pool deck with steps leading down to a private beach. They must have had sand brought in, because it's fine and there are no rocks or other lake debris. My heart aches for home.

There's a large bonfire with several people around it either standing, sitting in beach chairs, or lounging on blankets. Tristan introduces me around; Otto seems to know everyone already.

I stay close to Tristan throughout the evening, trying my best to connect with him physically, but his attitude toward me continues to be politely indifferent. Otto, on the other hand, is getting more irritated by the minute. I'm not sure what his deal is. Someone at the party must be pissing him off.

A wind has kicked up, causing the temperature to drop

while Tristan and I talk by the water. I lean against him to get warm.

"You're shivering." He wraps an arm around my shoulders, pulling me into his side, then slides his hand up and down my arm, attempting to warm me.

Finally! "Yeah. I should have brought a jacket."

"I've got a sweatshirt in the car. I'll go get it."

"No, this is okay. Your body is a perfect temperature."

He laughs. "It will only take me a minute."

"Oh, okay. Thanks." My teeth chatter when he lets go and disappears into the house.

"So, you and Tristan, huh?" a voice whispers in my ear. I whip around, coming face to face with Chase.

What the hell is he doing here? I move further down the beach, away from prying eyes. He stumbles along with me, obviously drunk.

"We're just friends," I say.

"Friends like you and I were?" He runs his fingers down my arm, making my skin crawl.

I smile sweetly at him, needing to maintain my previously crafted persona to get him to back off. "Otto's here too. The three of us are just hanging out."

He slides a hand around my back, pulling me into him. "Well, then we should party together. I remember how much fun you were."

Crap. "You had your chance," I whine, sounding dejected. I drop my lower lip. "You never called me. Remember? Your friends were more important than I was."

"My mistake," he says, leaning in to kiss me.

I reach up and push his face away. "I need some breathing room." But he grips my chin and crushes his mouth to mine.

"Stop!" I scream against his lips while attempting to shove him away.

Suddenly, he's ripped from my body. "What the hell are you doing!" Tristan yells at him, his eyes livid and wild.

Chase stumbles back but regains his balance and lunges at Tristan with his fist cocked. Tristan side-steps, and Chase hits the ground.

"Fuck!" Chase screams before jumping to his feet, sand flying in every direction.

"Chase! Stop!" I lunge at him, but Otto appears by my side. He grips my arm and pulls me back.

Chase squares off with Tristan, then steps forward, throwing a wild punch, which Tristan easily dodges. Tristan follows it with a hard right to the jaw, sending Chase sprawling once again.

"You are so dead!" Chase yells as he scrambles to his feet, ready to attack again, but several guys grab hold of him.

"Enough!" one guy yells as Chase struggles against his hold.

"It's time to go," says another as they drag him toward the house. "You're not even supposed to be here."

"You better be watching your back, Tristan. I'm coming for you," Chase rants as he's pulled away, stumbling up the stairs. "She's not even worth it!" he hollers from the top step. "Just white trash like her mother!"

Otto releases me to charge after him, but I quickly clamp down onto his arm, stopping him in time. "Don't! Just let it go." I don't want to see Otto getting hurt over this. "The guy is a total dick."

"Yeah, stay with the slut, Spaceboy. You know I'd only kick your ass and embarrass you like always."

"Get the hell out of here, Chase!" Tristan yells, shaking off the guys restraining him. "We both know I can make you regret you were even born."

"Hey!" I shout at Tristan. "You're not helping!"

"Bring it on," Chase taunts, but Tristan turns his back to him and starts talking to the guys at his side.

Otto's eyes continue to blaze with fury as he watches Chase fight against the hands that restrain him and forcibly pull him into the house.

"It's okay. He's just white trash with money," I tell Otto, hoping to lighten the moment. "The filthiest of all the rich—beyond garbage." Otto's body remains rigid. I take his hand. "Hey, it's okay, they're only words." He stares into my eyes for a moment, then touches his forehead to mine.

"It's okay," I whisper to him.

"I know." He breathes deep before straightening. "I'm just so sick of him and all his crap."

"I know, but there will always be some jackass, thinking they can push you around. They do it because they're weak, messed up, and insecure. You're not, so screw 'em."

He nods in agreement, then lifts our joined hand and kisses my fingers. "Thank you."

I look over at Tristan and find him staring at us.

"Are you okay for a second?" I ask Otto. "I need to check on Tristan."

"Yeah. Sure." He turns abruptly and walks away.

I stare after him a moment and wonder about his shift in attitude. I can't seem to figure him out.

"You okay?" I lean against him, cradling his cheeks in my hands. "Thanks for that."

"Thanks for giving me a reason. I've been wanting to deck

him *forever.*" He smiles down at me, making my knees go weak. "Besides, what are friends for?"

I instantly step back, slapped by the clarification. "Yeah, right . . . friends." I've never been put in the friend zone before. That's usually *my* line.

We move to the fire. I'm really chilled now, and the heat feels amazing.

"Hey," Otto says, coming up next to me all smiles.

So he's fine again? I'm so confused.

We drop Otto off first. I'm not giving up on Tristan. There is no way he just wants me for a friend, that's just not how it works with me. But as soon as the thought is completed, my once relied-upon confidence crumbles into uncertainty. I've been dealing with too many unwanted feelings lately.

"Thanks again for standing up for me."

"I'm sorry he was even there."

I take his hand from his lap and squeeze it. "It's my fault. I played a game and lost, giving him the wrong idea from the beginning."

"Doesn't matter. He had no right."

"You know . . . you can get scary."

He leans toward me with his forearm on the center console, laughing. "So I've been told. My grandmother says it's from her Irish side of the family, Grandad says it's his Scottish ancestry. They like to make me feel better." He winks. "I don't like it when I lose it like that. One minute I'm fine and the next I'm raging mad, and it all goes black—I lose control."

I minimize the space between us. "My hero." I wait for Tristan to close the distance, hoping for the kiss that puts us past the friendship level. Instead, he kisses my forehead and straightens in his seat.

"I should go," he says. The words I least want to hear.

"Oh, okay." I try to smile, feeling utterly rejected.

"Text me when you're off next so we can take another ride on the boat. You can bring Harlow again."

"Sure. I could do that." I open the car door and slide out onto my feet.

"Kylie?"

I turn back, hopeful. *"Hmm?"*

"I had fun tonight. Thanks for coming with me."

"Sure," I say, brightening. Maybe he's just shy or old-fashioned. The thought gives me a bit of my pride back.

I all but skip my way up the sidewalk to the house as he drives away. *He had fun!* I stop when I reach the stairs and give my head a shake. Of course, he did.

Oh, look at the lilies! They're blooming. Time to find some more flowers to plant. I pull out my phone to text Otto, then stop. I'm surprised that I didn't think of Tristan first, but then remember gardening with Otto the other day and it makes perfect sense.

I touch the screen and notice a text from Agent Walker wanting to know if I'm okay. I look up and down the street, wondering if I'm under surveillance or it's just a random question. I haven't noticed anyone.

I text back that I'm fine and ask why. She says that she was just concerned after our meeting the other day and wanted to reiterate that if I need to talk about anything, she's available. I text her a thank you, look around one last time and head inside.

19

OTTO PICKS me up in his old, beat-up Toyota truck. I laugh to myself as the door creaks open—total hunk of junk, and I'm actually getting into it.

"Do you know where you want to go?" he asks.

"That's why I called *you.*"

"Mom goes to the greenhouse at the edge of town. I don't know why she bothers . . . just about everything she plants, dies."

The first thing I notice when we get there are all the rows of tables loaded with color—how does anybody pick? I think I'll preview everything before making any decisions. Mom added some of her money to mine, but I want to stretch it as far possible.

"Are you okay? You know . . . from the party," Otto asks when I stop to look at the name of some vibrant pink flowers.

Petunias. Pretty. I'll keep them in mind. "I was going to ask *you* that, but yeah, I'm good. Thanks for standing up for me."

"I didn't do much. Tristan did most of it as usual."

"Isn't that why you keep him around?" I jab an elbow into his side, teasing. Otto's face falls. *Crap.* "Sorry. I didn't mean it like that. He just seems like that kind of person—the defender of all those in need."

From a flat of purple flowers, he pulls out the small plastic stake with care instructions. He skims over it, then puts it back. "No. I know what you mean. He's always been there for me, at least during the summers. But when he's not around . . ." He shrugs a shoulders. "I'm just not that guy! I don't fight or play the tough-guy role."

"It's not a big deal. Not everyone can be, and you shouldn't feel the need to. Chase, and people like him, are a waste of space, Otto. You're an intelligent, gentle, caring person. We need more people like you and less dickhead bullies like him." I stop in front of a large selection of roses.

"Thanks." He gives my hand a squeeze before quickly releasing it. "Roses?"

"Yeah, roses." I rub my hands together in glee. "They're so beautiful." There are so many shapes, colors, sizes, heights—it's overwhelming.

Otto waits patiently while I look through them, reading their tags as I go. It's so hot in here. I'm melting.

"So have you thought anymore about school in the fall?" Otto asks. "You know, where you want to go or what you want to take."

"It's always been University of Southern California, but with my dad missing . . ." *Crap!* I was so wrapped up in the flowers. "I didn't—"

He cuts me off. "You don't know where your dad is?"

"Well . . ." I desperately try to think of a cover story, but my mind is blank. I sigh in defeat, my shoulders drooping. "It's a long story."

"You don't have to tell me if you don't want to."

He's said those words to me several times, never pressing for more than I wanted to give. No. The timing's right. I look around and see a bench tucked into a flower display. "Let's talk over there."

I fill him in from the morning the feds showed up to everything Sherice told us.

"Are you safe?"

His concern gives my heart a little tug. Having someone genuinely concerned about me is a novelty—well, other than Harlow and Mom.

"Yeah." I touch his arm, a simple gesture, but the intimate feeling of his skin has me dropping my hand and mentally shaking my head at myself. "We're okay. He's never abused me, only my mother."

"He beat your mother?" He looks horrified.

"Shit! Sorry. No." I roll my eyes toward the corrugated roof. "My brain is out to lunch. He was mentally abusive, but there's a lot more to it."

"Hey, I've got all day."

"Another time." I'm not sure Mom would appreciate me sharing the details of her humiliation.

"Fair enough."

"Can we get back to the flowers?"

"Sure. Let's do it." He stands up. "Thanks for confiding in me. I know it's not easy for you to let your guard down."

"Thanks for listening." He shrugs off the compliment. "No, really. Thanks."

I feel better talking about it. And I trust him completely. My strange reactions to him are another matter.

"*Sooo.*" He claps his hands together in a loud *smack.* "What's it going to be?"

I pick out a rose bush with fragrant, medium-sized yellow flowers with a touch of pink around the edges. Otto finds a trolley and we load it along with a jillion annuals—they're super cheap and bloom all summer. Mom, can help me figure out locations for everything when I get home.

"So you want to go to a movie with me tomorrow night?" Otto asks.

"In Chatwell?"

"No. Here in town."

"I'm confused. Tristan said there wasn't a theater here."

"There isn't. But on the last Sunday of every month, one of the local farmers plays old movies against the side of his barn. He's done it for as long as I can remember."

"Oh, wow, *that's* different. Does he charge admission?"

"No. It's just something he does. Usually there's a fundraiser going on with baked goods for sale. Your great-grandmother was the previous organizer. She liked to bake like you do."

"Really? I didn't know that. Mom never said anything. How does mine compare?" Just curious.

"Definitely just as good, if not better."

"Really?" I beam.

He laughs.

Maybe I can help out sometime . . . do a fundraiser.

A fundraiser . . . seriously? *Pull it together, Kylie.*

Otto helps me unload the flowers—some in the front and the rest in the back—before he leaves. He insisted on buying me the rose bush when I came up short at the register. I might have gone a little overboard.

I look up when I hear the back door slam. It's Mom. "Wow! You got lots!"

"There's more in the front. I had fun picking them out."

"Do you mind coming for a drive with me and Harlow? I want to show you two something."

I look down at the flowers, eager to get planting. "What is it?"

"Where I used to live."

It was never a thought, but now that she brought it up . . . "Definitely!"

I realize, as we cruise out of town, I haven't explored the area since moving here. I've stuck to the need-to-be locations.

We pass well kept, medium-sized homes built on acreages, then turn down a dirt road that goes from flat and smooth to unkempt and bumpy. The houses are smaller here and turning shabby.

"Look at all the horses," Harlow says in awe.

The ten or so horses remind me of Frank and June. "Nice. Maybe we can come back sometime with some carrots."

She leans forward between our seats. "Can we?" she asks, sounding excited. "Mom, do you think that would be okay?"

"Are you still in your seatbelt?"

She sits back. "I am now. But can we?"

"I don't know." She pauses. "I don't see why not? They look like they've been put out to pasture."

"What does that mean?" Harlow asks.

"Just that they're old." We hit a huge pothole and go flying. Our heads would have hit the roof if we weren't belted in. She turns to me, then looks at Harlow in the rear-view mirror. "Sorry about that."

"It's okay," I say, thankful Mom made Harlow put her seatbelt back on.

The car slows down, almost to a crawl, as Mom pulls off the road onto an overgrown driveway. We park in front of a dilapidated structure that might have been a house at one time.

"This is what's left of where I grew up."

I stare at the ramshackle dwelling, then at Mom. "No way!"

"Yep. This is it." The corner of her mouth lifts, then falls.

"Look at all the land you had," Harlow says in awe. "You must have had fun with all that room to run and the horses nearby to play with."

"Sometimes," Mom says as we all step out of the car. "I liked to hide in the pasture and feed them grass. They could get it themselves, but I liked the feeling of their muzzles nibbling against my hand."

The word 'hide' is not lost on me, and I wonder about the horrors she had to deal with.

We follow Mom toward the house. The roof has partially caved in the middle. It's so small. Smaller than most sheds in our old neighborhood.

"I hated this place," she whispers. "All I ever wanted to do was get away."

"Why are we here, Mom?" I ask.

"I'm not sure. I guess I wanted to see what was left. I didn't want to do it alone."

Harlow takes Mom's hand, sensing the need for support. I wonder if Mom filled her in on the details of her childhood or if she's just that intuitive. Maybe she's always known, and I'm the last one to find out? The thought stings.

"Can we go check it out?" Harlow asks.

"Sure. But we have to be careful."

There is debris all over the yard—if you can call it that. Windows are smashed or missing, and the front door is hanging to the side by a lonely hinge which looks like it could give at any moment.

Harlow runs ahead and leans in. When she takes a step forward, Mom yells to wait. "Let me make sure it's safe first."

We look over Harlow's shoulder when we come up behind her. It's filthy. The old linoleum floor is peeling up and missing in places. Time has torn this house apart piece by piece, scattering its existence. Harlow moves aside and lets Mom go in first.

"Everyone, follow close behind me." Mom looks up at the roof then tests the strength of the floor, first by stepping, then bouncing lightly. "Seems solid. Amazing. Let's stay close to the walls. I don't trust the roof."

"Okay," we say in unison.

The main area is an open space with a small kitchen off to the left and a short hallway to the right with two other rooms— most likely bedrooms.

The kitchen consists of a couple of cupboards over a small metal counter with a sink and an old wood-burning cookstove off to the right.

"What's that red thing over the sink?" I ask.

"It's a water pump," Harlow, the smarty pants, explains.

"Why do you have a pump in the kitchen?"

"For water." Mom grins.

I stare at her, unbelieving. "But what about the rest of the house?"

"That's all there was."

"How did you go to the bathroom?"

"Outhouse."

"No way!"

"No electricity either," she laughs.

"Oh my god, Mom. That's crazy."

"You were living off the grid." Harlow says. "A lot of people are doing that now. They have a whole TV show on it."

"*Why?*" I ask, perplexed by the idea. "Why would anyone want to live without all the modern amenities?"

"More economical and better for the environment," Harlow replies.

I shake my head. "To each his own, I guess."

We follow Mom as she backtracks to the other side of the house. One room has a leftover metal bedframe with a destroyed, thin blue and white-striped mattress laying sideways across the top. She turns to the other, placing both hands on the doorframe, effectively blocking us from entering. Her knuckles are white from her grip as she stares forward with a blank expression. "This was my room."

Harlow peeks under her arm, me over the top. Mom's not moving, as if she's frozen solid in the doorway.

I place a hand on her shoulder. "Let's go. There is nothing for you here but bad memories."

"You're right," she says, barely above a whisper.

"Who's in the mood for ice cream?" I ask. "Who wants to go raid the freezer at the store?"

"*Meee!*" Harlow races out of the house.

Mom turns to me, looking sad. "Thank you."

"You survived, Mom. That's all that matters."

She doesn't look too sure. "Maybe I shouldn't have come back here. I can still feel it all—hear all the yelling, see the violence. I didn't expect the memories to still be haunting this place."

"Well, you faced them and now you can move on, right?"

"Right." She wraps her arms around her waist, like she's holding herself together just in case.

"Maybe we should burn it to the ground," I say as we near the car.

"The thought did cross my mind. I wonder who owns the land?"

"Does it matter?"

She laughs. "It's tempting. More as a screw-you, you-didn't-destroy-me moment, but *eh* . . . it's not worth getting charged for arson. Let's get out of here."

"Yeah. It's friggin' hot."

Harlow's chanting—"ice cream, ice cream, who wants some ice cream?"—when we get to the car. That child could raise anyone's spirits.

20

OTTO PICKS me up for the movie. I'm a little worried he might think this is a date. I can't see why he would, especially after our talks and me going out with Tristan. Besides, it's not like he got all nervous and goofy when he asked.

"So what movie is playing?"

"*Terminator.*"

"The first one?"

"Yep."

"Nice."

He follows a trail of cars and pulls off the road into a field. The cars line up side by side, parking with the experience of many years behind the tradition. The whole town must be here. The parking area is packed.

Otto opens the trunk and takes out several blankets. "Here, let me carry those." I hold out an arm. "Where are your glasses? Did you leave them in the car?" He's hottie Superman again.

He drapes the blankets over my arm. "Contacts. I'll get the cooler. I brought us some snacks."

"If you have contacts, why are you always wearing your glasses?"

"Laziness."

"I like being able to see your eyes."

"Really?" He looks genuinely surprised.

Great. He's going to think I'm flirting. How can the removal of a pair of glasses cause such a transformation in someone? Now all those late-night feelings I had after we went boating are back and there's no superhero T-shirt to shield me from my thoughts.

We weave our way through a loose patchwork of blankets, sheets, and quilts laid out in disjointed, colorful patterns all over the grass—some contain people, others are empty while their owners walk around visiting with friends and neighbors.

"How's this?" Otto asks, stopping at a small empty space in the middle of the kaleidoscope.

"Sure. Works for me." I notice the makeshift screen on the side of an enormous red barn. So cool!

He opens the largest blanket, spreading it out. "I brought extras in case you get cold."

It's like a hundred degrees out, but it was thoughtful anyway. "They'll make good pillows," I say.

"That too."

He opens the cooler. "Diet or regular?"

"Diet."

He hands me a diet cola and pulls out a plastic grocery bag filled with popcorn.

"You've done this before."

"Yeah, the family does this a lot."

Now I'm even more cautious about maintaining the friend zone. "Are they here? They should sit with us."

"Normally they would, but Olivia isn't feeling well. And this movie may be too much for her. She's not one for violence."

"Totally opposite of Harlow. She'll watch anything and everything."

"She's a brave kid. And smart too. I enjoy talking to her when she visits Olivia. Hey, did I tell you they discovered—"

"I didn't know you two were coming?" We both turn, surprised by the sound of Tristan's voice.

"What are you doing here?" I ask, concerned he'll misinterpret my being here with Otto.

"My grandparents don't like to drive if they can help it, so they asked me to bring them. Do you mind if I hang out with you guys?" He directs the question to Otto.

"Not at all," I answer for him, doing my best to sound casual. *Yep, just friends here, hanging out.*

"No problem," Otto says, sitting on the blanket, his expression blank.

"Awesome. Now I don't have to watch the movie with the old folks."

"Why do your grandparents have so many cars if they don't like to drive?"

"I asked Grandad that once. He said it was important to have a reliable car. I told him he only needs one. And he replied, 'Says you.' I learned long ago there's no point in debating with the man. Honestly? I think he has loads of money and changes his mind like the weather. How he justifies it to Gran? I haven't a clue." He lets loose a boyish grin that sets the butterflies loose in my belly. "Do you want to meet them? They knew your great-grandmother well, and they've been wanting me to bring you by."

"Really?" I'm thrilled at the idea of being mentioned.

"Come with us, Otto. They love seeing you."

"I just got settled." He pops a few kernels in his mouth. "You two go."

"Okay." Tristan reaches into the bag and scoops up a handful of popcorn. "We'll be right back."

"Are you sure you don't want to come?" I feel bad, like I'm ditching him, which I'm not because we're just casually hanging out. Not a big deal.

"No, it's fine." He picks up his phone. "I'm sure they'd love to meet you."

"Come on," Tristan says, taking my hand, pulling me away. "We'll come right back." He guides me, weaving us through people and blankets.

Having him hold my hand, staking a claim in front of everyone, feels like a victory. Eventually, we stop in front of a cute old couple sitting in lawn chairs.

"Gran, this is Kylie. Remember I told you about her? Grace is her great-grandmother."

She wags a finger at him. "I remember who she is, you silly boy. My mind is still sharp as a tack."

"Yes, ma'am."

She holds her hand out to me. "I'm Brigid, and this old man next to me is Calum."

I shake both of their hands.

"Old, my foot," Calum says with a twinkle in his eyes. "Who kicks your fanny at the golf course on a daily basis?"

She gently smacks his arm. "Oh, now." She looks up at me. "You sure are a pretty young thing. Just like your mother. How is she doing?"

"Mom is good."

"We sure miss Grace. She was always getting us involved in

one of her charity projects. Did you know she started a program at the elementary school that provides hot breakfasts to kids in need? Fact is, a lot of families around here don't have a pot to piss in. If you ask me, you shouldn't be havin' kids if you can't feed 'em."

"*Okay*," Tristan says, shifting nervously on his feet. "You don't want to get Gran started. She has strong opinions that not all people agree with."

"What is wrong with a lady speaking her mind?"

Calum pats her arm. "Now, lass, don't get your knickers in a twist."

She smiles at him with the love and familiarity of forty-plus years behind it.

"We should go," Tristan says. "Otto is waiting for us."

"Where is that lovely boy?" Brigid asks.

"Just over there on the blanket," Tristan responds.

Brigid looks confused. "Come now, boy. Did you steal Otto's date from him?"

"No, no." I step in. "Otto and I are just friends. He invited me, and then we ran into Tristan."

"You two aren't fighting over this girl now, are you?" Calum teases.

"No, Grandad. We're all just friends."

I'm beginning to hate that word, especially when he says it.

"Kids today. When I saw your grandmother, pretty as a bright spring day"—he smiles at her, and she pats his hand—"I knew she was something special and started courting her right away. Wasn't going to let anyone else have time with her, didn't want some randy bastard snatching her away from me." He looks between Tristan and me expectantly.

Yeah . . . you tell him.

"Well, a lot has changed in the last hundred years, Grandad."

"Oh, you." Calum tries to get up. "Help me out of my chair, Tristan, so I can give you a swift kick on your backside."

Tristan laughs and backs away. "Not a chance. You're strong as an ox. You could probably still take me."

"You bet your sweet *aaa* . . . bahookie." He kicks a leg out, which Tristan easily dodges. We all laugh. They're so cute. It's hard to believe that a self-righteous snob, like his father—Tristan's description—could come from these sweet people.

"I'm going to sit with Kylie and Otto. I'll come get you after the movie."

"Alright, boy," Calum says. "Kylie, it was a pleasure meeting you. This is a fine boy standing here before ya." He winks at Tristan.

"Yes, he really is," I reply, giving Tristan a sideways glance and a smile with a side of wistful.

I follow him back to the blanket—no hand holding this time. Maybe I overplayed the need.

"Sorry," Tristan says as we come up to Otto. "You know how they like to go on."

"No problem."

Otto takes a sip of his pop and holds the bag of popcorn up to us. Tristan grabs a handful before sitting on the blanket. I shake my head as I kick off my sandals and place myself between them. I hate getting kernels stuck between my teeth, especially when there isn't a mirror nearby to fish them out.

While we wait for the movie to start, we talk about aimless stuff, joke around, and Otto updates us on the latest celestial discoveries.

With no city lights and the dark coming quickly, a star

called Betelgeuse becomes the next topic in the queue. I ask Otto why they named it after a character in a movie. He laughs and says it isn't spelled the same, that it actually translates to the armpit or the hand—something like that—and points to the red supergiant at the top right portion of the constellation Orion. I never understood how someone could have seen random pinpoints of light in the sky and decided they look like images.

I was nervous when I first sat down, Otto always seems to get my mind in a twist in one way or another, but the conversation's been easy and the previous tension is gone. I'm having fun.

The film starts, and the bright light has us all squinting to readjust.

I forgot how cheesy this movie is, but still . . . I'm glad I'm here.

I find myself looking at Tristan's profile, wondering how anyone can be that beautiful and still be single, then at Otto's, and my heart beats a little faster, my body's reaction confusing me as usual. This is so messed up.

To prove to myself that Tristan is the one, I casually lean back in a way that has our shoulders touching, then spread my fingers so a couple of them overlap his. He gives me a brief smile, before turning his attention back to the movie. He doesn't take the hint. Maybe it's because of Otto.

Somewhere in the middle of the movie, I take one of the extra blankets and casually lay it in Tristan's lap, then rest my head on it. To balance the action, I put my feet in Otto's lap. I'm not trying to create an issue. I just want to get closer to

Tristan—getting comfortable at the same time is an added bonus.

Tristan doesn't move. Otto looks over at me and smiles, then pulls my legs against him and starts rubbing my feet, sending tingles everywhere.

Okay. Shit! This was not how I saw this moment unfolding. I stare at Otto, surprised. The kid's got skill.

When the rubbing stops, I pull my legs up and curl on my side. *Just repositioning myself.* The ground is hard after all, plus it allows me to disconnect from the sensory onslaught triggered by Otto's touch.

Tristan twirls the ends of my hair around his fingers. I'm in heaven, but then guilt creeps into my blissful moment.

Why am I feeling guilty?

Because I'm being a shit, that's why. I came here with Otto. Friends or not, flirting with Tristan feels wrong. I sit up.

"You have to tell her." Otto leans over me, quietly hissing at Tristan. "It's not fair to her!"

Tristan returns with an icy glare.

A shushing sound comes from behind. "Otto?" I whisper. "What are you talking about?" A sick feeling comes over me. "Tristan?"

He breaks eye-contact with Otto and focuses on me. "Otto is mad at me because . . . because he likes you, and he thinks I'm leading you on."

"*Butt out*, Otto!" Wait . . . He likes me?

We get shushed again. Otto gets up and walks away.

And how is Tristan leading me on? He hasn't done anything —*that's* the problem. Maybe he has a girlfriend back home. Otto never answered my question on that subject. And being my self-assured, conceited self, it never occurred to me that it would be an issue. He would dump her to be with me.

Could that be why he's been so evasive? He's been battling the guilt of wanting me over his commitment to someone else. That does make sense. He's a guy with morals.

But what's with Otto? He's never let on that he liked me—I mean, he *should*—but he hasn't. His behavior is odd at times, but he's kind of socially awkward, so it's hard to tell with him. It's not like I'm into him, anyway. I don't know . . . I'm so confused.

The movie ends, and Otto still hasn't come back. "What did Otto mean about leading me on? Do you have a girlfriend?" I'm amazed I made it through the entire movie without asking. Maybe I wanted to avoid the answer a little longer.

"No."

Whew! "Then what?"

"Yeah," Otto says from behind us, surprising us both. "Then what?"

By now, most people have cleared out.

"Otto." Tristan stands up. "Let it go."

I'm on my feet, in an instant. "Tristan! What's going on?"

"Can't you see she's totally into you?" Otto says to him. "She doesn't stand a chance!"

"Are you married?" I ask, mortified. It's the only other obstacle I can think of. He's young, but people do it.

"*No.*" Tristan looks uncomfortable, like he's trying to figure out how to deal with the situation. I want to punch Otto for turning it into one.

"Would somebody tell me what the hell is going on?" I shout.

Maybe his family is pressuring him to marry, but he's in love with me. Oh, god. It's because I'm poor. His family won't accept me. *Uhhh*, I groan inwardly. It's my mother's life all over again!

"I'm not into girls."

My internal rant comes to a complete halt. "What?"

"Well, I like girls. I'm just not attracted to them sexually." His expression is apologetic.

I look at Otto, whose face is blank, then back at Tristan, trying to process. "You're asexual?"

"I suppose that would be easier, but no."

I continue to stare at him utterly perplexed. "I don't understand. How could you not be attracted to girls?" None of this fits into any of my theories. Then it hits me. "You're gay?" He nods. "But, we . . . you . . . you and I . . ." The reality hits me like a one-ton truck.

"You jackass!" I yell at Otto.

"Huh?" He looks at me, stunned. "Why am I the jackass?"

"You knew this whole time and didn't tell me!" I yell at him. "You watched me make a complete fool of myself."

"It wasn't my story to tell," he fires back.

"And *you!*" I point an accusing finger at Tristan.

He places a hand on my arm, which I shrug off. "Look, I'm sorry. I know you're mad, and I'll be happy to explain later, but I need to find my grandparents. They're probably waiting for me by the car, and I don't want them worrying. I have the keys."

"*Whatever.*" I'm humiliated to the core. I'd rather not look at him, anyway.

"You could have at least hinted," I say to Otto when Tristan is out of hearing range. "I thought we were friends."

"We *are* friends, but no one knows about Tristan except me, and I wasn't about to break his confidence."

"You must have been laughing your ass off." My eyes narrow into angry slits. "That's the worst part. I can totally handle the fact that Tristan is gay—it explains a lot—but *you* just sitting back watching the show while some rich bitch from Cali gets what she deserves . . . that's so messed up. *Ahhh!* You could have trusted me!" I storm off, walking in the direction of the cars.

"Come on, Kylie," Otto calls out, pleading.

I ignore him and keep walking. What a dick move! I run through my time spent with Tristan . . . yeah, it all makes sense now. Then I remember Otto's reactions whenever I spoke of him. His attitude wasn't because he was socially awkward or jealous. He knew the entire time! And his smirks. . . He was laughing at me.

Man! I want to slap the crap out of him right now.

When I get to the parking lot, most of the cars have left. I look around, thinking maybe I'll ask someone for a ride, but I doubt they'd let a girl with a murderous expression in their vehicle.

Shit!

Screw it. I'll walk home.

But it's so far away.

Defeated, I wait for Otto by his truck. I don't want to see him, but what choice do I have?

Eventually, he shows up with all the stuff. Without a word, he chucks it all in the back of the truck, unlocks the doors, walks around to the driver's side, gets in, and starts it up.

Asshole! I look around one more time, debating my alternatives. There aren't any, so I get in.

The silence continues on the drive home.

Tristan is leaning against a Mercedes sedan when we pull up to my house.

"I'm sorry," Otto says as I get out of the truck.

I slam the door, ignoring him, the tears already brimming as he drives away.

"Leave me alone." I walk past Tristan, but then round on him. "How could you do that to me? Let me believe we had a chance?"

"Look. I know. I'm sorry." He runs his hand through his hair. "But don't be mad at Otto, okay? He was just being a loyal friend."

"Otto? Your only concern is for Otto?"

"No. It's just—"

"Why did you even ask me out?"

"You're beautiful, fun, high energy. I like hanging out with you."

"Didn't you think I might like you more than a friend?"

He reaches for my hand, pulling me closer. "Yes. But I thought if I made it clear enough . . ."

"How did you make it clear?" I raise our joined hand. "You held my hand to meet your grandparents. We went on a date!" I drop my head. "*Uck*. I feel so stupid. I've basically been throwing myself at you since the beginning."

"Basically?"

My head snaps up, and I punch him in the chest. "You ass!" He could have left me with at least a *shred* of dignity.

"Look, I'm sorry. I've never been in a situation where I've liked a girl this much. I was afraid if you knew, you'd blow me off. It was selfish of me."

"You think? You know I come from California, right? It's a pretty liberal state."

"Yeah, I suppose."

We stand facing each other in silence as my mind works furiously, trying to make sense of it all. "If you like me so much, maybe you're just . . . you know . . . confused?"

He laughs as he stretches his legs out on either side of me. Leaning forward, he grips my hips, pulling me between his thighs. I drop my forehead against his chest, breathing him in.

He strokes my hair, then lifts my chin with his fingertips, until my eyes meet his. "If there was *anyone* I wanted to be straight for, it's you."

"If that's true, maybe you should just try. You might change your mind . . ."

He regards me a moment, then slowly leans in, my heart racing as he kisses me softly on the lips, testing, then touches his lips to mine again before leaning away. "Nope."

This time, I punch him hard. "You jerk!"

"Ow!" He laughs, rubbing at the sore spot.

I take a step closer, flattening my body against his. "Maybe you need a little more convincing. Want me to give you my smolder kiss? It's a sure-fire male knockout. From there on, you'll be putty in my hands."

"Oh, god no!" He looks horrified.

I step back. "This is so unfair!"

"I'm sorry. I can't change who I am."

"I know." I sigh, deeply disappointed. "Hey, you need to be happy, whatever your happy is."

"Thanks. I appreciate that."

"It just . . . well, you know." I step into him again. "I really like you." I run a finger over his lower lip.

He nips at it, then circles my waist with his arms. "What am I going to do with you?"

Oh, I could think of a lot of things. My body flushes hot. "We could be friends with benefits—everything but the sex? Look how natural this is." I motion to the intimate position we're in. "You must get lonely for physical contact here alone all summer. It's one of the basic human needs. Maslow says so."

He grins, shaking his head. "You never cease to amaze me, but Maslow's Hierarchy of Needs? Really?"

"It's a sound argument."

He laughs. "It is and you're right. I would say yes, but I think I've hurt Otto enough."

"Otto needs to mind his own business."

He gives me a look.

"Fine!" I pout. "I get it. Sort of." *Not really. Screw Otto!* He could have at least hinted, then I could have drawn my own conclusions. "So what was the deal with you introducing me to your grandparents?" I ask, my mind swirling.

"I'm a chicken-shit, hiding behind a pretense, what can I say? My parents are horrible people. I thought if my grandparents told them about you, they'd stop pressuring me to make contact with girls from prominent families they deem acceptable. It's exhausting. When I graduate college, and I'm on my own, then I'll tell them."

"You used me?" The thought is like a cold bucket of water.

"No! Not really. Maybe a little. I mentioned to my grandmother that you moved here. She loved Grace and wanted me to bring you by."

"You suck."

"I know."

"Well . . . my father is on the run from the FBI who claims he embezzled millions . . . if that makes you feel any better."

He looks at me like, *that was random.* "Why would that make me feel better?"

"I don't know. Maybe my family is more screwed up than yours?"

He thinks for the briefest of seconds and chuckles. "Nope, I can top it. But I'm not at liberty to discuss the details. Gag order and all."

"Really?"

"Yup."

His dimpled smile gets my nerves humming again. "Quit doing that!"

"*What?*"

I exhale loudly, rolling my eyes to the sky. "Smiling like that. You're making me crave you all over again!"

His smile slants to the left, making him look even more irresistible.

I cast him a dark look.

He ignores me. "So, hey, um . . . Otto . . . he's a great guy."

"*Ugh!* I know, but I don't see him like that."

"Give him a chance. He's an amazing person. If he was gay, *I'd* totally go for him."

"He's not my type. You are," I say, almost pleading, like *come on . . . you can change for me!* Even though I know he can't.

"Did you ever think maybe your guidelines might be a little off?"

I roll my eyes. "No." He tilts his head to the side, questioning. "Well, maybe a little, but it's only a recent realization."

"Give Otto a break. I know you're mad at him, but he didn't do anything wrong."

I sigh. "I know, but I'm beyond mortified . . . *and* hurt. Not because he didn't tell me, it's the way he acted every time I talked about you. I don't like being laughed at. I trusted him! And I can't say that about many people in my life—Harlow, and maybe you, but with Otto . . . it's different somehow." He raises an inquisitive brow. "Fine! I'll text him." He kisses my forehead. "*Why?*" I moan.

He laughs and sets me away from him.

"Okay, fine," I sulk. "I'm going in. Let me know if you change your mind about the friends-with-benefits thing. You could definitely fill *my* basic needs."

He turns me around and smacks my butt, sending me toward the house. "Down girl!"

I stick my tongue out at him and saunter into the house, turning over my shoulder at the last moment to say something witty, but he's already in the car, totally missing the show.

Mom's sitting on the couch when I enter. "How was your night?"

"Enlightening." *To say the least.* "I'm going to go upstairs."

"Are you okay?"

"Yeah. It's just all been . . . too much."

"Well, when life gives you lemons . . ."

I hate that saying. "I'd much rather have a latte."

She laughs. "I'm sorry things have been so discombobulated. You and your sister shouldn't have to pay for my mistakes."

"It's not your fault, and it's okay. We're okay."

She gets up and pulls me into a hug. "I love you both so much."

I hug her back. "I know."

"I'm here if you need me."

"Thank you. But right now, I just want some privacy."

"Okay. Goodnight, baby."

I take a step toward my room but notice the attic door slightly ajar and change directions. Walking softly past Harlow's darkened room, I reach inside the door and flip on the light. I work my way up the steps, trying to avoid the creaks by staying close to the wall.

I can't believe he's gay! It's so unfair. At least I know that I'm not losing my touch. I was beginning to think there was something wrong with me. I guess you could say my record is still spotless . . . not that it matters, I guess.

I crank open the little window to get some air into the stuffy room and start going through random boxes.

Score! An old-fashioned apple peeler. I wouldn't have known what it was if an image hadn't popped up when I was searching for a modern one. This will really speed up the apple pie making process.

I set it at the top of the stairs, then sit down on a bench in front of a desk with a mirror. I guess it's not really a desk, more like a vanity.

I look at my reflection. "*Why?*" I whine. Tristan's perfect. He loves to shop, knows how to dress, his body, and those eyes . . . I groan, absentmindedly opening the side drawers. All empty. I tug on a smaller drawer right above my lap, but it sticks a quarter of the way open. I peak in but don't see anything lodged in the way, so I duck my head underneath to have a look. There is a letter taped to the bottom. I carefully detach it.

It's addressed to Charles and sealed.

I turn it over in my hand, then hold it up to the light to see if any of the writing is visible. I can make out a few words and know immediately that it's Nana's unique style of penmanship.

Isn't there something about steam softening the glue? I mean, shouldn't I read it first, before deciding if I should give it to him? What if it's bad? The man's a grouch, but I wouldn't want to hurt him.

My phone vibrates. Otto has texted me five times already, wanting me to call him. He must have been laughing his head off. No way I'm talking to him right now. I don't care what I said to Tristan.

I take the letter downstairs and place it in my night table drawer till I figure out what to do with it. I turn on the light next to my bed and take the diary over to the window seat. There's a nice breeze blowing. I lift my face to it, letting it cool me.

September 14, 1942

I haven't received a letter from Charles in three months. The war is bad. His father said that mail gets backed up and sometimes even lost when the fighting is heavy. He's been a great help and seems to be the only person who understands what I'm going through. He says the military won't give out information for strategic reasons, but he has some old friends with military connections that might be able to find something out. I've been helping him at the store. It makes me feel closer to Charles and, since his dad is all alone, I think it helps him as well. I'm trying not to think about it, but what if something's happened to him? What if I never hear from him again?

November 23, 1942

The mail came today when I was working at the store. When the General came out from the back, white as a ghost, I knew at once. They say Charles is missing in action. He said that doesn't mean he's dead, that he could have been captured, or maybe his platoon is trapped somewhere and hiding. I'm terrified. The General said he would use his contacts to get more information.

March 5, 1943

I died today. The General's contacts told him that Charles's platoon had been trapped during heavy bombing by the Germans. When the Allies went in, the destruction was total. Several of the bodies were buried under the rubble, so that's why they listed him as missing in action. They have no physical proof that he's dead, but the General's friend said that there were no survivors present. I must hold on with the hope that he escaped and will find his way home.

April 13, 1947

I waited for Charles like he asked. The war ended almost two years ago and there is still no word. Since they never found a body, I thought maybe he was being held captive in one of those horrible camps, but he would have made it home by now. He is truly gone. That is why I agreed to marry Richard. He is a very nice man. And although I don't love him the way I did Charles, I love him in my own way. I want a family. I've been broken for so many years and Richard helped me put the pieces back together. He was my saving grace, and I love him for it.

December 21, 1947

Charles came home today. I was in the store shopping, and I fainted the moment I saw him. When I woke up in his arms, I've never felt such happiness and devastation all at once. He kissed me in relief and, God help me, I kissed him back until he released me into the office chair and embraced his father. He told us how he had been in a prison camp, but it was months before he made it into a U.S. military hospital. He almost died from malnourishment, dehydration and disease. His dog tags were gone, and he was delirious for a very long time. They didn't know who he was. They felt there was no way he was going to make it, but after about four months, he finally began to improve. They told him it was a miracle. He said it was a long road to recovery and even longer before his memory returned. He'd been severely abused at the camp, the last being a traumatic beating to the head. He said that all his muscles atrophied so he could not walk and needed lots of rehabilitation. He was surprised the letters never made it home. He looked so thin, a shell of the man that left me behind. The General excused himself, said he needed to deal with a customer, then he was going to close the store. He shut the door behind him. I had to tell him about Richard. When I did, he looked at me like I'd shot him. He told me I was what helped him survive the prison camp, that I was the only reason he was able to fight off death in the hospital, the reason he suffered all the pain during physical therapy. I felt so ashamed. He yelled at me and said horrible things. I guess I can't blame him. I should have waited. If I'd only known. If the letter had only gotten through . . . Now, I'm pregnant, and if it wasn't for the baby, I would probably leave Richard. I know that's crazy talk, but I feel like I am going crazy. I told Richard when I got home, and he held me while I cried. He knows that he can never replace Charles.

January 6, 1948

I haven't been able to go back to the store. I'm so glad Richard understands. We've been going over to Chatwell to shop. I feel broken and torn. I'm thankful for this baby that is growing inside me. It gives me a reason to go on.

May 17, 1948

Charles came by the house today. He asked how I was feeling and apologized for the hateful things he said to me. He told me that Richard came to see him. I get the feeling Richard forced him for my sake. I haven't been able to keep weight on and I know he is worried about the baby. Charles told me he hopes that I will be happy, but I didn't get the feeling that he was sincere. But I will try to believe he was. How can I ever be happy again? We talked, but only about mundane things. What else is there to say? I'm married to another man, pregnant with someone else's child. And talking about the past or future isn't healthy for either of us. It should not be like this. I have this beautiful being growing inside of me, and it should be his. I still love Charles so deeply. I only learned to love Richard. He saved me, and I am loyal to him for it. I have to put Charles away somehow, but how can I? How do I move past when, every time I see him, I die all over again?

July 20, 1948

Hope was born early this morning, and she is the most beautiful baby. Richard is proud as a peacock. I realize, looking down at her, that she is my reason for living now and Richard gave me this gift. This is my family, my life, everything else is in the past. It's time to move on. Poor Richard has suffered so much since Charles came back. He doesn't deserve it. So this is my last entry. I'm closing this part of my life and tucking it away because it is a story of a different path, one that could not be finished. I am letting go.

Tears roll down my cheeks and drip on to the page. Her pain. I can't imagine how heart-breaking this must have been. Mom needs to read this.

I tiptoe down the hall and feel a slight sense of relief at the light coming from under her door. I knock softly, not wanting to wake Harlow.

"Come in," Mom says. "Kylie, what's wrong?" She startles the moment she sees me.

I climb up next to her, put my head on her shoulder like I used to when I was a small child, and let loose. I cry for my father, for the life that I knew, Tristan, for never having the chance to meet Nana, and for Charles and their lost love. I don't think I've ever been so completely overwhelmed—felt so low and broken, so totally lost.

Mom lets me get it all out, stroking my hair until I've cried myself out. "Are you ready to talk about it?" she asks when the uncontrolled sobs quiet into a final, shuddering intake of breath. "Here." She reaches over for a tissue and waits for me to blow my nose, ultimately handing me the entire box. Moms are so smart with little details like having a box of tissue next to their bed.

I tell her about Tristan, Otto, the diary. I start off tentatively, expecting to be interrupted and chastised, but she remains quiet until I finish.

"I should have given the diary to you sooner. I thought it would be silly teenage stuff. I'd read it, get a few laughs, and pass it on to you. And it mostly was, until tonight."

She runs her hands along the quilt. "It's okay, I understand. Thank you for giving it to me now."

"I need to warn you. It's going to be a shocker. Do you want me to give you a synopsis, or do you want to just find out as you read?"

She's quiet for a moment. "I'll just read it as you did."

"I love you, Mom. I'm so sorry for the way I've treated you. I just didn't know." I choke on a sob. I didn't think I had any tears left.

She takes my hand. "It's okay, baby. We are where we need to be now—that's all that matters."

"I'll leave you so you can read." I wipe under my eyes and head for the door.

"Kylie?" I turn. "I'm sorry about Tristan, and I understand why you're mad at Otto. But I don't think he would do anything to intentionally hurt you. He doesn't strike me as that kind of a person."

"No. I suppose he isn't."

"Maybe don't leave it too long. I'm sure he is hurting too."

I know it's mean and vindictive, but part of me wants him to hurt, at least for a little while. "Okay." I stall at the door, suddenly afraid to leave her—afraid things will go back to how they used to be.

No. If I want things to stay this way, then it's up to me. "Night, Mom."

"Night, baby."

21

Mom looks exhausted in the morning. Her eyes are red-rimmed and puffy. It doesn't look like she got much sleep.

"Did you not have to work today?"

"Luckily no. Dr. Taylor attended a conference over the weekend and is coming back today. I would be dead if I had to make it in this morning. I barely slept."

"Do you want me to make you an omelet?" I ask, feeling for her.

"That'd be great." She looks at the clock. "Wow, I really slept in. Where's Harlow?"

"Joanne stopped by with Olivia, wondering if she could take her to Chatwell. I guess they have a water park. I didn't think you would mind. Harlow was super excited."

"Good," she mumbles to herself. "That's good."

I pour her a cup of coffee and place it in front of her. "So? What did you think?"

She takes a deep breath, blowing it out through pinched lips. "*Wow.*"

I lean against the kitchen counter. "I know."

"It's weird to think, if the war never happened, or he didn't get caught, I may not be here. Neither would you."

"True."

She takes a sip of coffee. "Life has a lot of twists and turns. I guess we do the best we can with the direction we choose." I don't think she's talking about Nana anymore. "Kylie . . . I know you don't like it here, but thanks again for trying to make it work."

"It's not *that* bad." I think of Tristan and Otto. *Ugh.* Memories of last night flatten me with embarrassment. Otto only texted me once this morning. Maybe he's given up, *the shit.*

I pull out ham, onion, mushrooms, cheese, and eggs from the refrigerator. I need to think of something else. Nana and Charles. That's just crazy. "So what was it like living with Nana and her husband? I don't even know what to call him."

"Gramps."

"Did they fight?"

"No, never. They were just like water; they flowed over and around each other. They seemed as natural as breathing."

I chop up the mushrooms, onions, and ham. "Well that's good, I guess. They were happy in their own way."

"They seemed to be. I don't think there is such a thing as a cookie-cutter relationship. I think a lot of people attempt to fit into the molds. They have pre-conceived notions of how things should be, but end up fighting a losing battle because of it. Expectations are poisonous."

Mom's introspective this morning. I'm used to "hi," "bye," and "where are you going," not her philosophical outlooks on life. I kind of like it. It makes her real, as opposed to the nagging robot-of-a-human that I was used to. I guess when you have to live in survival mode like she did, maybe that's all a person is capable of. To be fair, she's been a lot better lately. I'm sure being away from my dad helps, and so have our conversations. Well, *and* me not being a total bitch to her all the time.

I set the vegetables and ham in the frying pan to cook while I whip up the eggs. "When did Gramps die?"

"About two years after I left town. I couldn't make it for the funeral. I wanted to, but somehow your dad talked me out of it. He said it wouldn't be good to travel with you, being that you were so young." She shakes her head. "I deeply regret not being there. He was the closest thing I had to a father."

"How come you never came back here for a visit?" I pour the eggs over the other ingredients, sprinkle some cheese, then cover the pan, turning the heat on low.

"Your father said I should let go of the past. He can be very persuasive."

"That wasn't right."

"No, it wasn't." She drops her head into her hands. "I'm so ashamed. I should have been stronger." When she looks up, there's deep regret and pain in her eyes. "I didn't even know Nana was sick." I move to her side and wrap an arm around her shoulder. "She died, and it was her lawyer who told me. It shouldn't have been like that." She looks up, her red, puffy eyes spouting fresh tears.

I slide a hand up and down her back. "He's a manipulator, Mom."

"I know, but I should have seen it. It was so subtle though, the way he separated me from my family. I didn't even realize it was happening, and then I didn't have anyone but him. Kylie . . . she was always there for me, and I let her down. Your dad wouldn't let me go to her funeral either. He said that it was a stressful time for him at work, and that he needed me at home."

I move to the stove and fold the omelet over. "Maybe he was afraid if you left, got away from him, you'd never come back? I'm sure you would have taken us with you."

"Probably. I would have wanted to."

It makes me sick. I was the perfect pawn. "From what you've told me, he needed control. He used me to control you."

"I suppose he did. I never let myself process any of it. You learn pretty quick that ideas can be dangerous and you're better off not allowing yourself to contemplate anything. I don't think it was a conscious choice, that's just the person I evolved into. It was pure survival." She shakes her head, looking bewildered. "Even if I'd let myself acknowledge that he turned you against me to manipulate and control, I don't think I would have had the strength or the confidence to get you back. *Uhhh!* I'm so pathetic." She groans, wiping more tears from her eyes.

I flip the omelet over. "You're not pathetic. He contaminated our relationship the same way he did with you and Nana. A person is easier to control if they're isolated, and I didn't see it either, Mom." I slide the omelet on a plate and place it in front of her.

"This looks great. Thank you. Logically, I know you're right. The guilt is just so . . . *suffocating.*"

I know how she feels. Guilt, shame, regret . . . I busy myself cleaning the mess I made.

"Hey, there's a lot here. Do you want to share it with me?"

My stomach rumbles, and I realize I haven't eaten yet. "Okay." I pull out an extra plate from the cupboard and place it in front of her. She cuts the omelet in half and slides it onto my plate. "There's nothing we can do about the past. So, I guess you make your peace with it and move on, you know? Why dwell?"

"Kylie . . . thanks for listening. I really appreciate it."

I smile and sit in the chair facing her. "No problem." I feel the need to change the subject. "So . . . do you think we should give Charles the diary to read?"

"I don't know."

My phone chimes. It's Otto. I turn it on silent.

"Is that Otto?"

"Yeah."

"He's a sweet kid, Kylie."

"I know." I take a bite. *Mmm* . . . I may have perfected the omelet.

"You should stop by the coffee shop and talk to him."

"I will." Changing the topic again. "Will you help me plant all those flowers I brought home? It will take me years to do it all myself."

"Sure. That'll be fun. Maybe if Joanne brings the kids back in a couple of hours, she can help us?"

"I don't know. Otto basically said that every green thing she touches, dies."

"I'm sure that's from improper care *after* planting. It's hard to mess up placing it in the ground."

"Yeah, but do we risk it?"

She laughs.

"Oh, I almost forgot. There was a letter. I mean, I found a letter addressed to Charles hidden away."

"Really?"

"Yeah, but it's sealed. It was taped to the underside of her vanity in the attic. Do you think she would want us to give it to him?"

"I don't know. You know him better than I do."

"Yeah, I guess. I was thinking about trying to steam it open, just to see if it's hateful. But I think I'll hold off for now."

After cleaning up, we move out to the garden. I think a lot about Otto while we work and come to the conclusion that I should at least text him something, but I left my phone in the house, so I'll do it when I clean up. Chances are I'll run into him eventually and texting him beforehand will make that first face-to-face meeting less uncomfortable. It's the chicken-shit way to go . . . but it's progress. The old me would never have spoken to him again. Besides, he works at the only coffee shop in town. I need my lattes, and Joanne needs her baking so . . .

"What are you two lovely ladies doing?"

My head whips around. Tristan walks out from the side of the house looking as mouth-watering as ever. I groan, knowing how crappy I look.

What is it with people around here thinking they can stop by whenever they want? A girl needs time to look her best. *Ugh!*

I stand up and attempt to smooth my hair back with the back of my forearms, since my gloved hands are filthy. "Hey. Mom, you remember Tristan?" I probably shouldn't have told her he was gay. Otto was the only one who knew his secret, and they kept it for a reason.

"Yes. Hi. It's nice to see you again. You know, I think Harlow may have adopted you as her new big brother next to Otto."

His broad smile has my belly tightening. "I'm honored."

"Would you care for some lemonade?" she asks him. "I was just going inside to make a pitcher."

"I'd love some."

Smooth, Mom.

"You okay?" Tristan asks when we're alone.

"Decent. Still stinging from the humiliation."

"I'm sorry. I hate that I hurt you."

I shrug my shoulders. "Realizing that it wasn't *me* you didn't want, but my sex in general, has helped my ego tremendously."

"That *would* be your concern." He laughs. "Could you please talk to Otto? He's driving me nuts."

"I will. Later, after I shower."

"Yeah, you look like you could use one. Smell like it too."

I manage to look as indignant as possible. "You can leave now." I kneel again, picking up my trowel.

"Do you want some help?" Tristan asks.

"Really? After that insult?"

"Don't be a baby."

I shrug. "Whatever. Do what you want."

"Well, if you're going to be that way . . ." He makes a turn to leave.

"On second thought . . ." I look him up and down, grinning. "I'd love to watch while you put those muscles to good use. And you should take your shirt off. You don't want to get it dirty."

He frowns like, *I thought we got this solved.*

Payback. "I'm kidding. Man, where's your sense of humor?"

"Bitch."

"Slut."

He kneels on the pad next to me. "I'm so glad we're friends."

"Me too. Now, get to work."

"Slave driver."

Working together helps to dispel the awkwardness as the day moves on. It's beautiful out and, so far, not too hot. When most of the planting is done, I say goodbye to Tristan with the promise of texting Otto after I shower.

With a towel wrapped around my head and a mind full of dizzying thoughts, I find Otto in my contacts.

Me: I get your loyalty to Tristan, but you didn't have to enjoy it so much.

I read through, press send, and wait. The response is immediate.

Otto: It seemed appropriate until I got to know you."

Me: Whatever.

Otto: But you changed. You have become so much more. I don't want to lose our friendship. I'm sorry.

Jerk.

His attempt at apologizing sucks. I shut off my phone and get ready for work.

22

THURSDAY COMES AROUND and I know I have to suck it up and bring the baking into Jojo's. I like having the extra income, and I will not let my issues with dipshit keep me from my spending money. Also, Harlow's been bugging me to see him. Knowing her, she probably senses something is up.

"Hey, Otto." I set a large pan of apple crumble on the counter.

He ducks his head. "Hey." With a sheepish smile, he moves the dessert to the back counter, then when he turns back, asks Harlow how she's doing.

"Good." She beams up at him.

"Things okay with you?" he asks me.

Here we go. That awkward moment. "Yep. I'm good." *Mostly*.

Seeing him, makes the hurt real again. I know what's what. I have it all squared away logically. Still . . .

"Do you want the usual?"

"Sure."

He loads the coffee into the filter holder thingy, then packs it before twisting it on to the machine. "Have you heard about Ultima Thule?"

"I haven't." Another one of his weird, random questions.

He presses the button to start the machine. "It's a nickname for Arrokoth—"

"Is that a new series on Netflix?" I tease.

"Uh . . . No." He stares at me a moment, confused, before continuing. "The New Horizons spacecraft flew by the distant Kuiper Belt and it was able to get a clear image of one of the furthest, most primitive objects in our solar system."

"Oh, right. Sure." I look over at Harlow, ready to give her an eyeroll, but she's wearing a look of fascination.

"It's a big deal. It's given scientists clues about the formation of planets and our cosmic origins." He places an iced latte and a black coffee on the counter in front of me.

"Good to know." I pick up the drink and turn to Harlow. "We should go."

"Did you get all the flowers planted?" Otto asks, stopping me.

"Yes. Tristan helped me with the backyard. Mom and Harlow helped with the front."

"Yeah, right. I guess he told me that." I turn to leave again. "Kylie . . ." He runs a hand through his hair, making it stand at awkward angles. Somehow he manages to make dorky look sexy. "Can we go for a walk later? When you're done with work?"

"Maybe. I'll text you." Adorable or not, the emotions are still raw.

"Okay." He looks dejected, and I hate it.

"Did you and Otto get into a fight or something?" Harlow asks when we're outside.

"I don't want to talk about it."

"Why?"

"Because you're only nine, and I don't want to."

She scrunches her nose. "Fine."

I mindlessly watch a dumpy, white truck pass until sudden recognition has me frozen in shock with both coffees spilling onto the sidewalk. I'm vaguely aware of the scorching hot and freezing cold liquid splashing up my legs as the truck continues to the end of the street and turns the corner.

"What's wrong? Are you okay? Kylie!" Harlow shakes me.

I regain control and grab Harlow by the hand. She must have jumped out of the way because she's not wearing the same mess I am. "Nothing. They just slipped." I continue to the store, coffees forgotten, walking quickly. "Hurry. I need to get this washed off."

Last time, when I saw the Mercedes, I thought maybe it was my dad, but there is no mistaking it this time. He looked right at me.

"Can you tell Charles I'm here?" I ask as soon as we're in the store. "I need to clean up." Harlow nods, and I run to the bathroom, turn on the light, and shut the door behind me. I grab a wad of paper towels and quickly clean off my legs. I'm scared. I need to call Mom and warn her, but decide to call Agent Walker first.

She picks up on the second ring. "Kylie, are you okay?"

"No."

"What's going on?"

"I just saw my father drive past the store, and I'm worried about my mom, that he might hurt her. He never has before, not physically, but I don't know now. She told me some stuff about him, and I'm worried for her."

"Kylie, it's okay. I have an agent in the area. I'll contact him and apprise him of the situation. Are you safe?"

It briefly registers that my suspicions were correct. Someone *has* been keeping an eye on us. "Yes. Harlow and I are at work. Mom is too, but still . . . can you please check on her and tell her what I saw?"

"Yes. Can you give me the make, model or color of the car?"

"It was a beat-up rusty white truck. A small one."

"Did you get a license plate?"

"No. I'm sorry."

"It's okay. I've already sent word to my agent, but I will confirm with him as soon as I get off the phone. *Do not* seek him out. If he's back, he's desperate. There is no other reason he would risk being seen near his family." She pauses, and I look at the screen to see if she's still on the line. "Kylie, my agent just texted that he's parked outside your mother's work. I will call and update her on the situation. Stay there until I contact you."

"She's supposed to be here to pick Harlow up in an hour."

"I'll inform the agent. He will take her to you, then bring you all home, and stay at the house. Please don't leave without letting me know."

"Okay but shouldn't someone be looking for the truck? Before it disappears or—"

"Your family's safety is our number one priority. I will contact the local police and apprise them of the situation. They can look for the vehicle. And Kylie . . . put my number on speed dial. I want you contacting me if he approaches you."

"I will," I say, then hang up.

"Kylie!" I hear Harlow scream. "Kylie!"

Fear rips through me. I race out of the bathroom, grabbing

a toilet plunger from the aisle as I pass, throwing it over my shoulder like a baseball bat. "Harlow!"

"Kylie!" Her voice is coming from the office. "He fell!"

"Are you okay?" I rush in to see Charles lying on the floor. "What happened?" I drop down beside him. "Charles!" I shake him. "What's wrong? Charles, wake up!" I shake him harder. I put my ear to his chest, but don't hear anything, then to his nose as I watch for the rise and fall of his chest. Still nothing.

"Harlow, there is a phone on the desk. Call 911."

"Kylie, I'm scared."

"I know, Bug. Just do it!"

I get into the CPR position like I've seen on TV and start pumping his chest. I have no idea if I'm doing it right.

"I don't think so," I hear Harlow say into the phone. "No heartbeat, right, Kylie?"

"Um . . . uh." I put my ear to his chest again. Nothing. "I can't hear it!"

"They say to squeeze his nose, tilt his chin, and give him two quick breaths."

As I'm getting positioned, I feel air against my face. "Charles?" His eyes flutter.

I grip him around his middle and hug him tight. "You scared the hell out of me! What happened?"

"I don't know." His voice is barely a whisper.

"He just talked!" There's a pause as she listens. "Okay," she says, then hangs up. "They said an ambulance is on the way."

I move into a position so he can rest his head on my lap. "Don't you dare die on me! Do you hear me, old man?" I yell at him. Harlow is standing next to me crying. "See. He's okay," I tell her. "Why don't you hold his hand."

She does as she's told. Charles closes his eyes and looks like he's gone again. "Wake up!" I nudge him. "Charles!"

"Stop yelling at me," he croaks out. "I was just resting. I'm so tired."

I lean over him. "You scared the crap out of me!" He tries to sit up. "Oh, no you don't. Stay down until the ambulance gets here."

"I don't need a *damn* ambulance."

"Charles?" Harlow's looking at him with frightened, tear-filled eyes. He turns his head in her direction and reaches up to touch the side of her face. "You look just like Grace when she was your age." He tries to get up again.

"Please don't get up," Harlow begs. "I'm scared."

"Okay, honey. I won't. You don't worry now. I probably didn't eat enough today. That's all."

"Did you hit your head?" I ask.

"I don't think so?"

"Harlow?"

"I don't know. I don't think so. He just crumpled."

"Can you run and grab a bottle of water? Just get it off the shelf."

She's back in a flash, handing it to me. I twist off the lid and lift Charles's head so he can drink.

"Thank you," he says.

"Here. Have a little more. Maybe you got dehydrated."

He does as he's told. In fact, drinks most of the bottle. That's a good sign, I think.

I hear the siren, faint in the distance. "Harlow, why don't you wait for the ambulance at the door and lead them here when they arrive."

"Okay." She kisses Charles on the cheek, then jumps up and runs out.

"But don't leave the building!" I yell after her. "Wait inside the door where I can see you."

"Okay!" she hollers back.

"Are you sick?" I ask him when she's out of hearing range. "Like is there something you should tell me?"

He closes his eyes.

"Charles!"

He looks up at me, his bright-blue eyes, glassy. "Kylie, I—"

The siren from the ambulance is crazy loud. It must be close.

"Well?"

We both turn toward the commotion. Harlow propped open the door and a paramedic is rushing toward us.

"Mr. Fitzwald," the paramedic says as he enters the office. "I heard you had a fall. I'm going to take your vitals." He wraps the blood pressure cuff on his arm and listens to his heart. "What meds are you taking?"

"What meds am I *not* taking?" he responds dryly. "Can I sit up now?"

"In just a minute. Do you have a history of heart disease?"

Charles looks up at me, then over at Harlow. "Do we have to talk about this now?"

A woman pushes a gurney close to the office door. "Girls. Can you wait outside? There isn't enough room for all of us in here, and we need to attend to Charles."

"Can you get me something to put under his head?" The lady hands me a blanket. I remove myself carefully, placing it under his head. "I'll see you in a minute," I tell him and step out of the office.

Tears are streaming down Harlow's cheeks as she grips me around the waist, burying her face in my side. I want to cry too, but we can't both fall apart. "It's okay. It's probably like Charles said . . . He went too long without eating. You know how busy he gets."

"Really?" she lifts her chin, looking hopeful.

"Yeah." No sense in worrying her until we know more.

I watch as they sit him up, then help him onto the gurney. Harlow squeezes me hard. This kid has had *way* too much to deal with.

"So what now?" I ask as they wheel him toward the exit.

"We will be taking him to the hospital in Chatwell for tests and observation."

Mom rushes in with the agent behind her, his hand resting on his holstered revolver. "Is everyone okay?" She looks terrified.

"We're good, Mom," I say. "Charles fainted. The medics are taking him to the hospital."

Mom's hand goes to her mouth as the agent closes his coat over the gun. Harlow rushes to her side, clinging tight.

"Charles?" Mom grips his hand as they wheel him past.

"I'm fine. Don't you start fussing too."

"Are you sure? Can we do anything?"

"We need to get him to the hospital, ma'am," the man says. Mom releases his hand and they continue to wheel him to the ambulance.

"Mom, it was horrible," Harlow says as we follow the medics out the door. "We were talking, then he got a funny look on his face and gripped his chest. He said he didn't feel too good, and then he passed out. Kylie had to give him CPR."

Mom's eyes go wide as she turns to me.

"Not exactly," I say. "I didn't know how. I was just guessing."

"It's a good thing you two were here."

"Kylie," Charles calls out. I run to his side. They are just about to lift him into the ambulance. "You stay here and mind the store."

"Like *hell* I will. I'm going with you."

He closes his eyes, looking exhausted. "*Sass...*"

Mom touches my arm. "I'll drive you to the hospital after you lock up."

"No one is going to listen to me, are they?" Charles sighs, then closes his eyes. "I've never closed the store early in my life."

"There's a first time for everything, old man."

"I'm fine," he grumbles as they load him into the back of the ambulance.

"You better be!"

"More sass. I get nothing but sass."

They close the doors, the warning lights go on, but no siren as they drive off in route to the hospital.

"I'll be right back." I run to Charles's office, grab the keys and lock up, then slide into the front seat where Mom and Harlow are waiting.

When we merge onto the highway, I turn and smile reassuringly at my sister before taking a quick glance out the back window. The agent is following. I figured he would be, but I wanted to make sure. As soon as I face front, it all hits me.

Mom looks over at me. "Are you okay?"

I hate hearing those words when I'm about to break apart. I can't do it in front of Harlow, so I swallow against the enormous lump that's formed in my throat and nod my head. I try not to picture Charles unconscious on the floor, but I can't. His skin was bone white—his body lifeless.

I need to learn CPR for real. I don't know if his heart actually stopped, or I missed all the vital signs. I've never been that scared in my life. I look out the window and feel Mom's hand squeezing mine. Death has never been something I've had to deal with. The thought makes me think of Nana, and I feel a deep sense of loss on top of everything else. The tears come quietly with me wiping them away before they can fall.

It's a waiting game at the hospital. I keep thinking about the diary and the letter Nana wrote to Charles. He needs to read them. But not yet. Upsetting him in his condition would not be a good idea. Maybe I'll start with the diary when he is feeling better. They had so much unfinished business.

"Is he okay?" Otto asks as he enters the waiting room.

I jump up and run into his arms. It wasn't premeditated, my legs just carried me there. "We haven't heard anything," I say against his chest as he rubs a hand up and down my back. I lean into him, just for a moment, absorbing a new feeling—safety, comfort, home—before reluctantly stepping away.

He takes my hand and leads me back to Mom and Harlow. Mom has a surprised look on her face. I give her a look like, *Get over it! We're just friends.*

He sits next to Harlow and pats her leg. "Hey, kiddo. You okay?" She gives him a small nod.

"How did you hear?" I ask him.

"I saw the ambulance and from what the bystanders told me . . . Well, I left for the hospital as soon as Mom could get to the café."

"Thanks for coming."

A nurse comes through double swinging doors and gives us all a smile that makes me think everything is okay. "Kylie?" I stand up immediately, suddenly terrified that the expression was a ruse to soften the blow about to come. "Charles would like to see you."

Oh man. The relief that washes over me . . . I've never felt so grateful in my life.

I follow her to a bed in a line with several others, separated by a curtain. "Didn't I tell you to stay and mind the store!" he barks at me.

"Yeah, well, I don't take orders very well. Especially from you." He must have forgotten he said it was okay to close up.

"See, what did I say?" he says to the nurse. "Nothing but sass."

I sit in a chair next to him. "Yeah, yeah. You hired me, so get over it." The nurse smiles and leaves. "What's wrong with you?"

"Apparently, I've got an old heart."

"Oh." I don't like the sound of that. "So now what?"

"Lots of tests. They want to keep me here a while. Can you take care of the store while I'm in this hellhole? I know it's a lot to ask, but I don't have anyone else." The statement hits me hard. I can't imagine not having family. He should have been with Grace. "You don't have any siblings?"

He shakes his head. "I was an only child."

"No worries. I've got it." I cross my arms over my chest and lean the chair back. "And I'll be sure to give myself a raise out of the cash drawer. There are some new Tom Ford sunglasses I've had my eye on." He narrows his gaze at me. "I'm joking." I let the chair down to rest on its remaining two legs and force out a laugh.

"You shouldn't tease an old man with a broken heart."

"Yeah," I say quietly. Once again, fighting back the horror of the day. "Hey. How am I going to visit you if I'm at the store morning till night?"

"You don't want to be in this place. It's depressing."

"Exactly." I attempt to sound bright and upbeat. "That's why you shouldn't be alone all day. I'll close at seven and then come see you." He starts to object. "I'll bring the books," I quickly add. "That way you can make sure the deposit is correct."

"I guess there's some sense in that. You can drop it in the night deposit box at the bank."

"Which bank?"

"There's only one."

"Right." I laugh to myself. "What does a deposit box look like?"

"It's next to the front door. Big sign. You can't miss it."

"Okay." I stare at him a moment. He looks so frail. "Charles. You're going to be okay, right?"

"Sure I am, kid. Now, why don't you run along. They probably have more poking and prodding to do, and I'm getting tired."

"Okay." I stand up and kiss him on the cheek. "Don't scare me like that, okay? We have a system going. You crab at me and I bite back. It's quirky, but it works."

He chuckles then closes his eyes.

Everyone has lots of questions when I get back to the waiting room, but I don't have much to tell them other than he looks a little better than he did.

"Can you drive me back to the store?" I ask Otto. "I left in a hurry, and I can't remember if I shut all the lights off, and I didn't close out the register. I need to put the money in the safe."

"No problem."

I turn to Mom, remembering Dad and the agent following us. "We can talk when I get home?" I ask, hinting at the sighting of my father.

"Yes," she responds with an affirmative nod as she stands.

"Can I come with you guys?" Harlow asks Otto and me.

"Maybe just stay with Mom. I'm sure you're hungry and she can fix you something to eat."

"I'm not hungry."

"I want to talk to Otto. I won't be long."

She looks confused a moment, then smiles big. Her thoughts must have gone to the impulsive display of affection, when I threw myself at Otto. That thought has been on my mind as well. It's not why I don't want her to come, but I'm happy to let her think it.

On the way back to town, I tell Otto about seeing my dad. I also tell him about Charles and Grace. He wasn't surprised. He remembered hearing something about it somewhere.

At the store, I take the money out of the register, fill out the banking slip the way Charles taught me, and place it all in the safe. He can check over both deposits tomorrow when I visit him after work. I check the back door, shut off the lights, and lock the front door.

When Otto pulls in front of my house, I notice the same nondescript car that's been following us parked across the street.

"Do you want me to walk you inside?"

"No, it's okay. But thanks. Will you text or call Tristan and tell him what happened? I don't know if he knew Charles that well, but he will wonder about me when he hears I was with him when he went down."

Otto looks down at his hands. "Yeah, sure."

"I'm over it, Otto—over Tristan. I'm glad I know the truth." I lean over and kiss him softly on the lips. I was aiming for his cheek, but I guess my lips had other ideas.

The sensation surprises me, and I find myself hovering a breath away, searching Otto's golden eyes for an explanation. When his hand reaches up and grips the back of my neck to deliver a toe-curling kiss, the reasons are no longer important.

I slide my fingers into his hair and grip tight as heat radiates through my body. I strain against the seatbelt to get closer to him. I've never felt anything like this.

He takes my face in his hands, breaking the kiss. "Kylie?"

I open my eyes slowly. "I . . . Wow! I wasn't expecting that."

"Me neither." He grins. "And I'd love to do it again when we don't have an audience." He motions to a lady and her dog doing its business at a tree just past my door. The little thing is barking incessantly.

"Oops." I sit back in my seat. "Guess I lost myself."

"Glad to hear it."

I unbuckle the seatbelt and step out of the truck.

He leans over. "Be safe."

"Will do." I shut the car door behind me, lift my hand in a wave as he drives away, then turn on wobbly legs toward the house. Definitely *not* what I was expecting.

An enormous man in a dark suit is sitting with Mom and Harlow. My sister looks worried. She knows.

He stands, towering over me as he hands me his card. "I'm Agent Tipton."

I sit next to my sister and put my arm around her. "Hey." She snuggles into my side.

"So, as I was saying . . ." The man returns to his seat. "Keep the door locked at all times. If he tries to make contact, call Agent Walker or myself immediately. Whatever you do, don't let him in. Desperate people do desperate, irrational things, especially when they know their future is behind bars." He looks at us pointedly.

I glance down at Harlow. She looks devastated.

When Agent Tipton leaves, we talk as a family. Harlow asks Mom a lot of questions—good ones—not that I'd expect anything less from my brilliant sister. Mom does an excellent job keeping the conversation focused on the charges against my dad and nothing more. As mature as Harlow is, she's only nine, and doesn't need to hear the whole truth of what and who our father really is.

This situation really pisses me off. She doesn't deserve any of this—none of us do—but especially her. She is so good—someone I think Nana would be proud of. I hope someday I'll be someone Nana would be proud of too.

23

"THE WHOLE DAMN town's been here. I haven't had a moment's peace," Charles grumbles while motioning to all the carefully worded cards and collections of balloons and flowers surrounding his hospital bed.

"Oh, be quiet. You're a historical part of Foxall."

"*Hrmph*. I'm not *that* old."

"Ha! Are you sure about that?" I say, getting a chuckle out of him. "Any word from the tests?"

"No. They want to keep me longer." He adjusts his blanket. "They just want my money."

"Is that why they've put you in a private room?"

He shrugs. "I know some people."

"More likely they had to isolate your cantankerous behavior, so you didn't infect the other patients."

His grey, bushy eyebrows shoot up. "I'm cantankerous? Girl, you are the epitome of the word."

"Only around you. See? You infected me with it."

He shakes his head, looking tired. "Did you bring the

deposits?"

I pull up a chair next to his bed and take the bank deposit book and ledger out of my oversized shoulder bag. "I still don't understand why you don't use a computer."

"It's worked since the beginning of commerce. No need to fix what isn't broken." He looks over my figures, then checks the deposit slip. "You sure you counted the money correctly?"

"Seriously?" I say, amused. "Money and I have a special bond. There's no fooling around with quantities."

"It's perfect, Kylie. Good job."

"Thanks." His compliment surprises me. "You sure you're doing okay?"

"Fit as a fiddle."

"*Uh-huh.*" I reach back in my bag and touch Grace's photo album, then the letter.

"Something on your mind?"

I pause a moment, deciding whether to show him one, or both, or just let it be. My hand grips the photo album. "I have something I want to show you. I found it in the attic at Nana's, and I thought you might want to see it."

"What's this?" He looks at me a moment before taking the book from my hands. He opens the cover and flips over the first page, not registering what he's seeing, then sucks in a breath. "Oh, my." He flips through the pages, taking his time with each one. There is a deep sadness in his eyes as he brushes his fingertips over the photo of him in his military uniform standing next to Grace. "To this day, she's still the most beautiful woman I've ever known."

"You want to tell me about it?"

"*No,* I most certainly do not."

"Well, I found her diary, so I know everything anyway." The

words pop out of my mouth involuntarily. I had planned on keeping the diary a secret. "I just thought you would want to give me your side of the story."

Rage burns in his eyes. If it was anyone else, I might cower, but I hold my ground. His bark has always been worse than his bite.

"This is none of your business, Kylie." He turns away, staring out the window.

"Maybe it shouldn't be, but it is now."

"Does your mom know about this?"

"Yes."

He turns back, his eyes still hot. "Kylie. This isn't something people need know about."

"It's not some dark and horrible secret. You had a relationship with my Nana. Big deal."

He drops his head. "Some things should remain in the past and left alone."

"Or maybe you've been holding onto this for far too long."

His head snaps up. "And what the hell would you know about it?"

"Not as much as you, but I've got my own guilt I'm dealing with. And I can see how it could eat at a person if you didn't work through it."

He closes the photo album, but remains silent, staring at the cover. I hadn't planned on delivering a shock and probably got his blood pressure up. *Crap!*

He should rest, but when I start to get up, he starts. "War was nothing compared to what I found when I came home. It devastated me." He swipes at the tears brimming in his eyes. "You would think after all this time I'd be over it, but it still hurts so damn much." He clears his throat. "A man's not supposed to cry." He reaches for a tissue, and blows his nose so loud, I'm tempted to cover my ears.

"That's so old-school. Anyone's allowed to cry. You know . . . gender equality and all." He stares at me, brows furrowed, looking confused. "Oh, come on. You know, like no discrimination of the sexes." My ridiculous attempt to goad him out of his pain. It hurts to see him like this.

"You're feeding me a load of bull crap." He coughs out a laugh and wipes his nose again. "I don't think they were talking about emotions."

"Why not?" I challenge.

He shakes his head like he knows I'm trying to cheer him up by irritating him.

"I've spent most of my life being bitter. First, I lost Grace, then my second chance at happiness when my wife and daughter were taken from me. I never loved her as much as Grace, but Mary made me happy all the same, and I was excited about the baby." He pauses. "I suppose I've been angry ever since."

"Plus you've been drinking that crappy coffee all those years. That's enough to make anyone crabby."

He chuckles. "Girl, you are a piece of work."

"Yeah, well . . . Hey, so . . . just curious, but why didn't you and Grace get back together after her husband died? You could have had some time together."

"I'm not exactly sure. I guess a person can get so bogged down with resentment that they forget to live. Maybe she didn't want me anymore." He drops his head back on the pillow and closes his eyes. "I've wasted so much time."

He's quiet, and I wonder if he's fallen asleep.

"Then *you* walked into my store with Harlow." A warm smile

spreads across his face. "She looks so much like Grace at that age, and so sweet. That little girl is an angel from above, I'm telling you, because just like that, the bitterness was gone."

"Could have fooled me."

"Sass."

"It wasn't Nana's fault."

"I suppose it wasn't, but it was damn hard not to blame her for all the pain. At times, the feelings were as raw as the day I came home. I loved her more than life. She was the only reason I made it home from the war, but when I returned to Foxall, ready to make her my wife, she . . ." He couldn't find the words, but I understood. I knew the story. "The bitterness may be gone, but the heartache will never go away."

I take his hand. "I'm sorry."

His other hand covers mine and squeezes. "Thank you for this." He pats the photo album.

"You're welcome."

"So . . . you haven't talked much about your father."

"I haven't talked about a lot of things." I lean back in my chair, not liking the direction the conversation is going.

"Want to tell me the real story?"

"Not at the moment."

His eyes hold mine. "Kylie, some people were just made wrong."

The description is a dead hit. "I guess."

"Do you talk to him?"

"No."

He waits for me to say more.

I'm not sure I want to tell him, so the stare-off continues. I'm half wanting to see how long he'll hold out, but *meh*, I'm over it. He's a friend, in an oddly dysfunctional way.

I fill him in, up to where he remains at large—I don't want him to worry him about the sighting—and finish with, "I hate that I was ignorant to my mother's abuse. And the horrible things I've said to her over the years. I . . ."

"I know, Kylie, but you're a good person."

"How would *you* know?"

"I've seen how you are with Harlow. That's the real you."

"Is it?"

"You put on that haughty exterior, but, yeah, *damn right* it is."

I smile. Maybe he's right. It was that simple all along. "Don't tell anyone," I tease.

He leans over conspiratorially. "I won't. So this guilt you mentioned. It had to do with your mother?"

"Yeah, among other things. I've had my eyes opened recently."

"You're young and still learning. Did you make amends?"

"Some."

"Well, do what you can and let the rest go."

"Same to *you*."

"Can you pour me a glass of water, please?" He points. "It's over there on the counter."

"Sure." I contemplate as I go. Do I give him the letter? What if it's hurtful? I think I've delivered enough excitement for one day.

"What?" Charles voice shocks the silence, startling me. "You're over there with your deep breaths and your sighs. Spit it out, girl."

I hand him his water. I don't know . . . No, it feels like the right thing to do. At least I think it is. Hoping I'm not making a mistake, I reach into my bag and pull out the letter.

"I found it by accident. It's addressed to you from Grace." He reaches for it, but I pull it back. "I didn't read it." His eyes narrow, assessing the truth of my words. "*I didn't*. But I'm worried that it will upset you, and in your condition . . . Charles, well, I don't think you were ever meant to read it, but maybe it's important."

He sits up straighter. "Give me the *damn* letter!" I hesitate. He regards me a moment, then softens. "Please."

I extend it out to him again. He takes it and holds it to his chest like it's the Holy Grail.

"Do you want me to sit with you while you read it?"

"No. I'll read it alone." He takes my hand and gives it a squeeze. "Thank you for giving it to me. And, Kylie . . . I'm glad you came into my life."

I can't resist. I wrap my arms around him and hug him tight. "I'll be by tomorrow." I reach down and pick up my bag. "I hope you'll let me read the letter. I'm dying to know what it says."

"Only if you bring me the diary."

"I don't know about that. Diaries are the window to a person's soul. You think you can handle it?"

"*Pfff*. A bunch of nonsense."

"Yeah, maybe. Can I bring you anything else?"

"No, just your smart-ass mouth, and your usual, less-than-satisfactory company. Oh, and maybe one of your treats?" There's that little kid behind the aged, blue eyes again.

I laugh. "Sure thing." I turn when I reach the door. "Charles?"

He has already started opening the letter but looks up. "*Hmmm?*"

"I'm glad I met you too."

24

My cell phone rings. I rush into Charles's office and dig it out of my bag. The alert says it's Sherice. "Did you find him?"

"No, but Agent Tipton found someone else creeping around your house."

"Who?"

"Someone named Chase."

"What the *hell*?"

"Is this the same guy that was hassling you at the party a while back?"

"How did you . . . Someone *was* watching me."

"Sorry, just a precaution."

"Yes. That's the dickweed."

"My agent has him detained at the moment. After they find out what he was up to, do you want me to have them scare some sense into him?"

"Can you do that?"

"The boy was sneaking around a house with civilians being monitored by the FBI. As far as I am concerned, he's hampering our investigation. Maybe your father contacted him and is using him to spy. How would I know?"

I laugh. "Then by all means. Question him, scare him. Do your duty to the best of your ability, Agent."

"I always do. Is Charles okay?"

"For now, I guess. They're still running tests on him. In the meantime, I will be taking care of the store, but you probably already knew that."

"Yes."

"So they haven't found the truck yet?"

"Not yet."

"It's an uglier than usual truck in a small town. How hard can it be?" I snap, then realize my mistake. "I'm sorry. Everything . . . This is all just stressing me out."

"It's okay. I understand how hard this has been on your family, then when you add Charles into the mix . . . That's a lot to take."

"Thanks for understanding. And being human. It helps a lot."

"You're welcome. I better call my people back so they can deal with the trespasser."

"Okay. I hope they scare the hell out of him. That arrogant prick needs to be set straight. He thinks he can have whatever and whoever he wants and doesn't care who he has to trample over to get it. He's a bully."

"Thanks for the profile. I'll have them proceed accordingly. Call me if you need me."

"Will do."

"Kylie?"

"Hmm?"

"We will get him."

"I know."

The call disconnects, and I realize the idea of my father being in jail makes me incredibly sad. I guess it's hard to help who you love.

I send a text to Otto, asking him to meet me at my house after I visit Charles. I haven't been able to get the dork off my mind. I finish stocking the shipment I was working on yesterday before all hell broke loose, then take the cash out of the register and fill out the deposit slip. Mom let me have the car today so I could drive to the hospital. She said Dr. Taylor would drop her off after work. Harlow has been spending the day with Joanne and Olivia. We are so lucky to have all these people to help us.

I wait on the front porch in the twilight of a beautiful evening, breathing in the fresh smells of summer—a welcome relief from the harsh disinfectant odors of the hospital.

I asked Charles about the letter from Grace, and he asked if I brought the diary. I told him I forgot, and he told me to mind my own business. He said it with a hint of a smile so the letter must not have been too painful. I know we had a deal, but I wanted to see how things went with the letter before I decided whether he should read the diary. I'll bring it by tomorrow.

Otto's truck parks in front of the house. I push off the chair, pausing a moment to watch him before meeting him on the sidewalk. He's wearing . . . a Pokémon T-Shirt? *Ugh*. How am I attracted to this guy? I don't get it.

I place my hands on his cheeks as I draw his lips to mine. I need this. I needed him. Cartoon shirts be damned.

"Wow!" he says when I release him. "Once again. Unexpected."

I smile. Taking his hand, I lead him up the porch steps to the wicker loveseat. "I wanted to see if yesterday was a fluke," I say, partly to myself. "I've decided it wasn't."

"Glad to hear it." He grins. "How's Charles?"

"Okay, I guess. Hopefully, we'll know more tomorrow."

A lot has changed since the last time I sat here with Otto on the porch, hungover and barely seeing straight. I stare at our linked fingers, feeling the warmth of his palm against mine, and wonder how we got here. The differences between us are numerous, but I can't discount how natural it feels to be with him.

"Otto . . ." I start. "This thing between us. Um . . . well . . . it's different for me."

"What do you mean?" He sounds defensive.

"No. I'm. I just don't. Well, I've never—"

"What? Never been with someone that isn't a trust-fund baby? Someone who isn't popular or owns a yacht? What?" He pulls his hand away from mine.

I gape at him. "No! I was going to say I've never been with anyone that made me feel the way you do."

"Oh." His cheeks burn red.

I punch him in the arm. "I can't believe you said that!"

He rubs the sore spot. "Sorry." He grips my hand when I start to get up, keeping me in place. "No, really, Kylie. I'm sorry. This is just all so . . . sudden. I'm a little lost. Surprised. You know?"

"I get that. I guess I'm a little confused myself."

"I never even thought . . . well, I dreamed of course." He

gives me an impish grin. "But I didn't let myself go there. I knew you were looking for someone . . . well, not like me."

"It's true." I sigh, giving my head a bit of a shake. "I came here with a different set of priorities. They were from a life I knew and understood. Now everything is different, and I guess I am too." I shift, turning to face him. "I love that you're not afraid to be who you are. You're smart, honest, caring, real, with no hidden agenda. And I know that when guys like Chase bullied you growing up, it made you angry, maybe a bit hurt, but you never let it define you. You're an incredibly strong person."

"I appreciate the acknowledgment. *Really*. It means a lot." He squeezes my hand. "But I can't help worrying that your interest in me might be temporary."

"What's that supposed to mean?"

"Well . . . I want this to be real, not part of some self-improvement strategy you've got going on."

I jump up. "Oh my god! *Seriously?* I just told you I care for you and you're slapping me with insults?"

He runs a hand through his hair. "*No.* I didn't mean it like that. *Shit!*" He stands up, takes a step toward me with his hand outstretched to touch me, but I move out of reach. "It's just . . . maybe you're confused, and you only *think* I'm what you want."

I lean my hip against the railing. "Okay. Fair. I can see why you would be concerned. None of this exactly makes sense to me either. Look, I'm still figuring my shit out, but I want to see where this goes. Don't you?"

"I do. It's just, I don't feel like getting my heart ripped out if you decide I'm not up to your standards."

"I understand." I pick at the loose paint chips. "We can go back to the way we were and . . . I don't know, be friends and see. If you think that's better?"

He shakes his head and comes to stand in front of me. "No . . ." He leans down and kisses me softly, then rests his forehead against mine. "I can't give this up, knowing how it feels."

I wrap my arms around his waist, pulling him closer. "Me either." I touch my lips to his. "Nope, definitely not. I guess we take it one day at a time?"

"Works for me. So does this relationship include first dibs on your baking?"

I bark out a laugh. "Of all the things a guy would want out of a relationship with a hot girl and *that's* where your thoughts go?"

He kisses my forehead, my cheek, my nose, then my lips. "They will go many places once I get used to the idea."

"Good answer." I take him by the hand, remembering the agent across the street. I didn't plan on giving him front row seats to the drama that just got played out, but I forgot he was there. "Come on. Let's go out back. I'll show you where we put all the flowers you and I bought."

At the side of the house, my phone vibrates in my back pocket. I stop and pull it out. "It's from Sherice, the FBI agent I told you about. She called me earlier to tell me they caught Chase lurking around the house."

"What the hell?"

"I know. That's what I said. But, it's all good. *Great* actually. I think they might have scared some sense into him." I read her text. "She says they apprehended him in the backyard. Apparently, Chase had been on a friend's boat drinking all day, got himself wound up, and decided to do a little damage to get back at me." I read a bit more. "Looks like I'll be taking the red bike from now on and . . . Shit!" I run to the massive oak tree near the shed. "Asshole!" He trampled all the flowers I planted. "I hope they smacked him around a little. What a jerk!"

Otto squats down to get a closer look. "I think we can salvage most of them. You'd be surprised how hardy these things are."

"Really?"

"Oh yeah. I've seen flowers come back after a wicked hailstorm. Go get the stuff. We can do it now before the roots dry up."

I kiss him on the cheek and almost spill out, *I love you.* Luckily, I stop myself in time and run off to the shed.

That could have been a disaster. I was swept up in the moment, feeling good. I wonder what he would have done if I said it out loud?

Do I love him?

Hell if I know. To even think it, is a big deal. I'll just file that away for now. I drop everything next to Otto and kneel down beside him.

25

IT'S BEEN one thing after another this morning. Between deliveries and people coming into the store asking about Charles, I haven't been able to get anything done.

When the front door chimes again, I sigh in frustration as I mess up my tally.

"Anyone here?" Tristan calls out.

"Where the hell have you been!" I jump up and run at him, catapulting myself into his arms.

He holds me tight, my feet dangling above the floor. "Whoa there. It's only been a couple of days."

"*So*. A lot has happened and you're my BGMF." I slide down his body back to the floor.

"What's that?"

"Best gay male friend which is much better than a BFF because there isn't any of the jealousy or pettiness."

"Hey. I could get jealous. What if we both like the same guy?"

I lift a brow. "A non-issue. If he swung both ways"—I slide a hand provocatively down the side of my body—"there's no contest. I'm irresistible."

He laughs. "You're something, alright. I'm not sure if irresistible would be the appropriate description."

"No need to squabble over semantics," I tease.

"Hey, I'm sorry to hear about Charles. I would have found you sooner, but I had to fly home for a few days. Family drama."

"Is everything okay?"

"Mostly."

"Have you talked to Otto?"

"Yes, just about every day."

"And?"

"And what?"

"I kissed him."

"*Nooo*, really?" He looks mildly astonished.

I narrow my eyes at him. "He told you, didn't he?"

"Of course. I'm his best friend."

"Never thought he'd be the kiss and tell type," I joke, considering I just did the same thing.

"It's a big deal to him." He sighs. "But I'm worried."

I frown. "He's a big boy."

"I know, but as the guy's best friend . . . go easy on him. You burn bright. I don't want you breaking him."

"I won't." Tristan stands waiting. "What do you want me to say?"

"I don't know. I'm just looking out for him."

Like always. "Don't worry. We're going to take it slow, see where it goes." He doesn't look convinced. "*Hey.* I like who I am when I'm with him, okay? And for some weird reason, I'm physically attracted to him."

"You're physically attracted to a lot of guys."

"And *you're* being an ass." He shrugs a shoulder in response. "Well . . . I've never been attracted to someone like him. So it's something different."

"Different doesn't get me all mushy inside."

"Give me a break! This all just happened."

The bells on the door jingle. I look around Tristan to see my mom entering. Her eyes are swollen and red. She looks devastated.

"What's the matter?" I run to her. "Is Harlow alright? Did something happen?" I immediately think of my father. Maybe he took her.

"No. She's fine." She chokes on a sob. "I'm sorry, baby. Charles. He didn't make it through the night."

"What? No . . . no!" I take a step back, feeling like someone punched me in the chest. "That's impossible. Mom! I just saw him yesterday. He was fine. He—he was giving me crap for not sending out the bills like he asked."

"Kylie, honey. His heart was severely damaged. There was nothing they could do to repair it."

"This can't be right!" I feel light-headed and grip Tristan's arm for support.

"Honey, I'm so sorry. I know he meant a lot to you."

I take several deep breaths. It helps. "Did I do this?" I wipe at the tears staring to fall. "What if the letter I gave him from Nana was too much for him?"

Mom puts a hand on my shoulder. "No, Kylie. Don't even think that."

Panic rises to my chest. "But what if it put him over the edge?"

"Nana was a compassionate woman and didn't have a vengeful bone in her body. I couldn't see her writing something hateful. Pained, heartfelt, but not hateful."

"What letter?" Tristan rubs a hand up and down my back.

"I'll explain it another time, okay? It's a long story."

"No problem. What can I do?"

"I don't know." I turn to Mom. "Where's Harlow?"

"I left her playing at Olivia's."

"Let's go get her. We need to tell her before someone else does."

"Do you want me to come with you?" Tristan asks.

"No. That's okay, but can you let Otto know? Tell him I'll call him as soon as I can."

"Absolutely."

Harlow is devastated as predicted. When all our tears are dried up, we move from the living room to sit at the kitchen table. Mom pours us all large glasses of iced tea.

"I remember one time . . ." Mom begins, sitting on the other side of Harlow. "I was picking up some cans of condensed milk for Nana. I had just handed my money to Charles when he hollers at two boys, accusing them of stealing. I nearly jumped out of my skin when he came out from behind the counter to chase them out of the store.

"After they high-tailed it out the door, Charles kicked over a display of animal crackers, sending boxes everywhere. He turned to me and yelled, 'What's wrong with you?' I'd never seen anyone get that mad before. My father, yeah, but not a stranger. Well . . . he wasn't a stranger, but you know what I mean."

"Yeah, Charles being legitimately angry would be an ugly sight." I chuckle despite the mood.

"I didn't know what to say. So he yelled at me again, demanding that I stop looking so terrified, that I had no right to look at him that way, that they stole from him. I remember my eyes being as big as saucers and doing everything I could not to cry. But then he did something that shocked me even more. He squatted down in front of me, took my hand in his, and apologized. It was genuine too. I could tell he felt bad.

"After that, he was always decent to me, nicer than he was to anyone else, which wasn't saying a lot, because he was a miserable human being. But still, it was something."

"Remember, Harlow? The first time we went into the store. How he snapped at you? What did Charles say when we were leaving? You never told me."

"He apologized for sounding harsh. That he got angry when he saw me hiding behind my sister because I was Grace's great-granddaughter and the thought of me being afraid of him nearly broke his heart."

"He said that? That doesn't sound like him at all."

"No, he did. I promise." The tears well up again.

I give her hand a squeeze. "It's going to be okay, Bug."

She wipes her eyes with the back of her hand. "He doesn't have any family. What about the funeral?"

"Oh, honey. How thoughtful, but I'm sure there are people who will see to that."

"Are you sure, Mom?" I ask. *He needs to be remembered.* "Who could we talk to? He's a longstanding member of this community. He should have a plaque or a gravestone or something."

"I'll talk to Joanne and John, *uh*, I mean Dr. Taylor. One of them should know who to direct us to."

I let the John thing go because of Harlow, but I get the

feeling there's something going on there, and I'm not sure how I feel about it.

There's a knock on the front screen door. "Hey, anybody home?"

I'm relieved to hear Otto's voice. After he consoles Harlow with hugs and reassurances, we move to the backyard where he pulls me in and holds tight.

The sense of loss . . . My heart aches. It's all so hard to grasp. He was there and now he's just gone? "It hurts." The tears swirl and fall again.

"I know." He runs a hand up and down my back. "When my grandmother died, we all felt it deep down. It's the worst kind of pain. It'll subside."

"I barely even knew him. I imagine it was worse for you."

"You knew him. Probably more than anyone, other than Grace. There was a connection there, between the three of you —a bond. But it was more than that. He didn't have anyone until you came. He really cared about you. I know you guys grumped at each other, but there was affection underneath it all, anyone could see it."

"I loved him." The thought brings fresh tears. "He meant so much to me, and I didn't see it until it was too late."

"That's not true." He leans me away, regarding me intently. "You may not have put the label on it, but you cared, and you were with him until the end."

I swipe at my wet cheeks. "Yeah, but still. I've only known him for about a month. That's kind of crazy."

"No it's not. You had something special. Time is irrelevant when it comes to emotion."

"And Harlow. She adored him. The way he was with her. He

treated her like she was his grandchild. She must be hurting so bad."

"It's a good thing she has you and your mother. You two will help her through."

I shake my head. "She's been through so much. First the truth about my dad is confirmed, and then Charles passes." I suddenly feel the need to seek her out. "Hey. Do you mind if I go check on her?"

"Not at all."

I rest my head against his chest and breathe him in while the reassuring beat of his heart sounds against my ear. "Thank you for being here." I squeeze him tight.

He kisses the top of my head. "I wouldn't want to be anywhere else."

"Me either." The truth of that statement is a big one—one that I'm not ready to deal with yet.

I find her in bed, reading. "Hey, Bug. Can I get you anything? Are you hungry?" I just realize none of us have eaten anything since . . . "When was the last time you ate?"

She sets her book down. "I'm not hungry."

"Are you sure?" She shakes her head. "Okay. Well, maybe later." I sit next to her. She looks so pale. "How are you doing?"

She shrugs her shoulders.

"Do you want to talk about anything?"

Her eyes pool with tears. "Why didn't he tell us he was sick? Maybe we could have helped him!"

"Maybe he didn't know. But even if he did, you know Charles . . . He's not the sharing type."

"I'm just going to miss him so much," she sobs.

"I know. I'll miss him too." I hate seeing her cry. It shreds me every time. "Hold on." I run and get her some tissue.

"We'll get through it." I push a wad of toilet paper in her hand. "Just one day at a time, I guess." I run my thumbnail up the bottom of her foot. She giggles, jerking it back. "When we feel sad, we'll look for something happy to replace it with and before we know it, we won't feel so bad anymore."

"That was good, Kylie"

I pick at her quilt, sniggering at myself. "Yeah, surprising isn't it?"

"No." She reaches up and touches my face. "I knew you had it in you."

I lean forward and hug her. I love that she sees the best in people. "How are you doing with the whole Dad thing?" I haven't talked about it since the agent came by. Charles kind of took precedence, but still, I wasn't looking out for my sister like I should have.

"I don't know . . ."

"Yeah." How does someone so young process something like this? *I'm* not even sure how to deal with it.

"I'm angry, I guess. How could he be so selfish?"

My question exactly. "How much did Mom tell you about it all?"

"What do you mean?"

It was a stupid question. Mom would never mention the abuse. Harlow doesn't need to know that about her father. "Oh, *uh* . . . I was just wondering if they told you they saw Dad at our old house?"

"Yeah. They think he was looking for money. It's just so hard to imagine Dad doing all this . . . stuff they're accusing him of."

"I know. I feel the same way."

"There is *still* a possibility that he's running from someone, right Kylie? Like the mob or something."

"Absolutely!" *I mean, innocent until proven guilty, right?* "We just have to wait and let the FBI do their job."

"Yeah," she says softly.

"Whatever happens, we'll be okay. We have each other and Mom, a roof over our head, and the bills are getting paid."

She launches herself at me, hugging me hard. "I love you, Kylie."

"I love you too, Bug. Now let's get you something to eat."

"I'm not hungry."

"I have those brownies downstairs. I could heat them up, add some ice cream." Not a heathy choice, but it's something.

"Do we have whip cream?"

I stand up and hold a hand out to her. "Let's go check."

26

I SLEPT like crap last night. And since I woke up before the sun with a brain that wouldn't shut off, I decided to come in and open the store. I wasn't sure if I was supposed to, but it's been a couple of days, and I know if Charles were alive, he'd be pissed that I kept it closed. Besides, I need to do something to stay busy until I have to be at the church. The funeral is today. It turns out Charles had all the arrangements in place with his lawyer being the executor.

As I unlock the door, I take notice of the key. It looks as old as the door and lock it fits into. Turning it over in my hand, I think about all the generations it's been passed down to. And now it stops with Charles. My heart sinks at the thought.

I look at the empty baking display by the register. I need to get on it. Jojo's needs some as well. I had a lady stop me on the way into work today to tell me she misses my apple tortes and asked if I take personal orders. Crazy.

I change the entrance display, placing a new item on sale. We have an excess amount of spices. It's one of those things people forget they need until it's too late. Next, I run a dust mop over the floors, straighten the shelves, then go sit at Charles's desk.

I don't know what's going to happen to the store now. They can't just close the doors. There's all this merchandise, and it's the only grocery store in town. People would have to drive all the way to Chatwell to get groceries. It's not like it's Siberia, but still.

I guess I could keep it open for now. Charles taught me everything I need to know. But it's summer, and what if I leave for school in the fall?

Who am I kidding? There's no money.

I sit at Charles's desk and pick up the pen he always used. It looks like one you would have to fill with ink. I pull open the desk drawer to my right and see an ink bottle. Yep. He liked to keep things old-school. *Real* old school.

Next to the bottle are pencils, pads of paper, paperclips, rubber bands, and a tape dispenser, all neatly arranged. I close the drawer and open the one below, flipping through papers absentmindedly until I get to the bottom. My hand touches on a small wood frame, and I pull it out. It's a photo of Grace—the one she took in the photo booth—the one he took to war.

I wonder how many times he came across the photo, taking an involuntary trip down memory lane? I don't know why he would keep it, torturing himself like that. The memories held so much pain, and to be reminded so haphazardly, it would be like a stab in the heart every time he came across it. Maybe the pain was self-inflicted punishment for the guilt he felt?

What am I? A psychologist?

I prop the photo against the framed picture of Charles and his wife. Life can be incredibly cruel sometimes. I lean back in the chair and notice a set of keys on the desk. I pick them up and make my way outside, locking up first, then start up the stairs to the second story.

It's like walking onto a set of an old fifty's movie. There's definitely a woman's touch, so it must not have changed since his wife died. The place is bigger than I expected, with two bedrooms, a bathroom, a kitchen, and living room all neat and tidy without a speck of dust.

There is a big comfy chair and a small table perfectly angled next to an enormous floor to ceiling window. I imagine it to be Mary's favorite place to relax, with its finely crocheted doily on the headrest, the vintage *Woman's Day Magazine* on the table, and the open view of Main Street. I sit in the chair as she would and flip through the pages, mesmerized by the fashions of the past, before replacing it to look out the window and the view below.

The town is coming alive. The salon lady across the street is unlocking her door. Her display window is trendy. I hadn't noticed it before. She must be late because a client is standing next to her looking impatient.

They've propped the door to the hardware store open with a tall box of colorful nylon windmills. Large flower boxes sit at either end of a long wooden bench where two old geezers sit, chatting away. A lady runs past pushing a sporty-looking baby stroller. The town is more than I expected it to be. The only thing missing is Charles.

It's almost time for the store to open. I better get moving.

. . .

I've never been to a funeral before, and I hope it's a long time before I have to go to another one. The weight of sadness everyone carries is awful.

It seems the entire town showed up to the little white church with its steeple and stained glass on this stifling hot day in the late afternoon.

Otto is next to me with his family. Mom and Harlow are on the other side. Tristan is sitting with his grandmother and grandfather on the pew behind us. He touches my arm, getting my attention. When I turn around, he leans forward and kisses my cheek. "How are you doing?"

"I'm okay."

"Damn shame," says Calum.

"We will miss him," says Brigid wistfully.

"Are we talking about the same man?" I joke, trying to lighten the mood.

She gives me a swat on the arm, chuckling, "Oh, you."

Otto clears his throat, like he swallowed a bug.

"What?"

Otto looks at the surrounding faces. "People may not understand the kind of relationship you two had."

I give Tristan a questioning look.

"I think they know." He places a hand on my shoulder. "Enough have heard their banter in the store."

I give Otto a smug expression. He rolls his eyes, tempting me to grip him by the chin and give him a loud smacking kiss on the lips. I know the timing is inappropriate, but I can't help it. Call it nervous energy or maybe an old habit of doing what I want when I want. He shakes his head, adding a stupid grin on his face that lets me know he wouldn't have me any other way.

. . .

When the man leading the service finishes, he asks if there is anyone who wants to come forward and say a few words.

I'm thinking, *oh, man*, this is going to be embarrassing— either no one will have anything to say, or the words won't be kind. But a fragile, elderly lady stands up and, with her walker, works her way up the aisle. A young man jumps up to help when she has to ditch her support for the few steps it takes to reach the podium. She's so tiny and frail you can barely see her over the pulpit, but her voice is strong and clear as she explains how her house is just around the corner from the store and that Charles has been mowing her lawn and shoveling the snow from her walkway since her husband died eleven years ago.

After that, a slew of people, all with interesting stories to tell, worked their way to the front of the church. Some were as ancient as the hills, talking about Charles as a rambunctious little kid, always making trouble. Others, who grew up with him, told tales of his wild nature as a teenager. A few even mentioned him and Grace. The funniest stories came from townspeople close to my mother's age who pulled off rebellious pranks in the name of retribution. One guy explained how he moved the store's garbage can down the street most mornings on his way to work. Another would hide his newspaper regularly.

I could see Charles grumbling to himself, fuming. Serves him right, being such a grouch to everyone.

I wouldn't have expected to hear people laugh at a funeral. And I honestly can't remember the last time I've laughed this hard, but it was oddly appropriate, and boy did I need it.

In between the humor, people talked about his generosity. He supported several programs in town but didn't want any recognition for it. One man said that Charles threatened to take away his contributions if he ratted him out. My first thought was that he was picking up Grace's charitable work after she passed, but the more people talked, the more I realized he had not only been backing her work for years without her knowing, but had taken on several projects of his own. I was so incredibly surprised. I think a lot of people were.

After the final tribute was spoken, I follow Mom and Harlow out of the church while holding on to Otto's hand. People don't disperse right away but visit with neighbors outside. Everyone is warm, outgoing . . . genuine. It makes me realize what it means to be part of a community. And I like it.

I notice Chase with his father, but he doesn't make eye contact with me. The dickhead is keeping his head down. *Good choice.* The FBI agent must have done their job well.

As the crowd thins out, Otto and I make plans for later. There's a small, out-of-the-way beach that not many people visit. He's going to bring his telescope. He said the moon won't be up tonight, so it will allow us to see far more than in town with all the bright lights. This will be the first chance we've had to be alone since we . . . connected. I'm looking forward to it. Me, Otto, and the stars. What could be better?

27

I'M SITTING at the kitchen table with Harlow and Mom eating lunch when we hear a knock at the front door.

"Wait here. Let me see who it is first." Mom inches out into the living room just far enough that she can see through the screen door. It must not have been my dad because she opens it.

We're all on edge, expecting my father to show up at the house. He'd be a moron to do it, which he's not, but still, it's important to take precautions. I haven't seen him since that day outside the coffee shop.

"Can I help you?" we hear her ask.

"My name is Donald Layton. I am Charles Fitzwald's lawyer."

Hearing Charles's name has me and my sister glancing at each other before rushing into the living room.

"Oh, please come in." She opens the door wider, letting the man in.

"Mom?" I question as we come up behind her.

"I'm Sarah." Mom points in our direction. "This is Kylie and behind her is Harlow."

"Nice to meet you all."

"How can we help you, Mr. Layton?"

"Call me Don, please."

"Would you like to have a seat?"

"Thank you."

Harlow and I sit next to Mom on the couch, eager to find out why he's here, while Don sits in a chair across from us.

"Can I get you something cool to drink?" Mom asks. "We just made some fresh lemonade."

"No, ma'am. That's quite all right. This won't take long. Charles contacted me after they admitted him to the hospital and asked me to come see you should anything happen to him." He picks up his briefcase, setting it on his lap before opening it. "I have been instructed to deliver these letters to you." He hands one to each of us. "You will have questions, I'm sure." He hands my mother a business card. "Call me when you're ready." He closes the case and stands up.

"Okay." Mom sounds as perplexed as I am but follows him to the door, anyway. After the goodbyes, she comes back and sits down. "Well? This is mysterious, isn't it?"

Without responding, I rip into the letter.

Dear Kylie,

Thank you for giving me the letter from Grace. I feel at peace for the first time since the war. If you are reading this, it is because I have passed away. I know it's silly, but I feel like my time is near, and I would hate not to have said the things that needed to be said. And don't you dare think by giving me the letter, you had anything to do with my death. As I said, it brought me nothing but peace.

I want your family to have the store. I own the entire building, which includes my living quarters above. My lawyer will take care of all the necessary arrangements.

"Say what?" I look over at Mom, who's still reading. My heart is beating so fast. "Mom!"

"*Shhh.*" She waves me off. "Hold on."

Harlow is still reading her letter, so I continue with mine.

We never know what paths our lives will take, and maybe this isn't yours, but in the meantime, I hope you and your family will run the store as my family did. You're not blood relatives, but you're Grace's kin, and that's as close to family as I've got.

I never got a chance to tell you how much you and Harlow meant to me. Having a part of Grace in my life, even for such a short time, was a gift, one I hardly deserve after the way I treated her. I was such an angry fool. But I am at peace now, and I hope Grace and I will be united again in spirit.

I watched you evolve in front of my eyes, and I want to tell you how much I respect the young lady you have become. I know things were hard for your mother, always had been, but she is a survivor just like the amazing woman who raised her and I know you and Harlow will follow in their footsteps.

One other thing. I made some good investments over the years and have set up a trust fund for you and Harlow. When you are ready to go to university, you won't have to worry about finances. I love your fire, as well as your sass and grit, and I know you will do great things, whatever it is you decide to do. I will miss your sass and Harlow's gentle spirit. I wish I had more time with you both.

Love,

Charles

Teardrops fall onto the letter as I fold it. I clear them away before looking over at Mom. She's staring at me with her mouth hanging open, speechless.

"He gave us the store?" Harlow exclaims as she wipes at the trail of tears streaming down her face.

"I guess so," Mom says.

"Mom. This is crazy!"

"I know. I guess we're in the grocery business." She laughs nervously. "I didn't get the opportunity to know him the way you two did. I'm sorry, girls. I'm sorry that he's gone."

Harlow crawls onto Mom's lap. She barely fits. When did she grow so big?

She must have had a growth spurt during all the chaos, and I didn't even notice it.

"I miss him," Harlow says with such sadness, it breaks my heart all over again.

I give her leg a squeeze. "I know, Bug. I do too."

Her eyes suddenly perk up. "Does this mean I get free ice cream from now on?"

Now *there's* the inner nine-year-old. "Haven't you always?" I tease.

"True," she says, looking sheepish.

My mind is racing with logistics. "We are going to be busy. Mom, you will have to quit your job." Her cheeks glow pink. Okay, seriously? What the hell? I stare at her a moment before continuing. "I can teach you everything Charles taught me."

"Yes. Right. Harlow, are you okay spending the day at the store with us when we both have to be there?"

"Heck, yeah! Charles showed me how to bag groceries. I'll teach you since Kylie isn't all that great at it."

"Hey!" I tug on her foot. "I am too."

Her expression turns serious. "You are supposed to layer heavy items on the bottom, softer ones on top."

"Is that so?" I tickle her as she squirms in Mom's lap.

"Stop!" she squeals.

"Well, girls. I guess our lives have changed again. You're both okay with it? He wrote that if I didn't feel this was in either of your best interests, I could sell the store and use the money for whatever I felt was appropriate."

"No!" Harlow jumps up. "You can't sell it. I love it there."

She turns to me. "Kylie?"

"No, I'm good for now. You can hire help if I leave for school, right?"

"I could do that."

"Mom? Are *you* okay with this?" I ask.

"I guess so. This is my hometown. More than California ever was. I know a lot of people here, and I like feeling part of a community."

Me too. The thought surprises me.

Harlow wraps her arms around Mom's neck and squeezes.

"Hey. What about me?"

She climbs over to my lap and hugs me hard. "So if Kylie doesn't want the store and you get too old, it's mine?"

I tweak her nose. "Yes. It will be *all* yours."

Her eyes light up. "I think we should have a section that sells books."

"Great idea. Hey, lift up." There were two letters in the envelope the lawyer handed me and Harlow's sitting on the second one.

Opening it, I realize it's the letter I gave him from Grace. "Here . . . scoot off," I tell Harlow. "I'm going out back." I motion with the letter, indicating that I want to read it in private. Mom nods with a smile that lights up her face. She's truly happy, and I realize that I've never seen her like this before. It warms me and hurts me at the same time.

I pull a chair under the big oak for shade. With the letter gripped in my hand, I take a deep breath and exhale, attempting to release some of the emotional overload that's gripping my chest.

The first thing we are doing with the money is getting air-conditioning and internet for the house.

Charles,

I never had the courage to tell you what I went through after you came home from the war, so I'm going to write it in a letter, seal it, and hide it away. I'm hoping by doing this I can be free of at least some of the pain.

I loved you more than I will ever love anyone in my life. The day they told us you were missing in action, that there was no chance you made it out alive after the bombing, was the day I died.

For years, I barely spoke, let alone left the house. I could barely get out of bed each day. I knew my parents were worried, and as much as I hated to hurt them, I couldn't break out of the darkness I fell into.

When the war ended, I held on to a tiny thread of hope that you would come home. I fantasized that maybe you had been in a prison camp and would be set free. I waited for years, but you still didn't come home.

I met Richard at a picnic my parents dragged me to. I was sitting under a tree, not really connected to the world around me. He didn't ask to sit down, he just did, then took my hand in his and held it. He seemed to understand the pain I was going through. I don't know how, he just did. I remember thinking his touch was a small comfort in the dark place where I had buried my heart.

Eventually, I looked up at him. I remember him smiling at me as if us sitting together, not saying a word, was as natural as breathing. The next day he came by the house and sat with me in the garden, holding my hand again, still not saying a word. Each day he would stop by after supper and take me for a walk, giving me his warmth until the day I finally spoke. I remember I commented on the gardens in the front of our house, the flowers of all things.

I know this is probably hard to hear, but he slowly, patiently, brought me back from the dead. I knew I could never love him the way I loved you, but being with him was the next best thing. He loved me and never expected anything other than what I could give him. So I agreed to marry him when he proposed. I wanted a baby more than anything.

Then you came home and were so angry at me. You had no idea what I went through, and you condemned me. I hated you for that. Then when Hope was born, I had a new purpose, and I began to live again. But seeing you at the store and around town, feeling your disdain, was so painful—you made me feel guilt for something I didn't do, a betrayal that wasn't my fault. You had no right.

I was happy when you found Mary. It released some of my regret, knowing that you had a chance for happiness. When she and the baby died, somehow once again I felt your pain was my fault. If I would have just waited a little longer, you and I would have never had to suffer the way we did.

Richard and I never made love again after you came home. Every time he would try, I felt like I was being unfaithful to you. I'm so lucky that Richard was the type of man he was, because he stood by me, regardless.

I am glad I wrote this letter. I hope I have finally found my peace, and one day, I hope you can find yours.

Grace

I look at the flowers and see some new weeds poking their heads through the soil—tenacious suckers. I walk to the shed, grab the garden gloves, trowel, and kneepad, and get to work, letting my tears fall into the soil.

28

I OPEN the store a little past nine. So I was a couple minutes late. The world isn't going to come to a screaming halt.

I unpack the new shipment from the day before, place the receipts in the file marked "Accounts Payable," and sit at Charles's desk. I guess it's my desk now. Harlow is with Olivia at a birthday party, and Mom working at the doctor's office.

I pull my computer out of my bag and hop on the internet. I'm borrowing the WiFi from next door. They said it was okay. It's just until the phone company comes and installs it. I've already got the appointment set up. I search for bookkeeping programs and download the one with the best rating. I can't wait to switch over, but I need to get through the tutorial first.

I hear the door chime, so I step out of the office. A man stands just inside the door, looking around, then takes off his ball cap and sunglasses.

It can't be . . .

He's dyed his hair dark brown from his usual blond—the recent growth of his beard is colored to match. The potbelly must be fake. My dad works out religiously. Ego would never let him get out of shape.

My adrenalin is pumping. "Dad?"

He looks around, making sure no one else is in the store. "Hey, baby. You're a sight for sore eyes."

"I saw you the other day. You drove past the store."

"I know. I saw you too."

"What are you doing here?" I look out at the street for the agent's car, but I don't see anyone. Crap, my phone's in the office. I should make an excuse and text Sherice.

"I just wanted to see my baby girl," he says, walking toward me. I take a step back. "What this?" He gestures at my action. "Come here. I've missed you so much." Reaching out, he grips my arm and pulls me in, squeezing me tight as my arms hang stiffly by my sides. He steps back, unaffected by my response. "How are you? I can't believe you're working in a *grocery* store." The distaste is obvious.

I glare at him. "It's not like you left us with any means to support ourselves."

"I know, I know . . . I'm sorry. Everything is so messed up. I came here to tell you what actually happened. I'm sure the FBI has been telling you all kinds of lies about me. And there is no use telling your mother anything, she's never been very supportive," he says bitterly. "The woman despises me. You know that."

"You better follow me into the back. There is usually an agent close by."

Why am I helping him?

I'm not. I just want answers before I turn his ass in.

"Sure, but I'm safe. They aren't as smart as they think they are."

"*Uh-huh.*" There's that huge ego. I must have been blind not to notice it before. I think about my phone again and wonder how I can tip Sherice off without him knowing.

After I get some answers.

He follows me to the back. "So, what's the story?" I try not to sound as hateful as I feel.

"Do you remember Jerry Goodman? He came to dinner at the house a couple of times?"

"Yes, you worked together."

"Yes, yes. So, I found out he was stealing from the company. Somehow, he got control of my work account username and password." He grips my arms, looking a little frantic. "Kylie, he stole millions from the company. He even planted evidence around my office so the FBI would have everything they needed to indict me. He also got access to my bank accounts and deposited money there."

I pull away from him.

"If I was stealing from the company, do you really think I would be stupid enough to deposit the money into my personal bank account? Kylie, it's been a nightmare."

He's right. My dad isn't stupid. I'm trying to remember if Sherice said anything about money in *his* account? I thought it was placed somewhere else, but I can't remember.

"Why would that Jerry guy do that?"

"He's never liked me. I think he always felt . . . I don't know, like I got the breaks and he didn't. Then when they made me CEO, it put him over the edge. He quit about two weeks before the FBI showed up. Oh, Kylie, it's been crazy."

From the beginning, I had a hard time believing that he could have done what they accused him of. It just didn't make sense. But after Mom told me all that stuff about him, it seemed possible. She made him out to be such a monster. But now . . . His explanation. It's exactly what I envisioned.

"What are you going to do?" I ask, concerned now.

"I'm not sure, but I had to see you. I didn't want them turning you and Harlow against me. You're too important to me."

My heart tugs. "But why didn't you text or try to contact me before? You could have picked up a disposable phone. Why now?"

"I didn't want to take the chance of getting caught before I could figure my way out of this mess. But now I'm out of options. Jerry has me buried deep, I'm not any closer to finding the answers, and I've been away from my girls too long. I had to see you." He places his hands on my shoulders. He looks so desperate and sad. "I needed you to know the truth. I obviously can't stay. I just wanted to see you in person, to tell you, but now I have to go. I will get this straightened out, Kylie. I promise. Just be patient a little while longer. And please don't tell anyone."

"Okay. Sure. That makes sense."

"Look, I better go." He replaces his glasses and cap. "Can you let me out the back door?"

"Yes. That's a good idea."

He hugs me hard. "I love you so much."

This time I embrace him back. "I love you too, Dad. Let me know if there is any way I can help." I lead him to the back door.

"Kylie," he says, stopping me. "Did the FBI confiscate your computer?"

I stare at him, puzzled. "No, why?"

"There might be a way for me to clear my name, but I need you to give it to me."

"Oh, sure. Yeah." I think about the computer sitting in the office. But something has me hesitating. Maybe it's the words shared by my mother or plain selfishness. Either way, I stay silent.

"Good girl. I knew you would never let those bastards take it from you. How did you get past them?"

I think about how I played dumb with the one guard and tried to seduce the other. To my credit, he really was cute, but still, I'm embarrassed at the person I was. I shake my head. I'm still glad I kept it. "Oh, you know. I have my ways." I smile half-heartedly.

"That's my girl."

The compliment doesn't make me feel the way it used to.

"How is my computer going to help you?"

"I think I can access my old files. When I realized what was happening, I had to leave the country quickly. I couldn't download the information I needed. Is your computer at home?"

"Ah, yeah, but I don't understand how—"

"Right, yes, okay." He taps a finger on his chin, cutting me off. "I'll have to figure out a way to get it. Could you bring it to the store early tomorrow, before it opens, around seven? You will need to sneak past that agent that is always around."

"Yeah, sure. No problem. But Dad . . . you could use *any* computer. Why do you need mine?"

He looks sheepish. "I borrowed it once. Sorry about that. When I was using it, I had to download the office user platforms, so I could gain access to the company's server. Your computer has everything I need." He kisses me on the cheek. "I will see you tomorrow unless something happens."

"Okay, Dad. Be safe. They're smarter than you think."

His grin says he's evaded them this far, and then he's gone.

I look up at the clock on the wall. Shit! I need to go. I'm supposed to meet Mom at the lawyer's office. I stuff my computer in my bag, along with all the other essentials, lock the front door and walk down the block, trying to process everything Dad told me.

"Are you okay?" Mom asks when she sees me.

"Yeah. Why wouldn't I be?" I snap, the familiar animosity rearing its ugly head.

The lawyer comes in and explains basically what Charles said in the letter. He left most of his money in trusts. He was being modest when he said he made some "good investments." Someone must have told him to buy stocks in Apple when it went public. He wouldn't have had a clue otherwise. He's never been into tech—no computer, cell phone, iPad, nothing.

We had to sign several documents. Don advised me to open a bank account. Charles requested that regular monthly payments be deposited to accounts for me and my mother. He also said that our names will be added to the business account, giving us signing power for everything involving the store, but that there will always need to be two signatures. Harlow's money will be held in a trust until she is eighteen, but my mother is supposed to use her money to give her whatever she needs. Don will be the executor of the trusts and said that if any of us need a larger sum other than our monthly deposits, to contact him. He used Harlow needing a car when she turns sixteen as an example. It's hard to imagine her driving. I told him *I* need a car. He said that when I find one to let him know and he would have a bank draft drawn up.

My head is spinning.

I leave as soon as the lawyer finishes his business with us, saying only a quick goodbye to my mother. Seeing my dad has sparked all the old anger and resentment toward her, and I just can't deal with that right now.

I walk back to the store in a daze.

"Hey," Otto says, stepping out of Jojo's as I pass.

I stop. "Hey."

"You okay?"

"Yeah, I'm just busy," I say, irritated by the inquiry.

"Sure. Okay. Do you want to hang out later, go for a walk, bring a blanket, find a nice spot at the beach? Maybe the same place we went the other night?" He pumps his eyebrows suggestively.

"I said I was *busy*. Don't you have some stars to map out or a paper to write?" He looks stricken, and my insides twist with guilt. "Otto—"

"No. You're right. I have been letting things get in the way."

"I'm sorry. It's just . . ."

"Don't worry about it. It was expected. I'm good. I'll see you around." He turns, opening the door to the café, disappearing inside.

I feel sick to my stomach. Why was this all dumped on me? I'm eighteen years old for eff sakes! I don't want all this responsibility. It's my summer after graduation. I'm supposed to be having the time of my life, not running a friggin' store. This is such bullshit!

I just about break the key in the lock trying to open the

door. I attempt to slam it behind me, but it's closes slowly on its hydraulics.

Frick!

I wonder if Dad would take me with him. Maybe I could help him clear his name?

Wait, I have money now. I can go anywhere I want. Maybe I'll travel to Europe? Mom can run the store and Dad can deal with his own mess.

I throw myself in the chair in the office. The picture of Charles and his wife, and the one of Nana stare back at me. "Why did you have to die?" I yell at the photo.

I wonder what Charles would say if I told him about my father's visit. Probably something like I'd be an idiot to trust him. But what does he know? I suddenly wish he was here so I could ask him.

"Eff this!" I grab my bag, lock up, jump on my bike, and peddle for home. Screw the store, the town, and screw my effing family. I'm so sick of all the crap that's been thrown my way.

I drop the bike in the front yard, not caring if it breaks, and let myself into the house. *Man, this place is a dump.* I go up to my room and see Grace's photo album on my bedside table and feel a hint of remorse at my contrary thoughts. I change into shorts and a tank, grab the album and her diary, and head back up to the attic.

I'm so sick of this heat! I miss California and its ocean breezes. I want to go home. Maybe I'll go to university back in Cali after all? I wonder if it's too late to sign up for classes? I could easily pick up with my friends, especially now that I'm loaded. And since I'm eighteen, I can do whatever I want. Mom and Harlow have each other—they'll be busy with the store—

and Otto . . . chalk it up to a summer fling. *Whatever*. I need to get out of here.

I open up the tiny window in this god-forsaken oven. The air is sweet and lends a small reprieve from the sweltering heat. Why am I even up here? I open the trunk and set the books back inside, sit on the floor, and lean against it. I stare at all the junk, then drop my face in my hands and cry.

"Kylie? Are you up there?" Mom calls up the stairs.

I must have fallen asleep. I sit up, soaked in sweat.

"Kylie? Oh, baby," she says when she sees me. "You better come downstairs. Let's get you cooled off."

"I don't need you babying me!" I'm grumpy, dehydrated, and feeling like a total bag of crap.

On the main floor, it's like a hundred degrees cooler. Ignoring my rant, Mom throws ice in a glass, fills it with water, and hands it to me. "I went by the store and it was closed. Are you okay?"

"If things were so bad with Dad, why didn't you just *leave*?"

She looks startled. "I told you, Kylie. I didn't have any money. And he threatened to take you and Harlow away from me. I'd rather be dead than live without you two. What's this all about?"

"Nothing," I mumble and take a sip. The coldness definitely helps, and before I know it, the glass is empty.

"Something's changed. What's going on? Did your father get in touch with you?"

My head snaps up. I glare at her a moment as my mind races. "Why did you dump all that shit on me about him? That was your problem, not mine. And what the hell is going on with you and the doctor? You suck at lying." Her face turns red. "Oh my god! You don't even know what's happened to Dad and you're already hooking up with some other guy?"

"Kylie—"

"Just leave me alone!" I storm out to the living room, jam my feet into my flip-flops, and head out the front door. Picking up my bike, I throw a leg over and peddle to the pier. I lean it against a tree and clomp my way down the wooden planks. I sit at the end and dangle my feet in the water.

It's a start. *I'm so damn hot.* Without thinking, I stand up and dive in. The cool water envelopes me in blissful relief.

I swim around until I feel goosebumps and begin to shiver. I climb the ladder and sit, dripping wet as I stare off in the distance. This whole situation sucks. I lay back with my hands behind my head and watch the clouds. I'm so tired. I haven't been sleeping well with all that's been going on.

Everything my dad told me makes sense, but all the things Mom said about him were true. As difficult as it is, deep down, I know she wasn't lying. But she did come from an abusive family, so maybe her perceptions are a little skewed and things were not as bad as she made them out to be? Dad did always say she wasn't the brightest person, and she can be a bit dramatic.

As I doze off, I think of Otto, and my heart aches. I ignore it, and then before I know it, I'm not thinking about anything at all.

I wake dry and see the sun has dropped low in the sky. Hopping on my bike, I head home. Mom's car is parked in front, so is the agent's. You'd think he would have followed me to see where I went. Maybe he did, and I didn't notice.

"Kylie?" she calls when I enter.

"I don't want to talk about it."

"Are you hungry?"

"Not really. I'm going up to my room."

"Okay."

She's not hassling me, which is a shock. In my room, with my door shut, I change into girly boxers and a tank, and wish for the air to cool, so I can get a decent night's sleep.

There is a knock at the door. I knew she couldn't leave me alone. "Go away!"

"Kylie?"

Shit. It's Harlow. "Sorry, Bug. Come in." She enters cautiously, which makes me feel awful. "How was your birthday party?" I climb onto the bed and lean my back against the headboard.

She sits at the end. "It was fun. All the kids were nice to me. I'm okay if we stay here in Foxall."

I wonder what would make her say that. It's not like she's going anywhere. "Something on your mind?"

"No. I don't know. I'm happy, and I want you to be happy too."

How could she possibly know I'm struggling? I doubt Mom would say anything to her. "I am. I'm just tired, and the heat makes me grumpy."

"Okay."

"Tell me what you did at the party. I want to hear all about it." It's important she knows I am always here for her no matter what.

She's animated as she fills me in. It's hard not to feel lighter when you experience things through a child's eyes.

. . .

I hear my door open late in the night. Disoriented, I slowly open my eyes, thinking Harlow had a bad dream or something. The tiniest bit of light from the streetlamp shines through the window. It's just enough to make out my father as he rifles through the bag I always carry to work. He grumbles something, then moves to the desk, quietly opening and closing the drawers.

"Dad? What the *hell* are you doing?" I say, sitting up.

"Oh, hey, baby. I didn't mean to wake you."

"Why are you here? I thought I was meeting you in the morning?"

"Change of plans. It's better if I get the computer now and get out of town. As you pointed out, the FBI are smarter than I give them credit for."

"Right." I start to get out of bed. "Let me wake Harlow so you can see her before you go."

He puts a hand up, stopping me. "No, I don't think that's a good idea."

"Why? Do you know how much she's missed you?"

"Kylie." His tone is clipped. "I don't have time for this."

"I thought you came here to see us?" The tiny suspicion I had earlier is growing.

"I did. But I don't have a lot of time. I'll be in touch as soon as I get this settled. I promise."

"So you thought you would break in, steal my computer and then go? How did you get in here anyway?"

He scowls. "Don't be so dramatic."

"Dramatic? How dare you say that to me! After everything you put us through."

"*Shhh*. You'll wake everybody up."

An icy rage washes over me at the thought of being

manipulated again. "What's on the computer, Dad?" I reach and throw back the covers to reveal it lying next to me.

"I told you." He eyes it, then returns his focus to me. "Just let me have it and I'll go."

"You know what pisses me off the most? I fell for it. All your bullshit. I believed in you."

"Kylie, you don't know what you're talking about."

"Oh, don't I? I'm guessing that you have all your off-shore accounts hidden somewhere on my computer." I see amazement flash in his eyes. "Oh my god, Dad! Seriously? Why? You had it all. What was it?"

"Kylie, there are things happening here I can't explain," he says through gritted teeth. His eyes search to the right, then left of me. "Now, honey, give me the computer. I told you when I get to a safe location, I will contact you. Then I can have a nice long chat with your sister."

"No."

"What do you mean, *no?*" He looks stunned that I would defy him. This was always my attitude toward my mother, never him. He walks to the side of the bed closest to the exit. "Give me the fucking computer!" He makes a grab for it, but I grip it close to my chest and roll off the other side. Grabbing my phone off the nightstand, I quickly hit my emergency contact. I only have one. I never thought I'd need to use it.

"Who are you calling?" he yells. "Hang up that phone right now!"

He walks around to stand in front of me. I'm cornered. He takes a deep breath, calming himself. "Baby, please. Let's not fight about this. I'll send for you and your sister as soon as I can. It will be like it always was. We'll spend entire winter months in the Caymans and summers in Canada or Europe. You can shop till you drop! Having to work for a living has been hard on you. I'm sorry about that—"

"Tell me why!"

"*Shit*, Kylie," he hisses out. "Lower your voice!" I give him a death glare. "Okay. Listen, I did it for you and your sister. I wanted you to have all the luxuries you deserved. I mean . . . what else could I do?" he pleads, looking totally sincere. "I didn't want to let you down."

"Cut the bullshit, Dad!"

His face twists in anger, all pretenses gone. "You were always so smart—so much like me. You want to know? Fine. Because your idiot mother got pregnant, my parents' cut me out of my inheritance—what was rightfully mine. I lost everything because of her."

"My god, why didn't you just divorce her?"

"It wouldn't have mattered. My parents' couldn't stand that I married white trash. They were embarrassed that the heirs to their legacy were of such low breeding. I was an only child after all. They're true blue bloods, Kylie. They come from old money. So they took away my trust fund and wrote me out of their will. All because I fell for your mother." He looks out the window, smiles and shakes his head. "Fell . . . *that's* a laugh. You should have seen her when she was young. The most beautiful woman I'd ever seen. I had to have her. Love had nothing to do with it."

The door opens, "Kylie." Harlow rubs her eyes. "I thought I heard—Dad? What are you doing here?"

"Harlow, sweetie. Come here." He opens his arms to her.

"Harlow, don't!" She stops short. "I need you to go back to your room right now."

In two steps he has her arm gripped in his hand, holding her firmly in place.

"Dad!" Harlow yelps. "You're hurting me!"

"Kylie. Give me the computer. Now!"

"Your threatening me with Harlow? Are you crazy?"

"Enough, Kylie!" he shouts, not caring who hears.

I lift the computer over my head, threatening to smash it to the floor.

The rage on his face is horrifying. Still gripping Harlow's arm, he charges forward, back handing me across the face. The blow has me stumbling backward, crashing into the nightstand, then falling to the floor along with the lamp. My vision is blurry from the impact of the blow, but I can see Harlow tugging against his hold, screaming to let her go as she tries to get to me. He throws her backward.

"Now look what you made me do," he spits out. "It didn't have to be like this."

I need to get to Harlow. I use the side of my bed to pull myself up just as a loud *crash* fills the room and my father's body falls limp to the floor in front of me.

I look up to see Mom, staring blindly at my father's unconscious body, holding what's left of the lamp from her bedroom.

I push myself up the rest of the way as she snaps to attention, grabbing a hold of Harlow and then me, positioning us protectively behind her as she backs us toward the door.

A commotion ascends the stairs. Mom holds our position, huddling us together in a death grip as Agent Tipton rushes into the room with his weapon drawn. He looks down at my father, crumpled in an unconscious heap on the floor, then tucks his weapon back in its holster.

"Are you okay?" he asks, looking to my mother then to me

and Harlow. We all nod our heads as he moves toward my father to check his pulse.

I should be hysterical right now, but I'm still in too much of a rage to fall apart.

Owe! I lift my hand to touch the side of my face, but halfway there, I change my mind. It feels like I've been stung by a swarm of bees and then belted with their beehive.

I separate myself from Mom and Harlow to grab my cell that landed on the floor. "Sherice?" I ask, lifting it to my ear.

"Are you okay? Are you hurt?" Her sincere concern almost tips the scales of anger to a place of devastation and a waterfall of tears.

"My face feels like it's going to explode, my ears are ringing, and I have a raging headache, but other than that we're all good."

She laughs. "You're a brave kid, Kylie."

"Not really. Just pissed off. I got tired of listening to his bullshit lies. Mom was the one who took him down."

"I heard Agent Tipton."

"Yes. Came in gun drawn, just like in the movies." He looks at me and grins. "Thanks for being there and believing in us."

"You bet. I had to fly to Washington yesterday. I will be back in Cincinnati tomorrow and will drive out to take your father into custody."

"He's not my father anymore. He is nothing to me."

"Okay." She pauses. "The police have been called. They're apprised of the situation and will lock him up until I get there with the appropriate documents and can arrange transport."

"Thanks. I'll let Mom know."

"Kylie, this will hurt for a while. Let yourself heal, talk to someone. Get help, okay?"

"Thanks, but it's going to be okay. I'm not letting that man control any more of my life."

"Good for you. Then look out for Harlow and your Mom."

"Always."

"Tell her I said thank you," Mom calls to me.

I relay the message and hang up. Harlow looks shaken, her face drained of all color. "Hey, Bug. Let's go make some chocolate milk and wait out back. Mom, is that okay? You got this, right?"

"Yes. I can take it from here." She eyes Harlow, then looks at me. "Thank you."

"No problem." As we walk toward the stairs, I turn around and smile at her. "Mom, this is done. It's over."

Her eyes fill with tears. "I love you so much. Both of you."

"I love you too," I say. "Come on, Bug. Extra chocolate for you." I wrap an arm tightly around her as we descend the stairs and grip the railing since we're both a little unsteady on our feet. Lights from the police cars are flashing through the front windows and door.

"Harlow, go into the kitchen. I'll be right there." She does as I ask, and I wait with the door open for the officers to make their way up the steps. "They're upstairs," I say. They nod their heads and disappear up the stairs.

I mix up the chocolate milk and fill a plastic bag with some ice—I'm sure my face is disgustingly swollen by now—and make for the back door as quickly as possible. She doesn't need to see them carry our father out of the house.

We sit in the chairs. Harlow sips her drink, staring out into the dark. I down mine, feeling the adrenalin drain from my body, leaving shock and loss behind. I'll have to deal with it later. I have more important things to worry about.

"Chug the milk. It helps." She does as I ask with no emotion, just stares off into the darkness. "Harlow, look at me."

Her eyes reflect her pain against the darkness. "I don't understand."

I reach out to her. "Come here." She sets her glass on the ground and sits sideways on my lap, placing her head on my shoulder. Charles's words come to me suddenly. "Some people just aren't made right."

"When I saw him hit you. I froze. I didn't know what to do," she chokes out.

"It's okay." I rub my hand up and down her back. "It's over now. We'll need to work this through as a family, okay?" I feel her nod. "It's been a hard month for you, but you're smart and strong and you will make it through. We'll be fine because we have each other."

"I love you, Kylie." She squeezes my neck hard, making my head pound.

"I love you too, Bug." I squeeze her back. "Hey, how about we call Otto and wake him up? He can hang out with us." I need him and having him here will help Harlow feel more secure. I know it.

She sniffs. "Can we call Tristan too?"

"Sure. Why not?"

They took my father away, but several police cars were still in front of the house when Joanne and Otto pulled up, followed by Tristan a few seconds after. There was a melee of concern, explanation, and hugs. And when everything settled down, Joanne and Mom got Harlow to bed with the stipulation that Tristan would stay with her. He happily agreed and was set up with lots of blankets and pillows on her floor. Tristan, the protector. Harlow saw it in him the day Chase tried to swamp us, so it makes sense that she would want him there.

Otto and I walk to the lake holding hands. The moon is bright and sparkles on the water in a rippling streak of white light before disappearing under the pier in front of us. "I'm sorry for what I said earlier. My father showed up at the store and got my head all twisted around. When you came up on me, I was angry at the world and took it out on you."

"Why didn't you tell me what happened? I could have helped." He sounds hurt.

"Maybe, but everything my father said screwed with my mind and nothing fit together anymore. It brought me back to who I was—the person I knew could handle anything. But it's no excuse for treating you that way."

Otto pulls me into his arms and buries his face into the side of my neck. The only sounds are the water lapping against the pilings and a mockingbird that doesn't seem to keep normal hours. We take in the moment, rocking side to side as we draw from our connection.

"When I got your call, I was shocked." He breaks the silence, regarding me warily. "But when I saw the police cars with their lights flashing in front of your house, I was terrified. And this . . ." He cradles the side of my face in his hand. When I wince, he quickly drops it. "I felt rage, *so* much rage. I didn't know what to do with it all. Then you wrapped your arms around me and held on tight, and even though I had so many questions . . . everything made sense. Somehow, I understood you better in that moment than all the secrets in the universe." He kisses my forehead. "And I forgive you."

"Thanks. But I might say or do something stupid again. I'm

still trying to figure myself out, but I'm glad I am doing it with you, Otto."

"Me too."

I step back. "What am I going to do now?"

"Now that you have the money . . . I guess anything you want."

"What if I don't know what that is?"

"Then we will figure it out together." He picks up my hand, flips it over, and kisses the inside, then points to the night sky. "Did I ever tell you about . . ."

Everything
I Knew
to be
True

RAYNA YORK

CHAPTER ONE

I stare in numb silence at my mother's casket, waiting to be lowered into its final resting place. Everything happened so fast, I've hardly had a chance to process it all.

A spilt second image of Mom sitting at our tiny kitchen table flashes through my mind—that's where we'd catch up on the daily grind. She had so many outrageous customers, Maria's antics, her daily goof-ups, but I guess that comes with being a waitress for thirteen years.

I know she tried hard to hide it from me—I can see that now. It started with her being tired all the time and then throwing up constantly—the weight loss was staggering. When she finally went to the doctor, they diagnosed her with stage IV pancreatic cancer. They gave her three to six weeks to live. Her name was Allora, and I still can't believe she's gone.

"Cassie?" Roxanne gently places a hand on my shoulder. "Are you ready?"

I look around, momentarily confused. There were so many people here. Where did they go?

I guess I've been pretty out of it the last couple of days, which is understandable considering. I swallow hard against the emotional lump that's jammed in my throat and tell her I need another minute.

"Okay," she replies solemnly. "I'll wait for you by the car. Take your time."

There's only a marker now. I guess the headstone comes later; at least that's what they tell me.

I leave for California tonight. Mom made arrangements for me to live with her closest friend—a person I never even knew existed until two weeks ago. I'd always assumed that Mom had grown up in New York—it's where her parents lived before they died. Apparently, I was wrong.

I begged her to let me stay here with Luigi and Maria—they're like family. At least then *some* things would have remained the same. Instead, she insisted I live with Roxanne and her family.

We drive back to the apartment so I can get my stuff. "I won't be long," I tell Roxanne, leaving her at the door looking bewildered. I feel bad being thrust on her like this. She doesn't even *know* me, and now I'm going to live with her. She seems fine with it, but still.

I can't believe how empty the place seems. Yeah, all our stuff's gone, but it's more than that. Mom was my best friend—my *only* friend. She made this dinky little hole-in-the-wall a home, made every day special no matter how hard things got—and there were some pretty tough times. How am I going to start over without her?

I step in to the tiny sunroom and stare out one of the many windows with my arms wrapped tightly around me. Mom surprised me on my thirteenth birthday when she turned it into an art studio. She built shelves and lined them with jars of paintbrushes, pens, and pencils. She even placed an easel in the corner next to the wall of windows, with blank canvases stacked next to it. I know it cost her a lot of money—money we didn't have to spare—but it was an amazing gift. Art was everything to me.

Now the walls are bare, the colorful murals painted over with coats of white paint, easily erasing all that I was—all that we were.

"Cassie, honey. I'm sorry, but we really have to go if we're going to make our flight."

I look over my shoulder at Roxanne, holding my small suitcase in her hands. "Yeah. Okay." I cross the room and pick up the backpack sitting at her feet, sling it over my shoulder, and take one last look around before closing the door on the only life I've ever known.

CPSIA information can be obtained
at www.ICGtesting.com
Printed in the USA
BVHW042239290820
587588BV00008B/525